PLANTS VS. ZOMBIES™

LAWNMAGEDDON

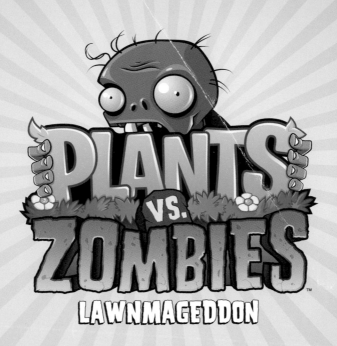

Written by **PAUL TOBIN**
Art by **RON CHAN**
Colors by **MATTHEW J. RAINWATER**
Letters by **STEVE DUTRO**
Cover by **RON CHAN**

DARK HORSE BOOKS

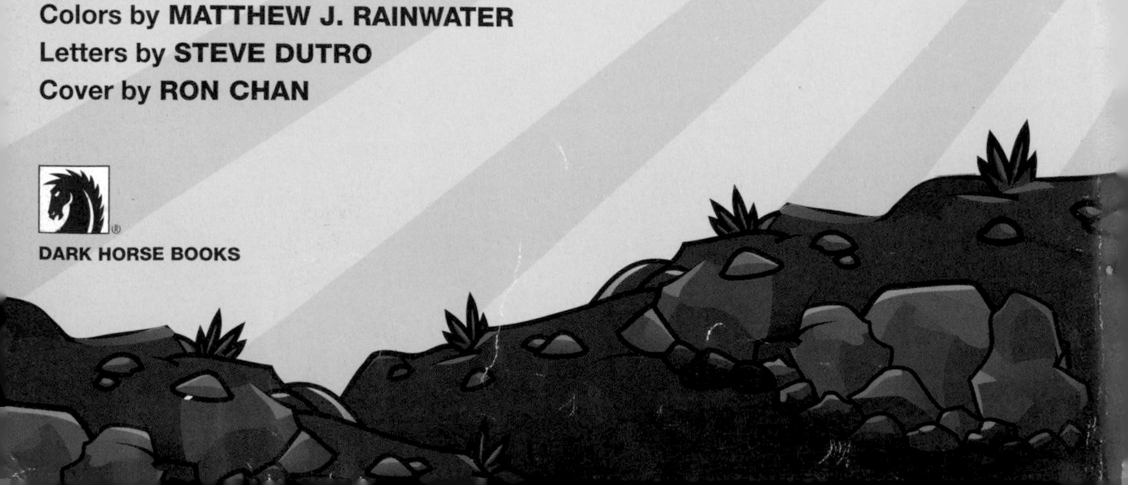

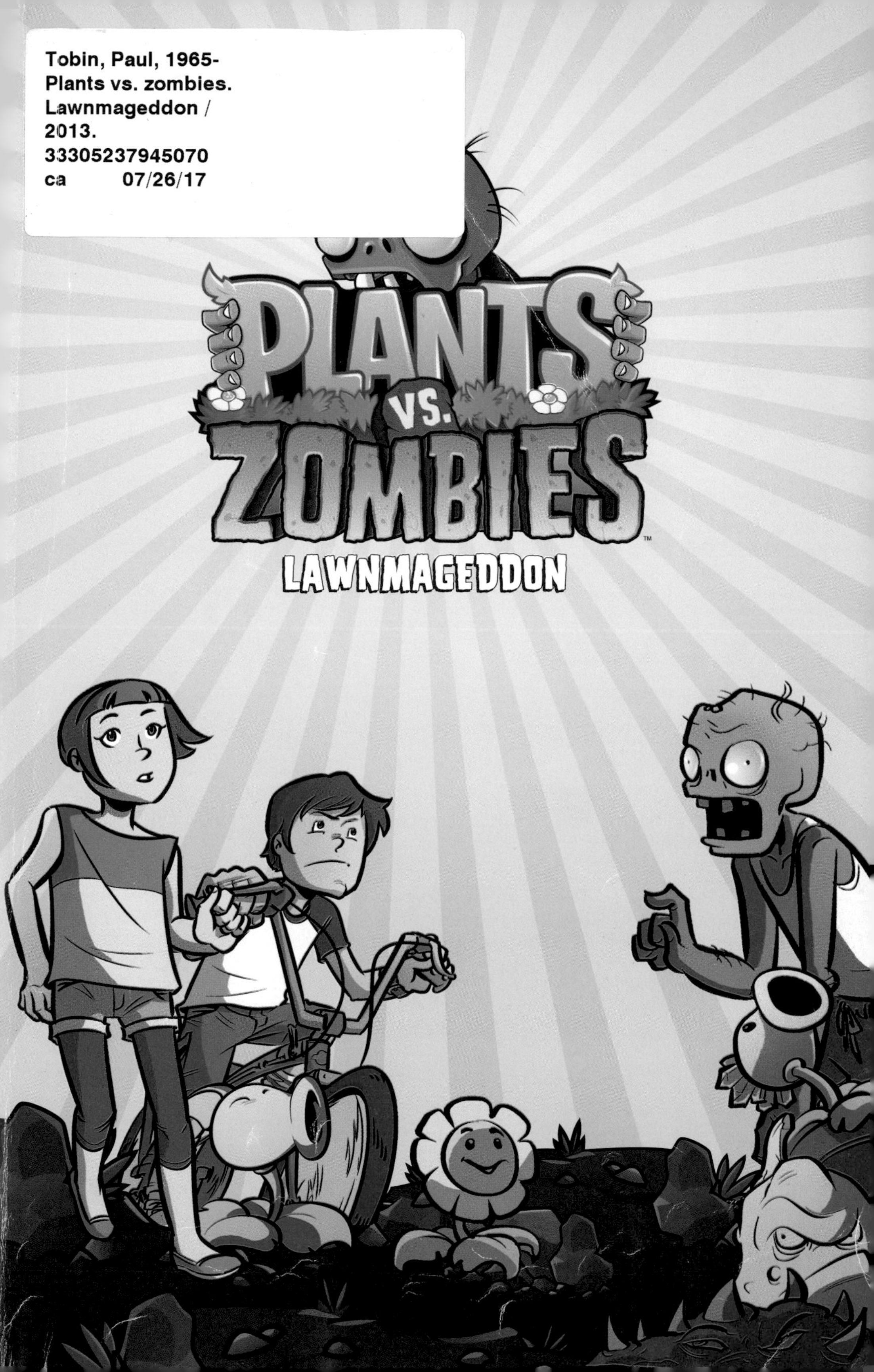
PLANTS
VS.
ZOMBIES™
LAWNMAGEDDON

Publisher **MIKE RICHARDSON**
Editor **PHILIP R. SIMON**
Assistant Editor **EVERETT PATTERSON**
Designer **KAT LARSON**
Digital Production **CHRISTINA McKENZIE**

Special thanks to SHANA DOERR, AMY
HEVRON, A.J. RATHBUN, PHILIP SMITH,
BRENNAN TOWNLEY, JEREMY VANHOOZER,
and everyone at PopCap Games.

This volume collects *Plants vs. Zombies:
Lawnmageddon* #1–#6, originally serialized
by Dark Horse Digital.

Published by Dark Horse Books, a division of
Dark Horse Comics, Inc., 10956 SE Main Street,
Milwaukie, OR 97222
International Licensing: (503) 905-2377

To find a comics shop in your area, call the Comic
Shop Locator Service toll-free at 1-888-266-4226.

Boxed-set edition: October 2015
ISBN 978-1-61655-192-6

10 9 8 7 6 5 4 3 2 1
Printed in the United States of America

▷ No plants were harmed in the making of this comic. Countless zombies, however, definitely were.

MIKE RICHARDSON President and Publisher **NEIL HANKERSON** Executive Vice President **TOM WEDDLE** Chief Financial Officer **RANDY
STRADLEY** Vice President of Publishing **MICHAEL MARTENS** Vice President of Book Trade Sales **ANITA NELSON** Vice President of Business Affairs **SCOTT ALLIE** Editor in Chief **MATT PARKINSON** Vice President of Marketing **DAVID SCROGGY** Vice President of Product
Development **DALE LAFOUNTAIN** Vice President of Information Technology **DARLENE VOGEL** Senior Director of Print, Design, and Production **KEN LIZZI** General Counsel **DAVEY ESTRADA** Editorial Director **CHRIS WARNER** Senior Books Editor **DIANA SCHUTZ** Executive
Editor **CARY GRAZZINI** Director of Print and Development **LIA RIBACCHI** Art Director **CARA NIECE** Director of Scheduling **TIM WIESCH**
Director of International Licensing **MARK BERNARDI** Director of Digital Publishing

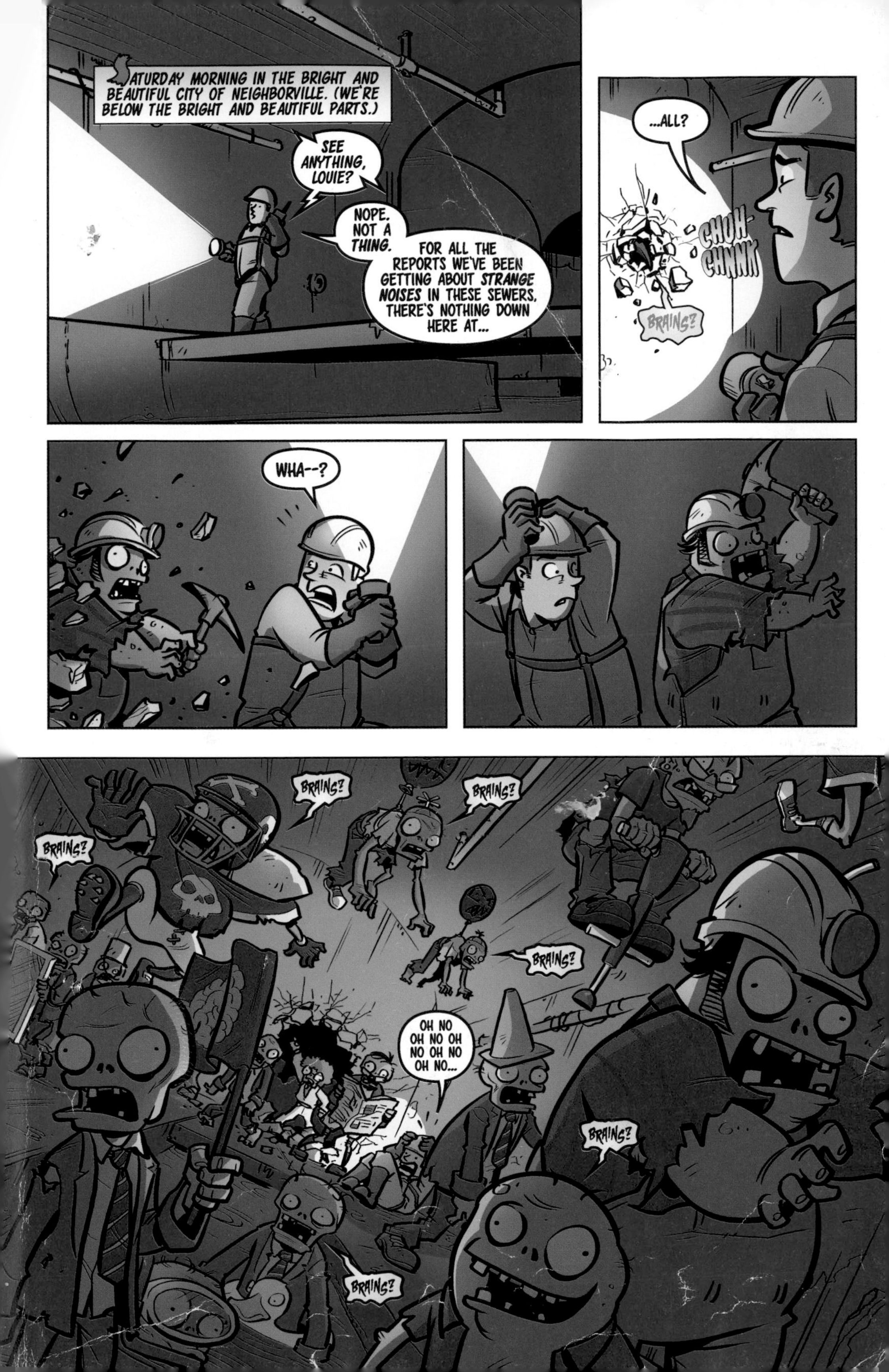
SATURDAY MORNING IN THE BRIGHT AND BEAUTIFUL CITY OF NEIGHBORVILLE. (WE'RE BELOW THE BRIGHT AND BEAUTIFUL PARTS.)
SEE ANYTHING, LOUIE?
NOPE. NOT A THING.
FOR ALL THE REPORTS WE'VE BEEN GETTING ABOUT STRANGE NOISES IN THESE SEWERS, THERE'S NOTHING DOWN HERE AT...
...ALL?
CHUH-CHNNK
BRAINS?
WHA--?
BRAINS?
BRAINS?
BRAINS?
BRAINS?
OH NO OH NO OH NO OH NO OH NO...
BRAINS?
BRAINS?

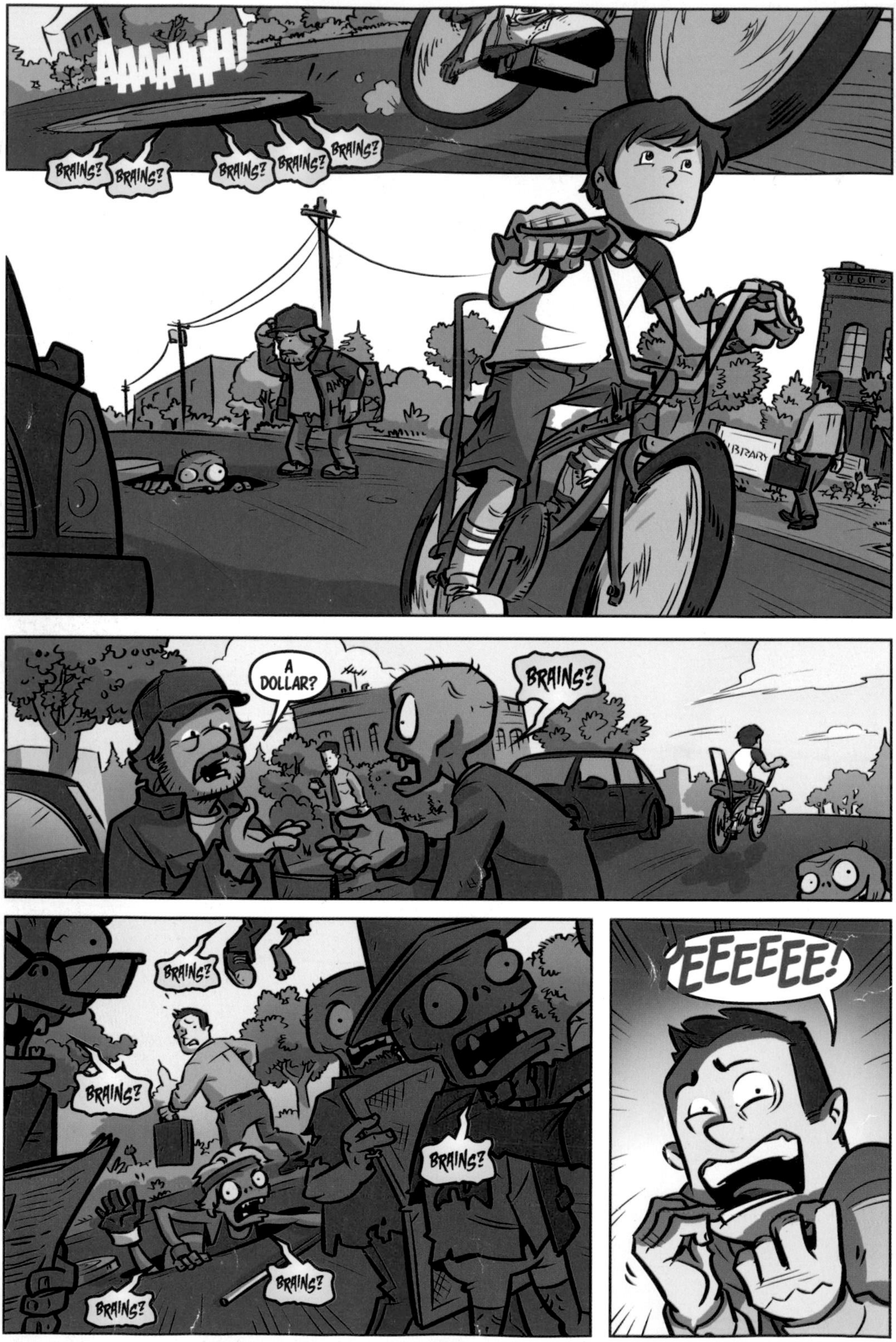
AAAAHHHH!
BRAINS?
BRAINS?
BRAINS?
BRAINS?
BRAINS?
LIBRARY
A DOLLAR?
BRAINS?
BRAINS?
BRAINS?
BRAINS?
BRAINS?
BRAINS?
EEEEEE!

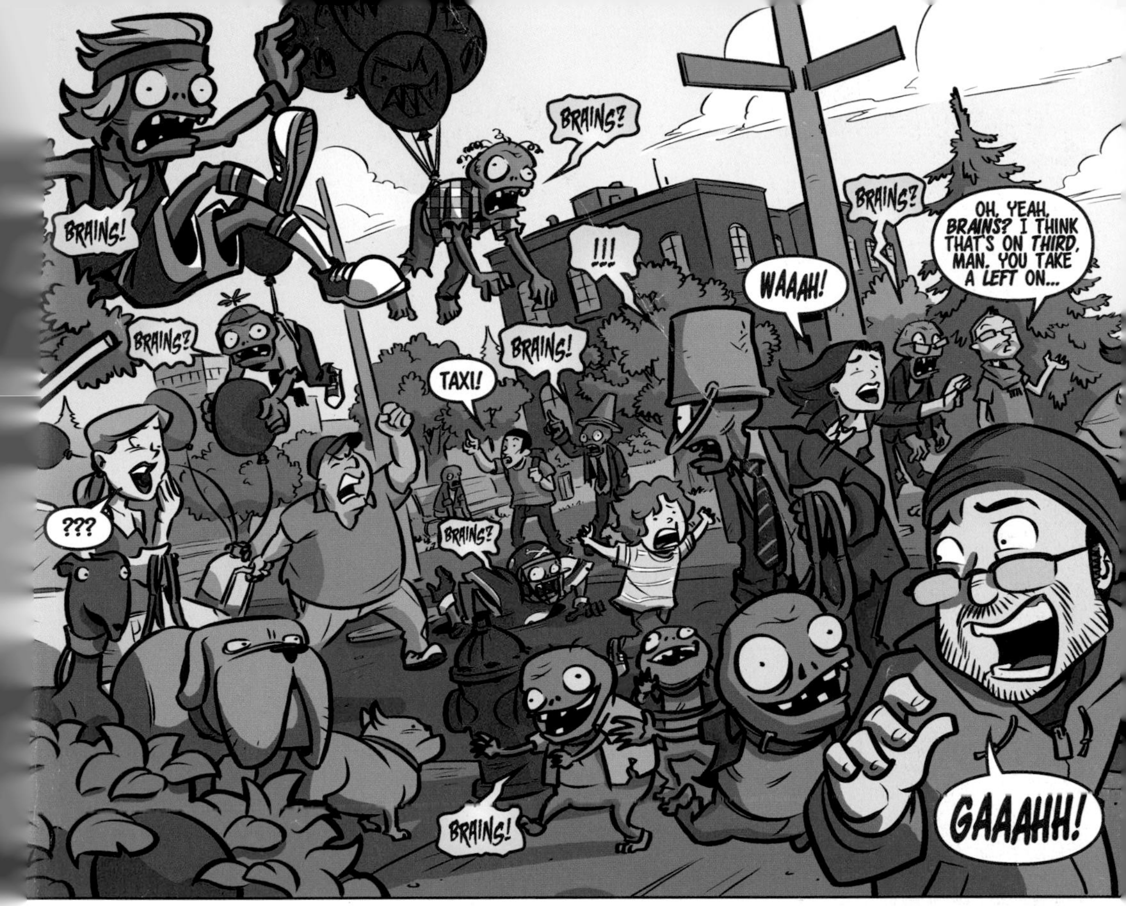
BRAINS!
BRAINS?
BRAINS?
!!!
BRAINS!
TAXI!
BRAINS?
WAAAH!
OH, YEAH, BRAINS? I THINK THAT'S ON THIRD, MAN. YOU TAKE A LEFT ON...
???
BRAINS?
BRAINS!
GAAAHH!

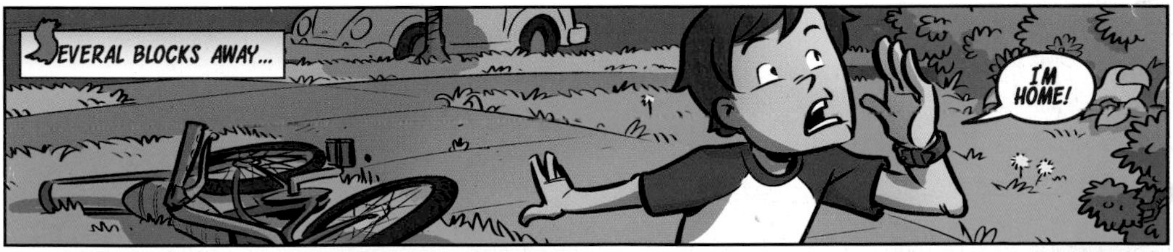
SEVERAL BLOCKS AWAY...
I'M HOME!

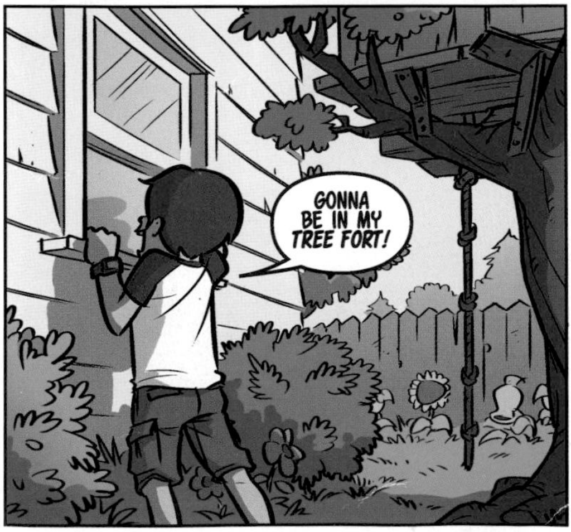
GONNA BE IN MY TREE FORT!

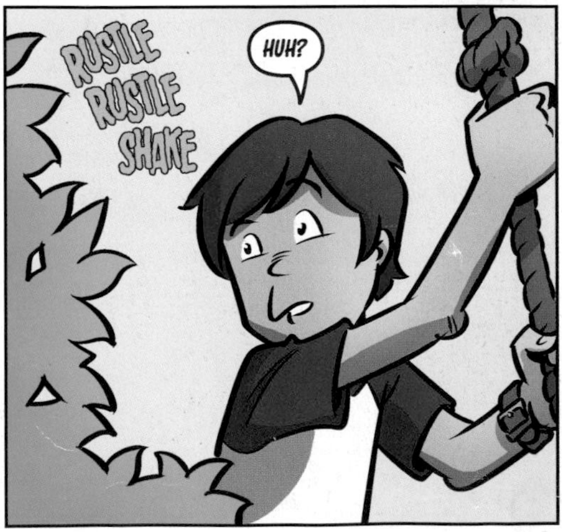
RUSTLE
RUSTLE
SHAKE
HUH?

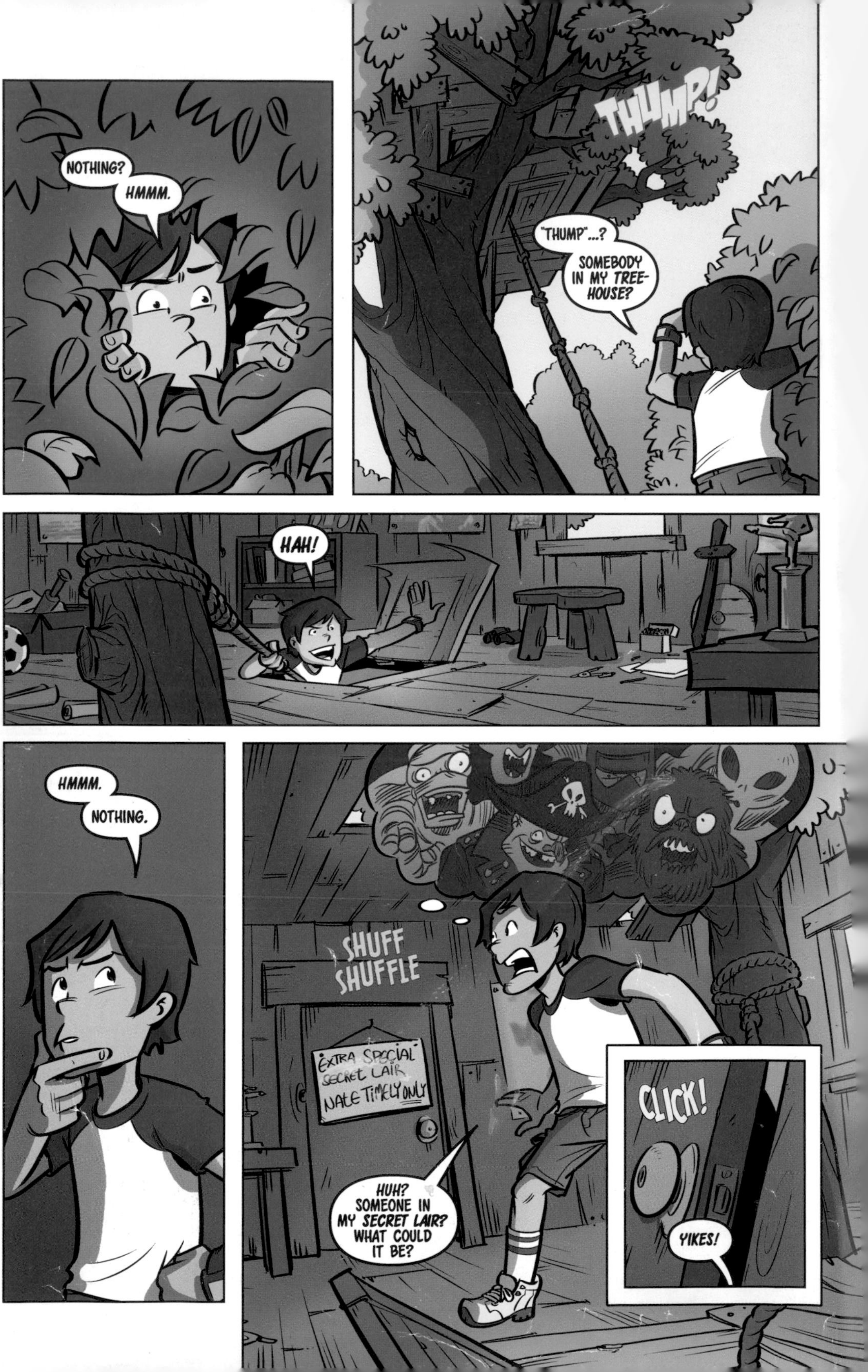
NOTHING?
HMMM.
THUMP!
"THUMP"...?
SOMEBODY IN MY TREE-HOUSE?
HAH!
HMMM.
NOTHING.
SHUFF SHUFFLE
EXTRA SPECIAL SECRET LAIR NATE TIMELY ONLY
HUH? SOMEONE IN MY SECRET LAIR? WHAT COULD IT BE?
CLICK!
YIKES!

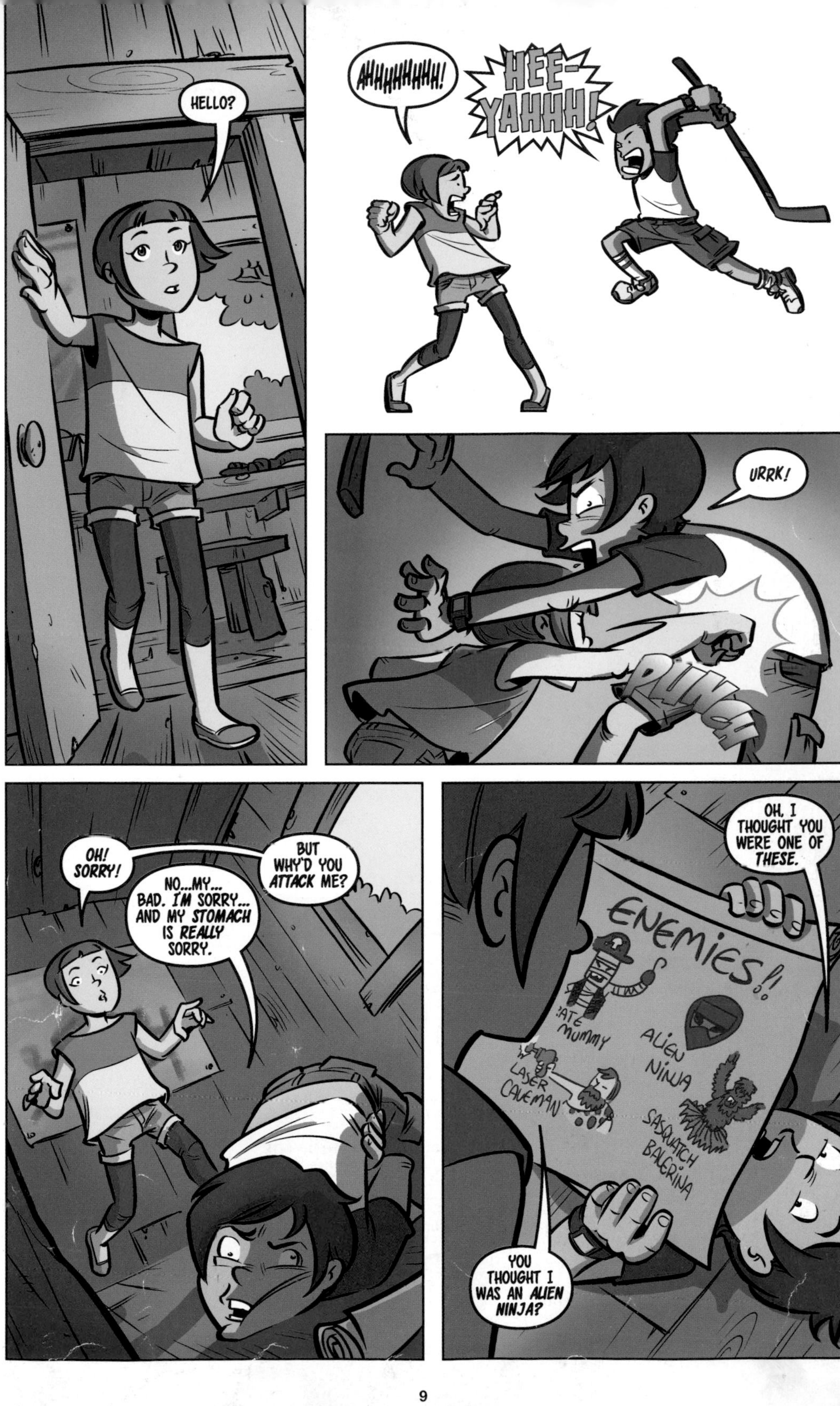
HELLO?
AHHHHHHHH!
HEE-YAHHH!
URRK!
PUNCH
OH! SORRY!
BUT WHY'D YOU *ATTACK* ME?
NO...MY... BAD. *I'M* SORRY... AND MY *STOMACH* IS *REALLY* SORRY.
OH, I THOUGHT YOU WERE ONE OF *THESE.*
ENEMIES!!
MUMMY
ALIEN NINJA
LASER CAVEMAN
SASQUATCH BALERINA
YOU THOUGHT I WAS AN *ALIEN NINJA?*

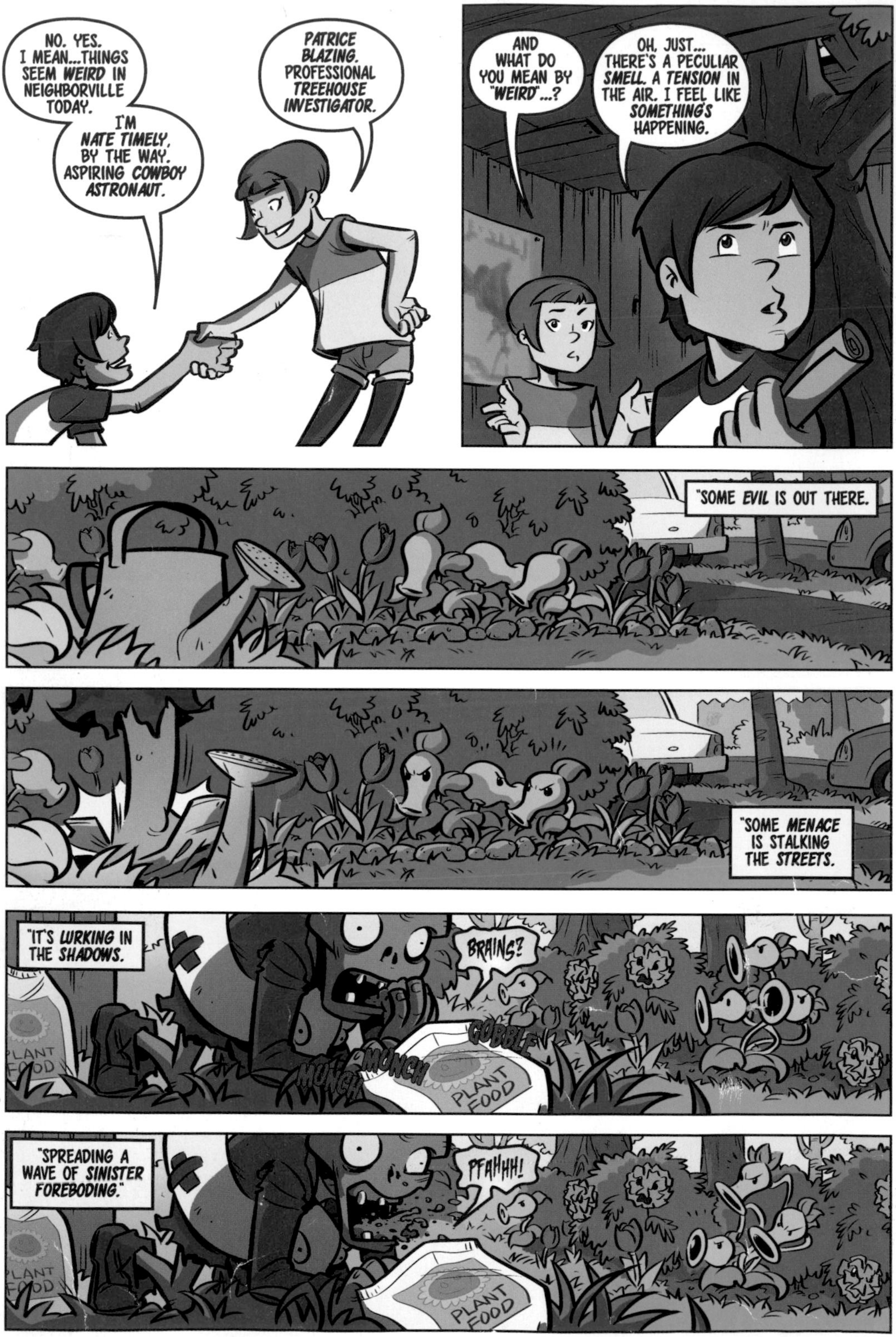
NO. YES. I MEAN...THINGS SEEM WEIRD IN NEIGHBORVILLE TODAY.
I'M NATE TIMELY, BY THE WAY. ASPIRING COWBOY ASTRONAUT.
PATRICE BLAZING. PROFESSIONAL TREEHOUSE INVESTIGATOR.
AND WHAT DO YOU MEAN BY "WEIRD"...?
OH, JUST... THERE'S A PECULIAR SMELL. A TENSION IN THE AIR. I FEEL LIKE SOMETHING'S HAPPENING.
"SOME EVIL IS OUT THERE.
"SOME MENACE IS STALKING THE STREETS.
"IT'S LURKING IN THE SHADOWS.
BRAINS?
PLANT FOOD
MUNCH
MUNCH
GOBBLE
PLANT FOOD
"SPREADING A WAVE OF SINISTER FOREBODING."
PFAHHH!
PLANT FOOD
PLANT FOOD

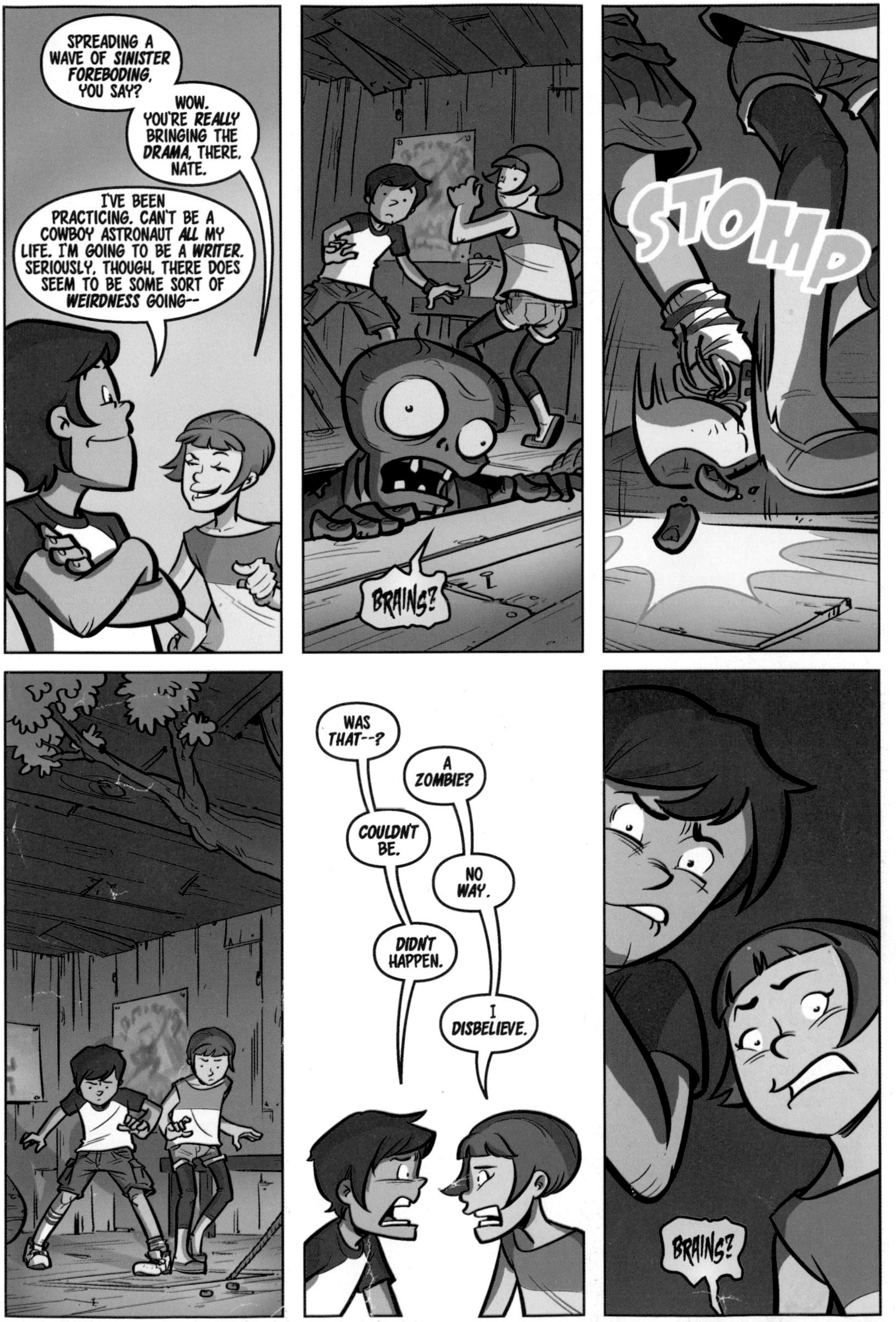
SPREADING A WAVE OF SINISTER FOREBODING, YOU SAY?
WOW. YOU'RE REALLY BRINGING THE DRAMA, THERE, NATE.
I'VE BEEN PRACTICING. CAN'T BE A COWBOY ASTRONAUT ALL MY LIFE. I'M GOING TO BE A WRITER. SERIOUSLY, THOUGH, THERE DOES SEEM TO BE SOME SORT OF WEIRDNESS GOING--
BRAINS?
STOMP
WAS THAT--?
A ZOMBIE?
COULDN'T BE.
NO WAY.
DIDN'T HAPPEN.
I DISBELIEVE.
BRAINS?

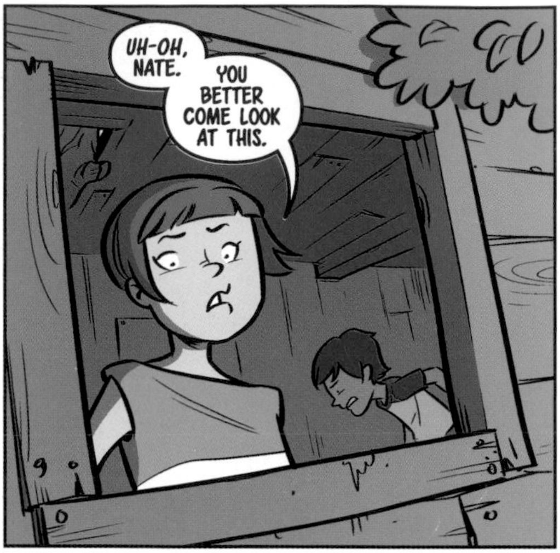
UH-OH, NATE.
YOU BETTER COME LOOK AT THIS.

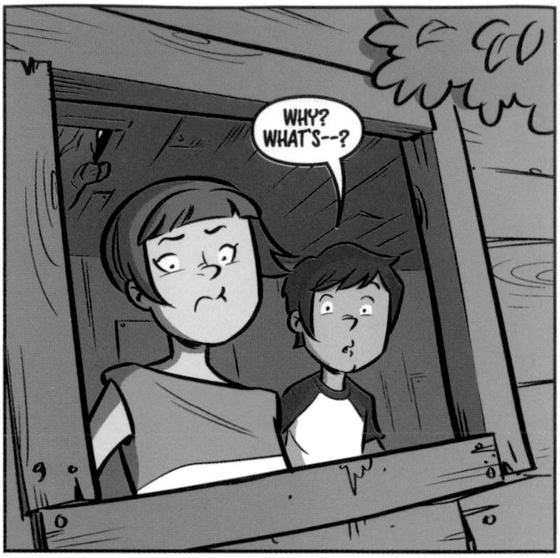
WHY? WHAT'S--?

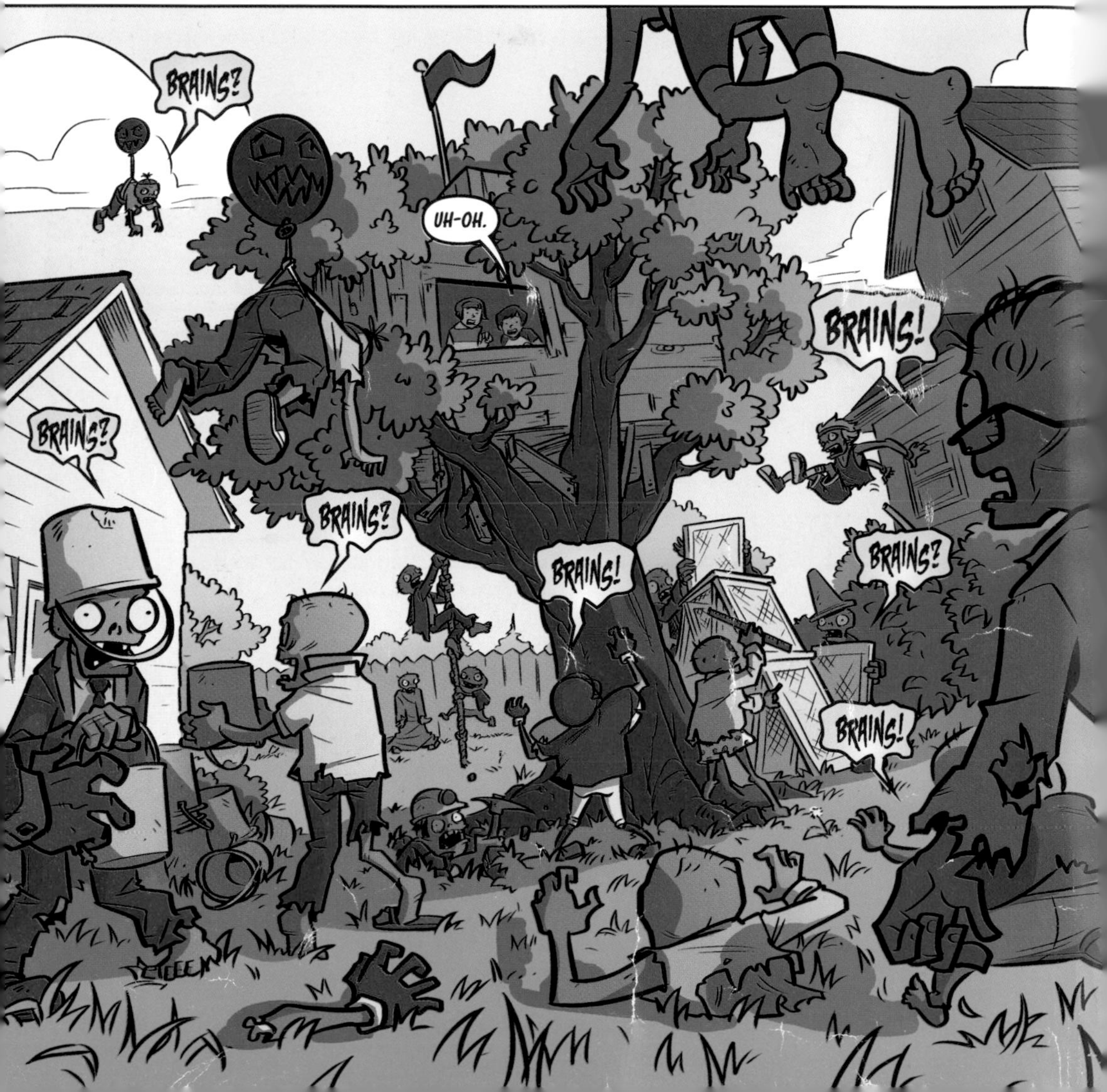
BRAINS?
UH-OH.
BRAINS!
BRAINS?
BRAINS?
BRAINS!
BRAINS?
BRAINS!

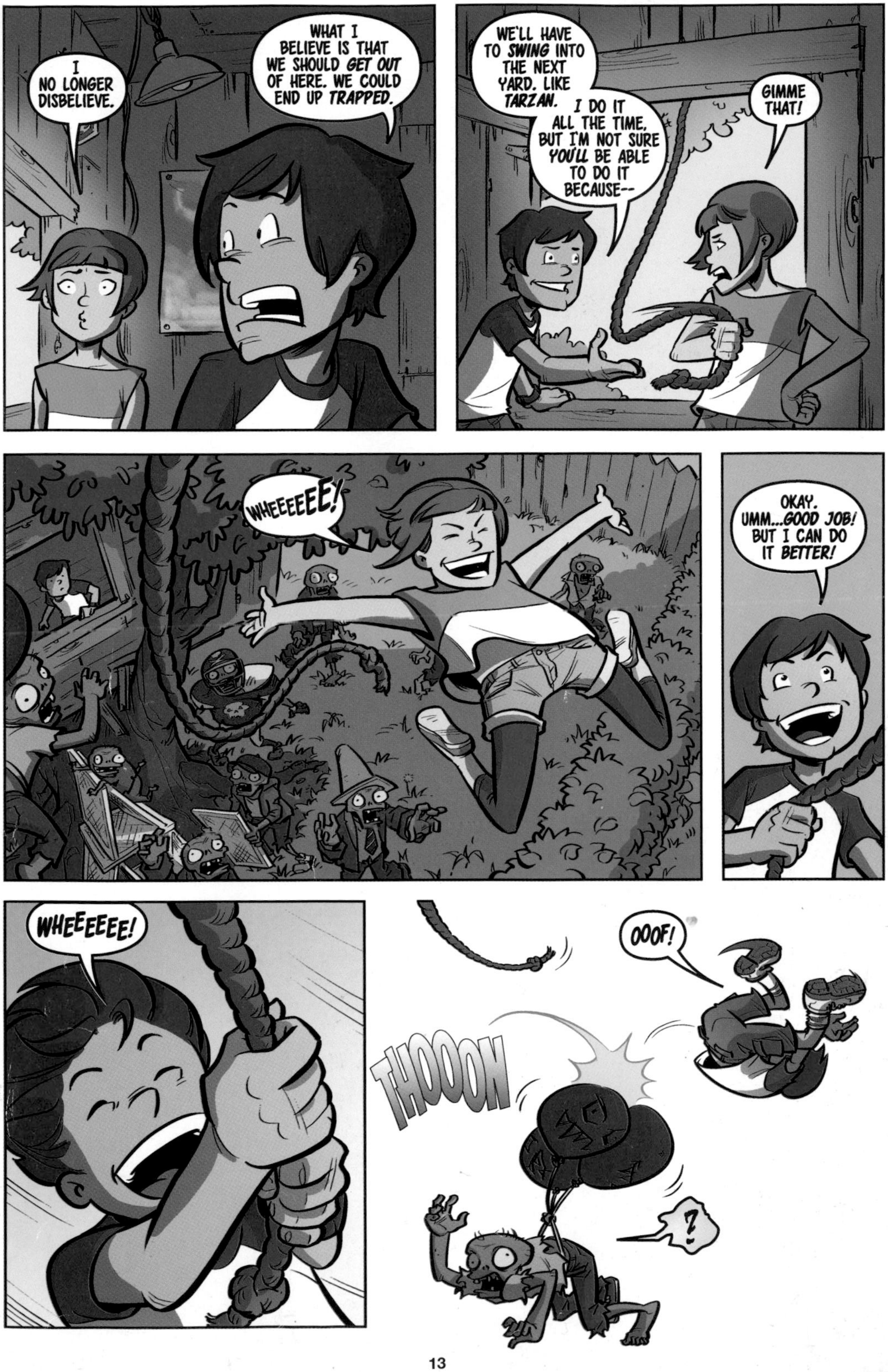
I NO LONGER DISBELIEVE.
WHAT I BELIEVE IS THAT WE SHOULD GET OUT OF HERE. WE COULD END UP TRAPPED.
WE'LL HAVE TO SWING INTO THE NEXT YARD. LIKE TARZAN.
I DO IT ALL THE TIME, BUT I'M NOT SURE YOU'LL BE ABLE TO DO IT BECAUSE--
GIMME THAT!
WHEEEEEE!
OKAY. UMM...GOOD JOB! BUT I CAN DO IT BETTER!
WHEEEEEE!
OOOF!
THOOON
?

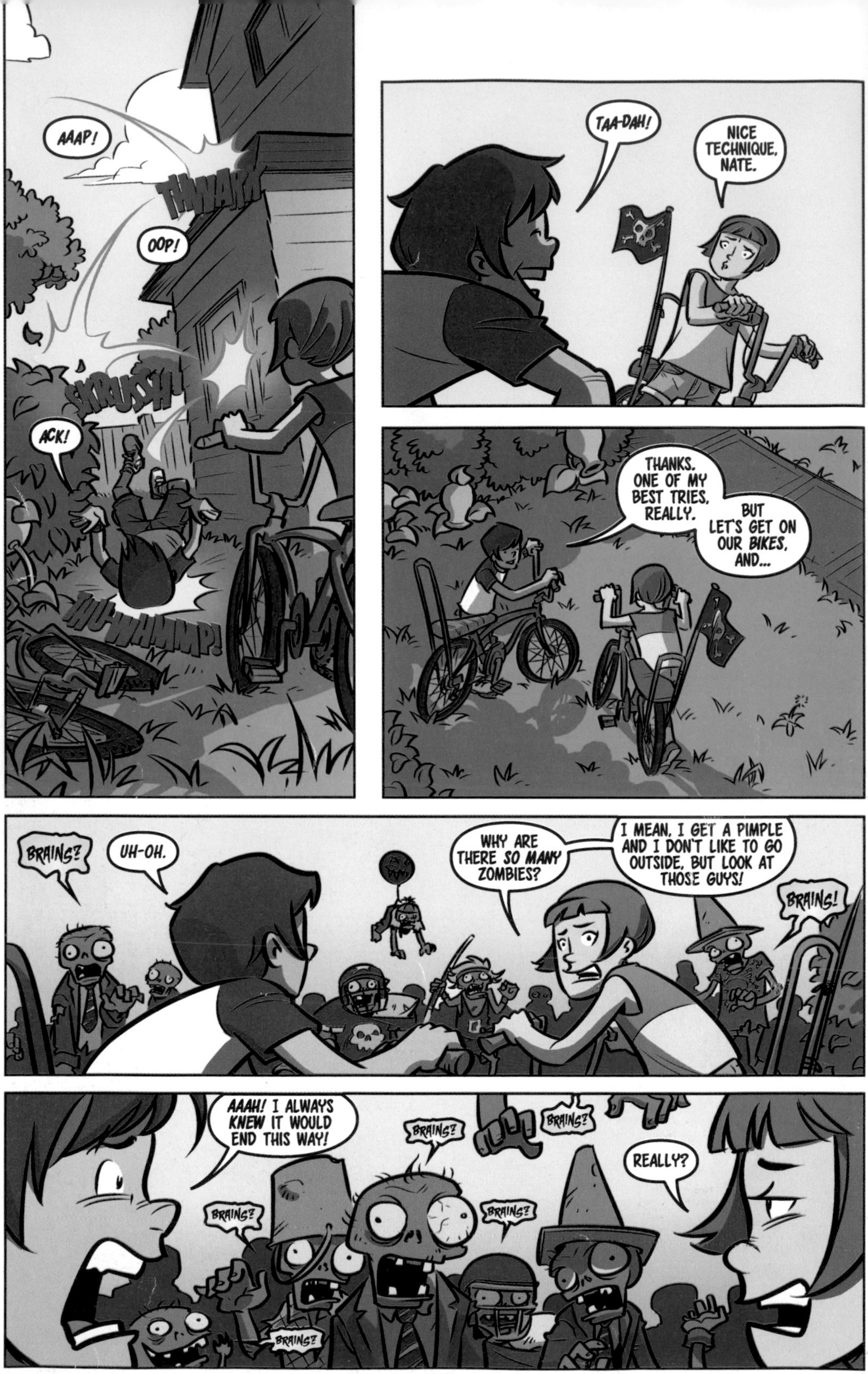
AAAP!
THWAK!
OOP!
SKRUSSH!
ACK!
THU-WHMMP!
TAA-DAH!
NICE TECHNIQUE, NATE.
THANKS. ONE OF MY BEST TRIES, REALLY.
BUT LET'S GET ON OUR *BIKES*, AND...
BRAINS?
UH-OH.
WHY ARE THERE *SO MANY* ZOMBIES?
I MEAN, I GET A PIMPLE AND I DON'T LIKE TO GO OUTSIDE, BUT LOOK AT THOSE GUYS!
BRAINS!
AAAH! I ALWAYS *KNEW* IT WOULD END THIS WAY!
BRAINS?
BRAINS?
REALLY?
BRAINS?
BRAINS?
BRAINS?

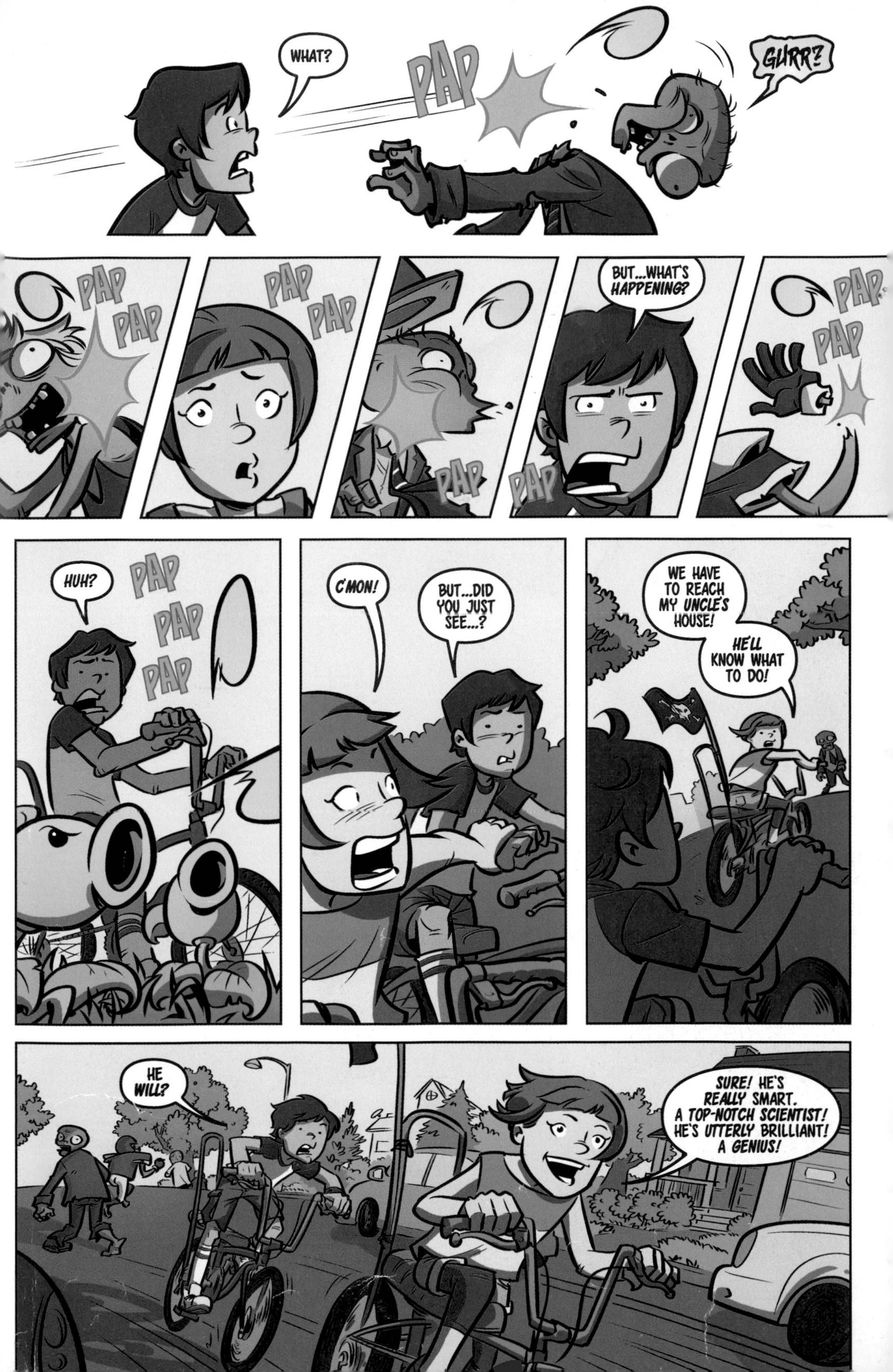
WHAT?
PAP
GURR?
PAP PAP
PAP PAP
PAP
BUT...WHAT'S HAPPENING?
PAP
PAP PAP
HUH?
PAP PAP PAP
C'MON!
BUT...DID YOU JUST SEE...?
WE HAVE TO REACH MY UNCLE'S HOUSE!
HE'LL KNOW WHAT TO DO!
HE WILL?
SURE! HE'S REALLY SMART. A TOP-NOTCH SCIENTIST! HE'S UTTERLY BRILLIANT! A GENIUS!

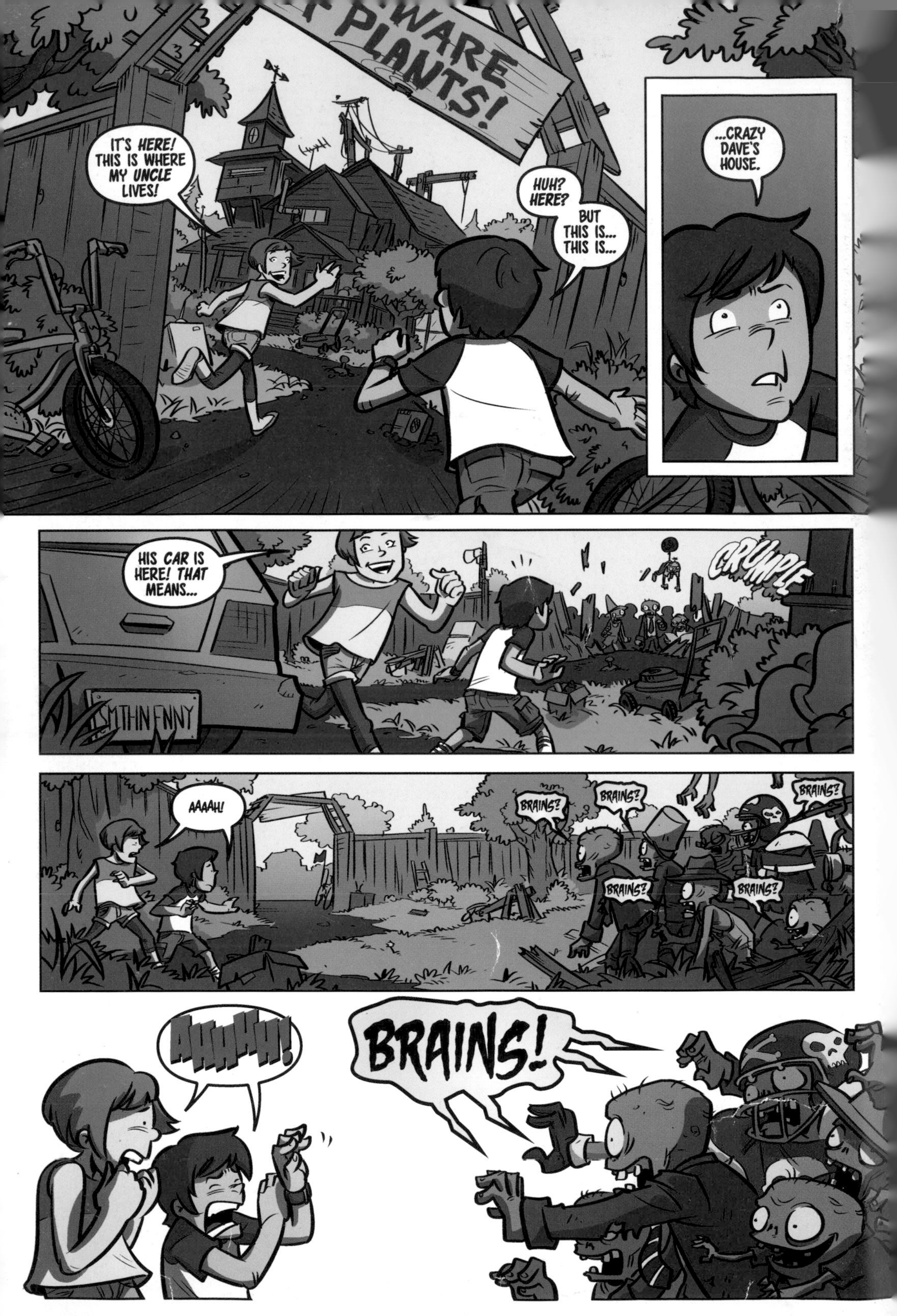
PLANTS!
IT'S HERE! THIS IS WHERE MY UNCLE LIVES!
HUH? HERE?
BUT THIS IS... THIS IS...
...CRAZY DAVE'S HOUSE.
HIS CAR IS HERE! THAT MEANS...
SMTHN FNNY
CRUMPLE
AAAAH!
BRAINS?
BRAINS?
BRAINS?
BRAINS?
BRAINS?
AHHHHH!
BRAINS!

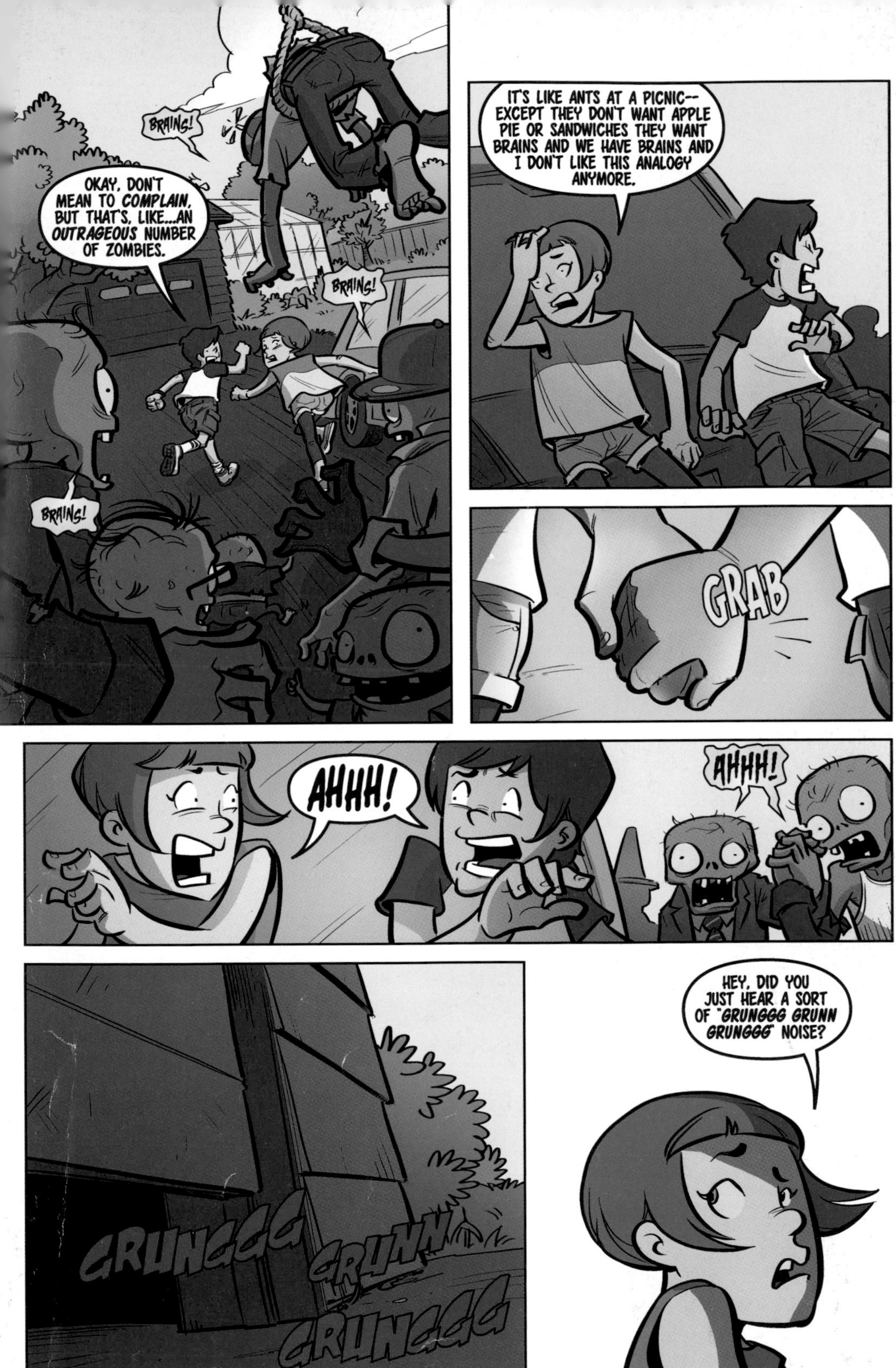

BRAINS!
OKAY, DON'T MEAN TO COMPLAIN, BUT THAT'S, LIKE...AN OUTRAGEOUS NUMBER OF ZOMBIES.
BRAINS!
BRAINS!
IT'S LIKE ANTS AT A PICNIC-- EXCEPT THEY DON'T WANT APPLE PIE OR SANDWICHES THEY WANT BRAINS AND WE HAVE BRAINS AND I DON'T LIKE THIS ANALOGY ANYMORE.
GRAB
AHHH!
AHHH!
GRUNGGG
GRUNN
GRUNGGG
HEY, DID YOU JUST HEAR A SORT OF "GRUNGGG GRUNN GRUNGGG" NOISE?

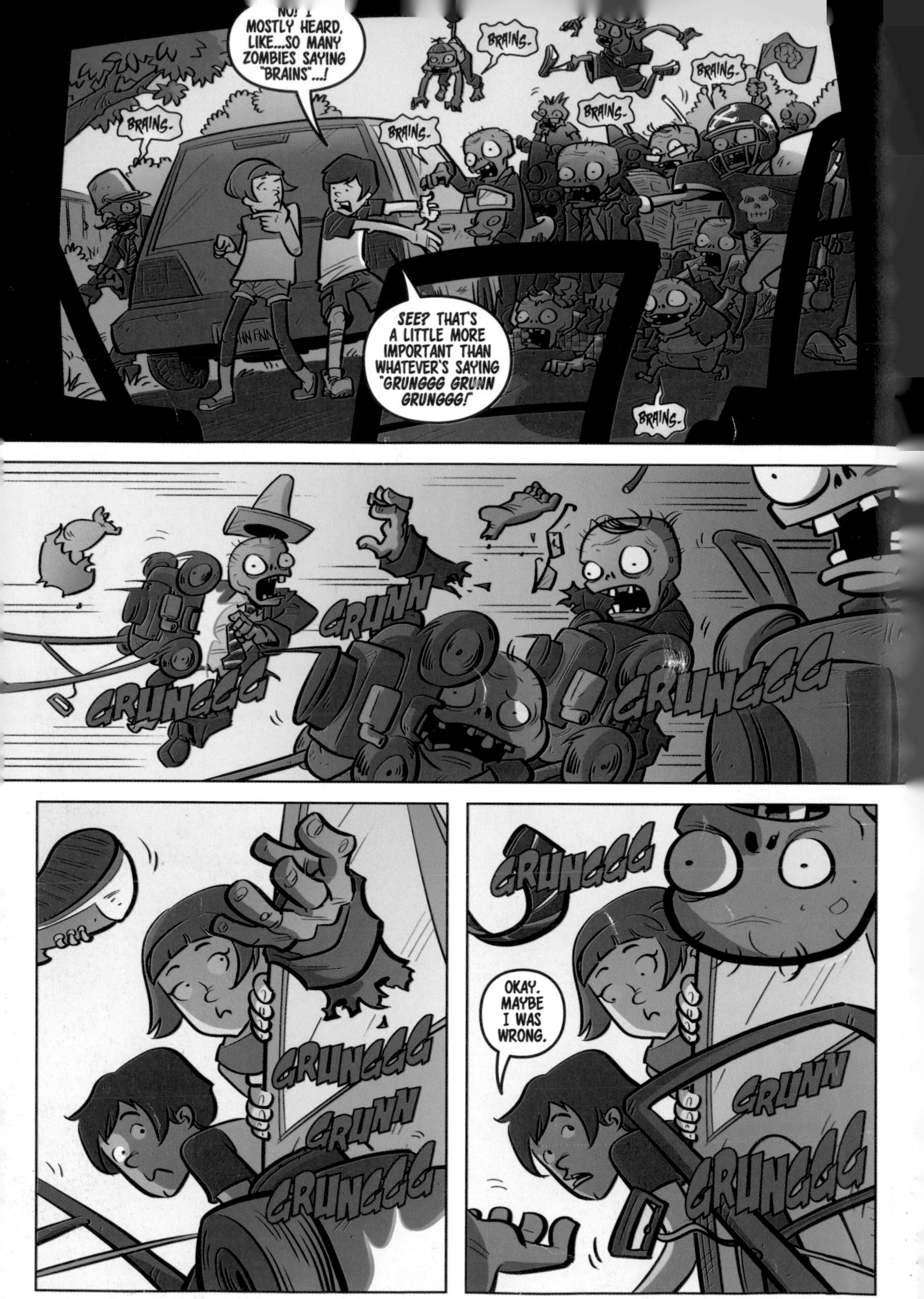
NO! I MOSTLY HEARD, LIKE...SO MANY ZOMBIES SAYING "BRAINS"...!
BRAINS.
BRAINS.
BRAINS.
BRAINS.
BRAINS.
SEE? THAT'S A LITTLE MORE IMPORTANT THAN WHATEVER'S SAYING "GRUNGGG GRUNN GRUNGGG!"
BRAINS.
GRUNN
GRUNGGG
GRUNGGG
GRUNGGG
GRUNN
GRUNGGG
GRUNGGG
OKAY. MAYBE I WAS WRONG.
GRUNN
GRUNGGG

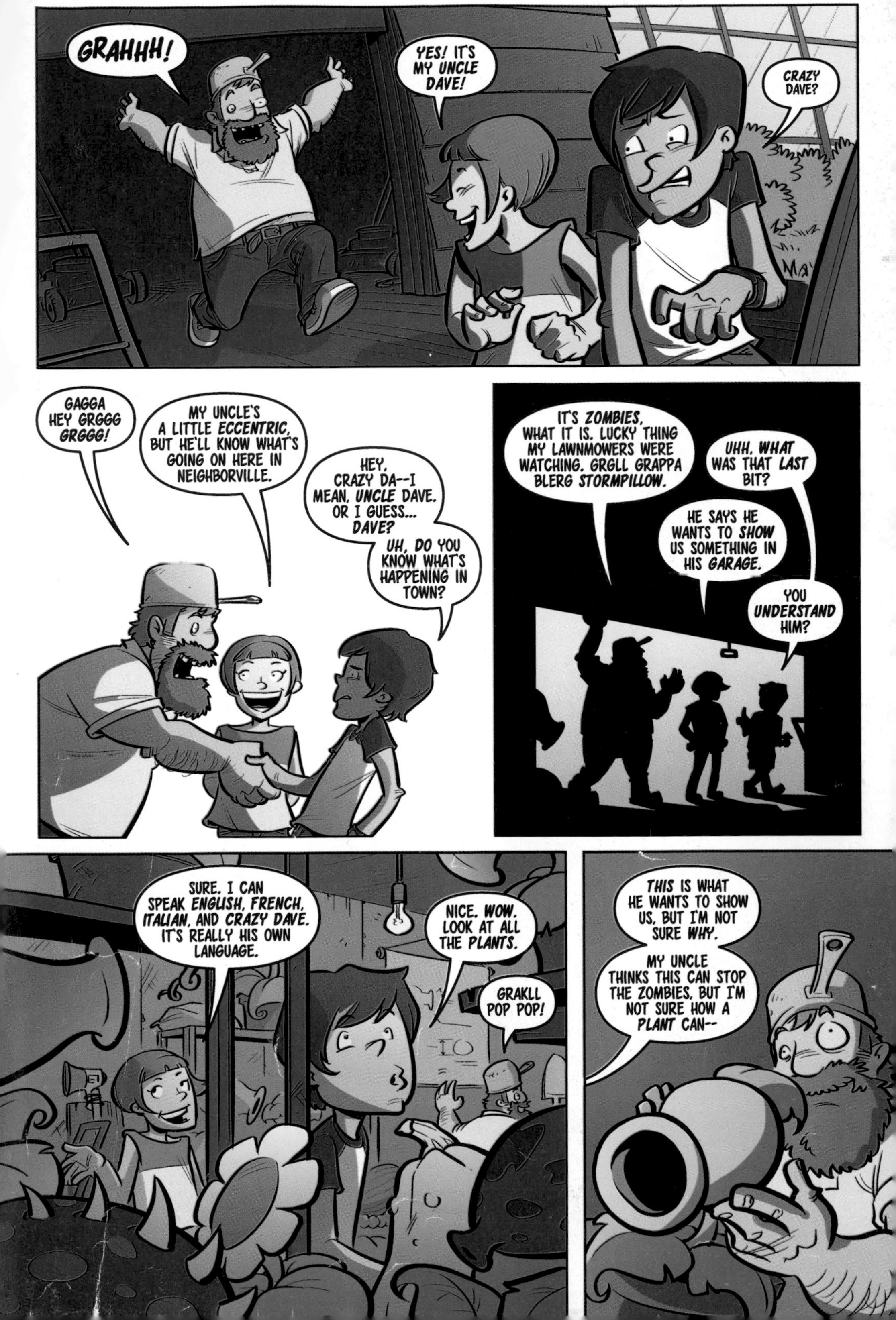
GRAHHH!
YES! IT'S MY UNCLE DAVE!
CRAZY DAVE?
GAGGA HEY GRGGG GRGGG!
MY UNCLE'S A LITTLE ECCENTRIC, BUT HE'LL KNOW WHAT'S GOING ON HERE IN NEIGHBORVILLE.
HEY, CRAZY DA--I MEAN, UNCLE DAVE. OR I GUESS... DAVE?
UH, DO YOU KNOW WHAT'S HAPPENING IN TOWN?
IT'S ZOMBIES, WHAT IT IS. LUCKY THING MY LAWNMOWERS WERE WATCHING. GRGLL GRAPPA BLERG STORMPILLOW.
UHH, WHAT WAS THAT LAST BIT?
HE SAYS HE WANTS TO SHOW US SOMETHING IN HIS GARAGE.
YOU UNDERSTAND HIM?
SURE. I CAN SPEAK ENGLISH, FRENCH, ITALIAN, AND CRAZY DAVE. IT'S REALLY HIS OWN LANGUAGE.
NICE. WOW. LOOK AT ALL THE PLANTS.
GRAKLL POP POP!
THIS IS WHAT HE WANTS TO SHOW US, BUT I'M NOT SURE WHY.
MY UNCLE THINKS THIS CAN STOP THE ZOMBIES, BUT I'M NOT SURE HOW A PLANT CAN--

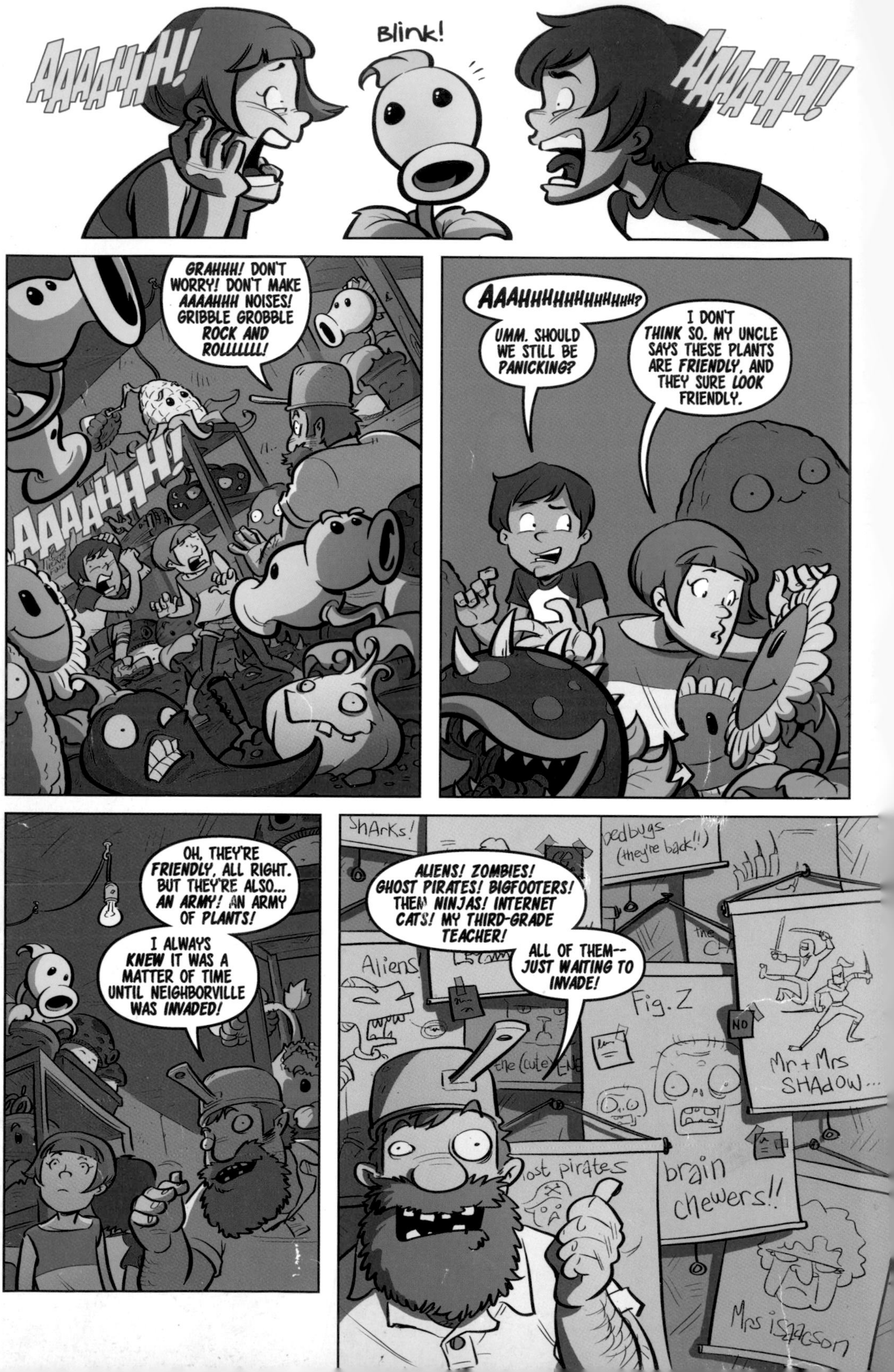
AAAAHHH!
Blink!
AAAAHHH!
GRAHHH! DON'T WORRY! DON'T MAKE AAAAHHH NOISES! GRIBBLE GROBBLE ROCK AND ROLLLLLLL!
AAAAHHH!
AAAHHHHHHHHHHHH?
UMM. SHOULD WE STILL BE PANICKING?
I DON'T THINK SO. MY UNCLE SAYS THESE PLANTS ARE FRIENDLY, AND THEY SURE LOOK FRIENDLY.
OH, THEY'RE FRIENDLY, ALL RIGHT. BUT THEY'RE ALSO... AN ARMY! AN ARMY OF PLANTS!
I ALWAYS KNEW IT WAS A MATTER OF TIME UNTIL NEIGHBORVILLE WAS INVADED!
ALIENS! ZOMBIES! GHOST PIRATES! BIGFOOTERS! THEM NINJAS! INTERNET CATS! MY THIRD-GRADE TEACHER!
ALL OF THEM-- JUST WAITING TO INVADE!
ShArks!
bedbugs (they're back!!)
Aliens!
Fig. Z
NO
Mr + Mrs SHADOW...
brain chewers!!
Mrs isaacson

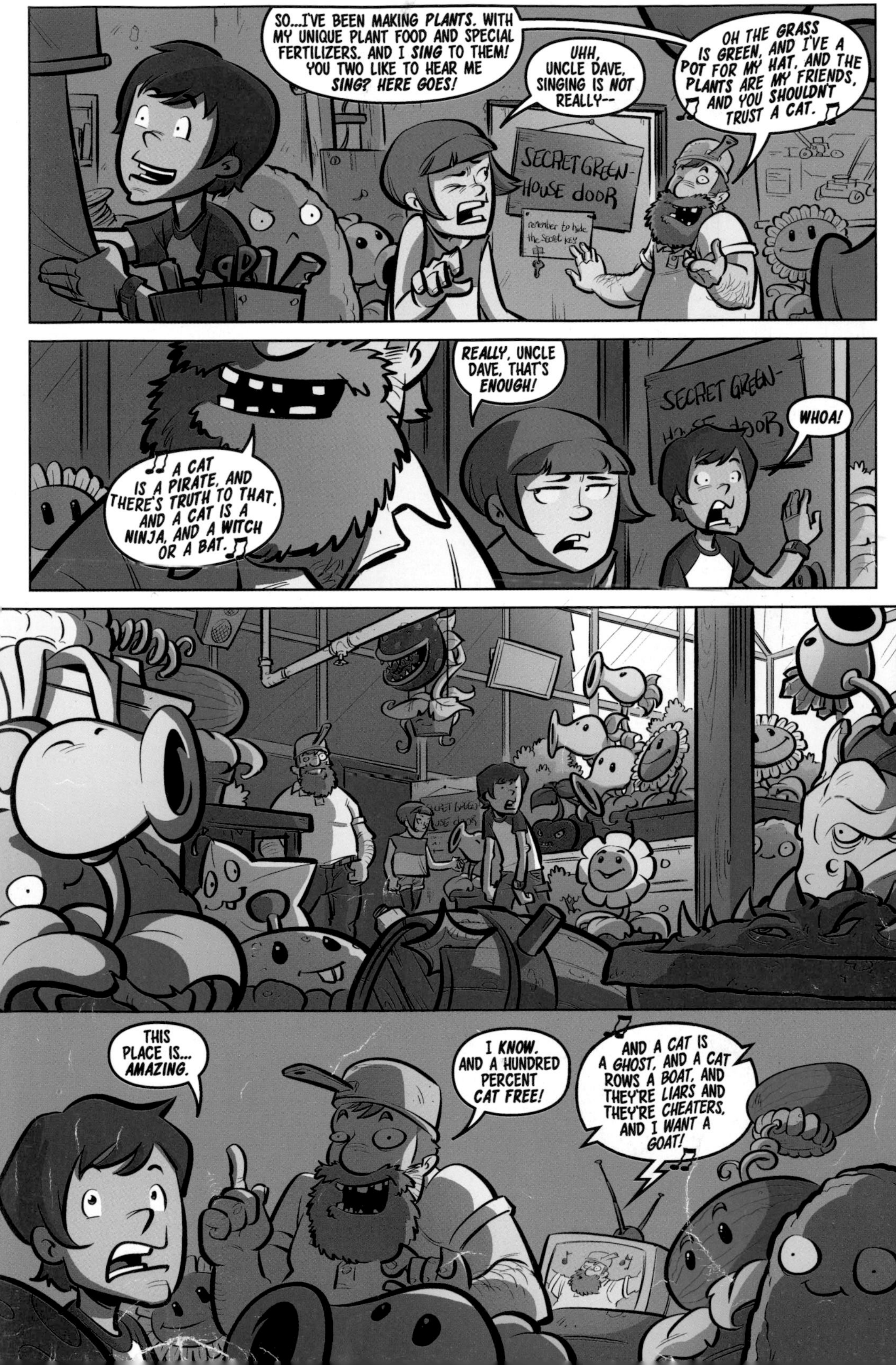
SO...I'VE BEEN MAKING PLANTS. WITH MY UNIQUE PLANT FOOD AND SPECIAL FERTILIZERS. AND I SING TO THEM! YOU TWO LIKE TO HEAR ME SING? HERE GOES!
UHH, UNCLE DAVE, SINGING IS NOT REALLY--
OH THE GRASS IS GREEN, AND I'VE A POT FOR MY HAT, AND THE PLANTS ARE MY FRIENDS, AND YOU SHOULDN'T TRUST A CAT.
SECRET GREEN-HOUSE door
remember to hide the Secret key
A CAT IS A PIRATE, AND THERE'S TRUTH TO THAT, AND A CAT IS A NINJA, AND A WITCH OR A BAT.
REALLY, UNCLE DAVE, THAT'S ENOUGH!
WHOA!
THIS PLACE IS... AMAZING.
I KNOW. AND A HUNDRED PERCENT CAT FREE!
AND A CAT IS A GHOST, AND A CAT ROWS A BOAT, AND THEY'RE LIARS AND THEY'RE CHEATERS, AND I WANT A GOAT!

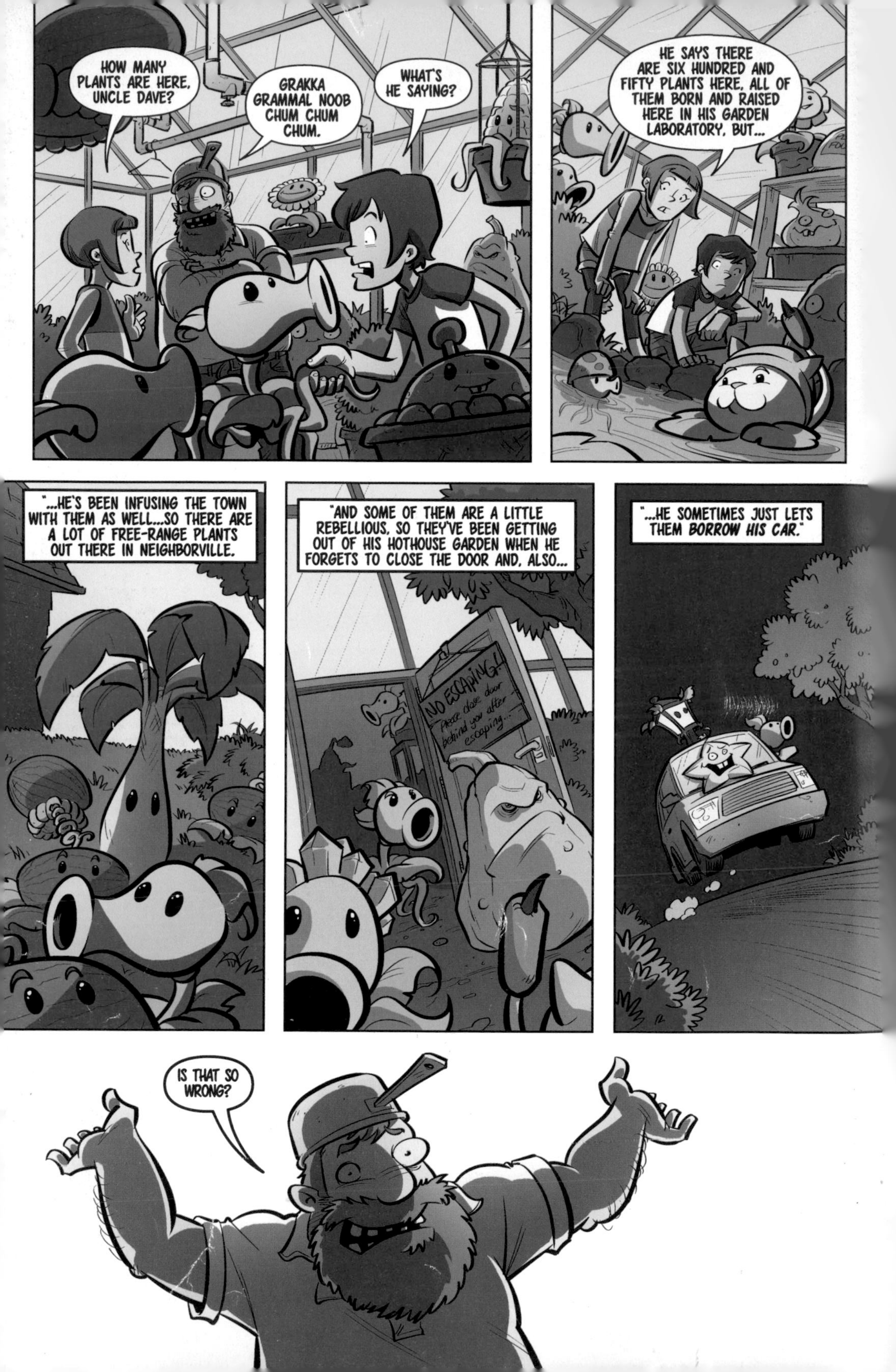
HOW MANY PLANTS ARE HERE, UNCLE DAVE?
GRAKKA GRAMMAL NOOB CHUM CHUM CHUM.
WHAT'S HE SAYING?
HE SAYS THERE ARE SIX HUNDRED AND FIFTY PLANTS HERE, ALL OF THEM BORN AND RAISED HERE IN HIS GARDEN LABORATORY, BUT...
"...HE'S BEEN INFUSING THE TOWN WITH THEM AS WELL...SO THERE ARE A LOT OF FREE-RANGE PLANTS OUT THERE IN NEIGHBORVILLE.
"AND SOME OF THEM ARE A LITTLE REBELLIOUS, SO THEY'VE BEEN GETTING OUT OF HIS HOTHOUSE GARDEN WHEN HE FORGETS TO CLOSE THE DOOR AND, ALSO...
NO ESCAPING!
Please close door behind you after escaping...
"...HE SOMETIMES JUST LETS THEM BORROW HIS CAR."
IS THAT SO WRONG?

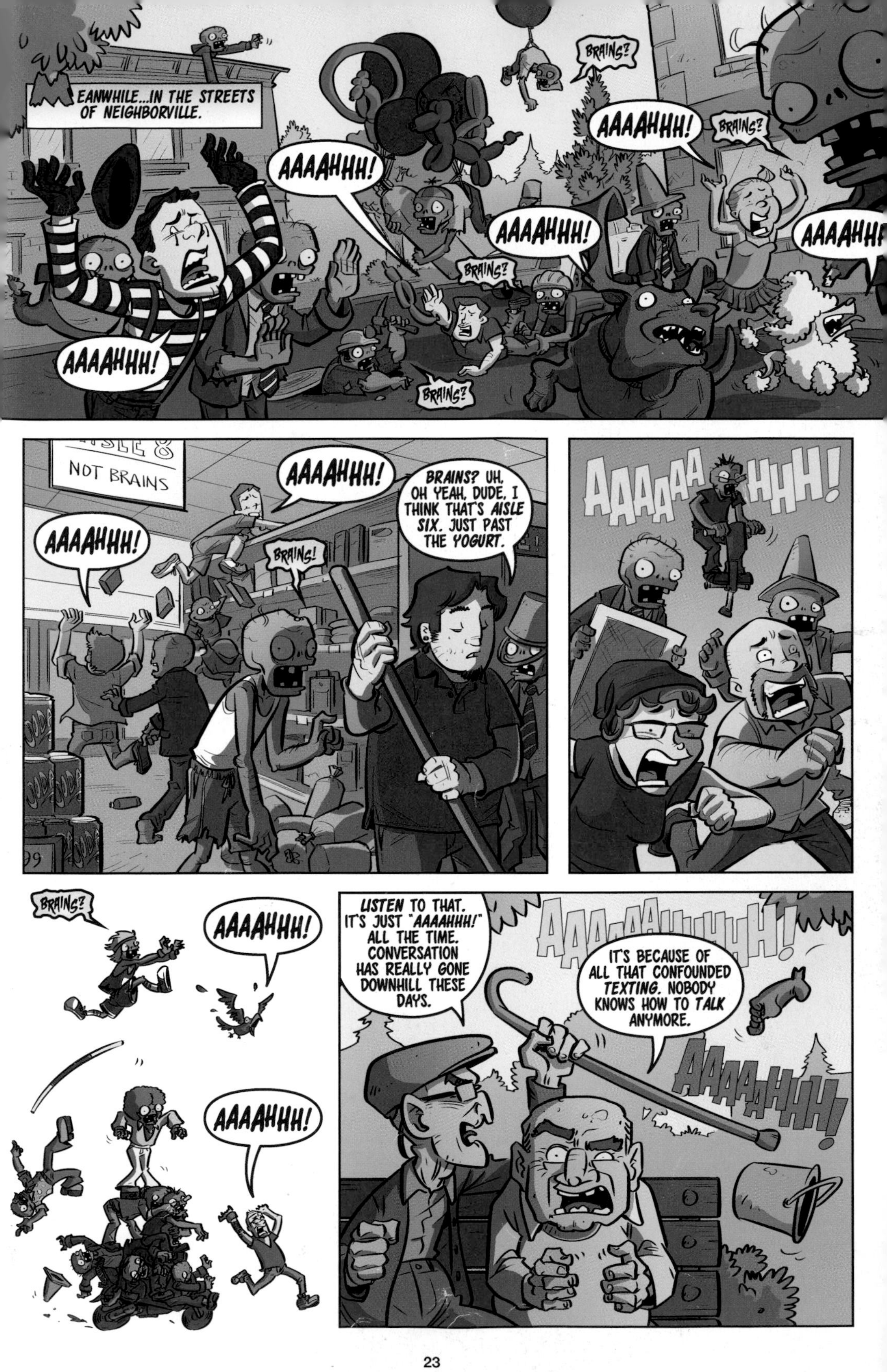
MEANWHILE...IN THE STREETS OF NEIGHBORVILLE.
BRAINS?
AAAAHHH!
BRAINS?
AAAAHHH!
AAAAHHH!
BRAINS?
AAAAHHH!
AAAAHHH!
BRAINS?
BRAINS?
AISLE 8
NOT BRAINS
AAAAHHH!
AAAAHHH!
BRAINS!
BRAINS? UH, OH YEAH, DUDE, I THINK THAT'S AISLE SIX. JUST PAST THE YOGURT.
AAAAAAHHH!
BRAINS?
AAAAHHH!
AAAAHHH!
LISTEN TO THAT. IT'S JUST "AAAAHHH!" ALL THE TIME. CONVERSATION HAS REALLY GONE DOWNHILL THESE DAYS.
AAAAAAHHHH!
IT'S BECAUSE OF ALL THAT CONFOUNDED TEXTING. NOBODY KNOWS HOW TO TALK ANYMORE.
AAAAAHHHH!

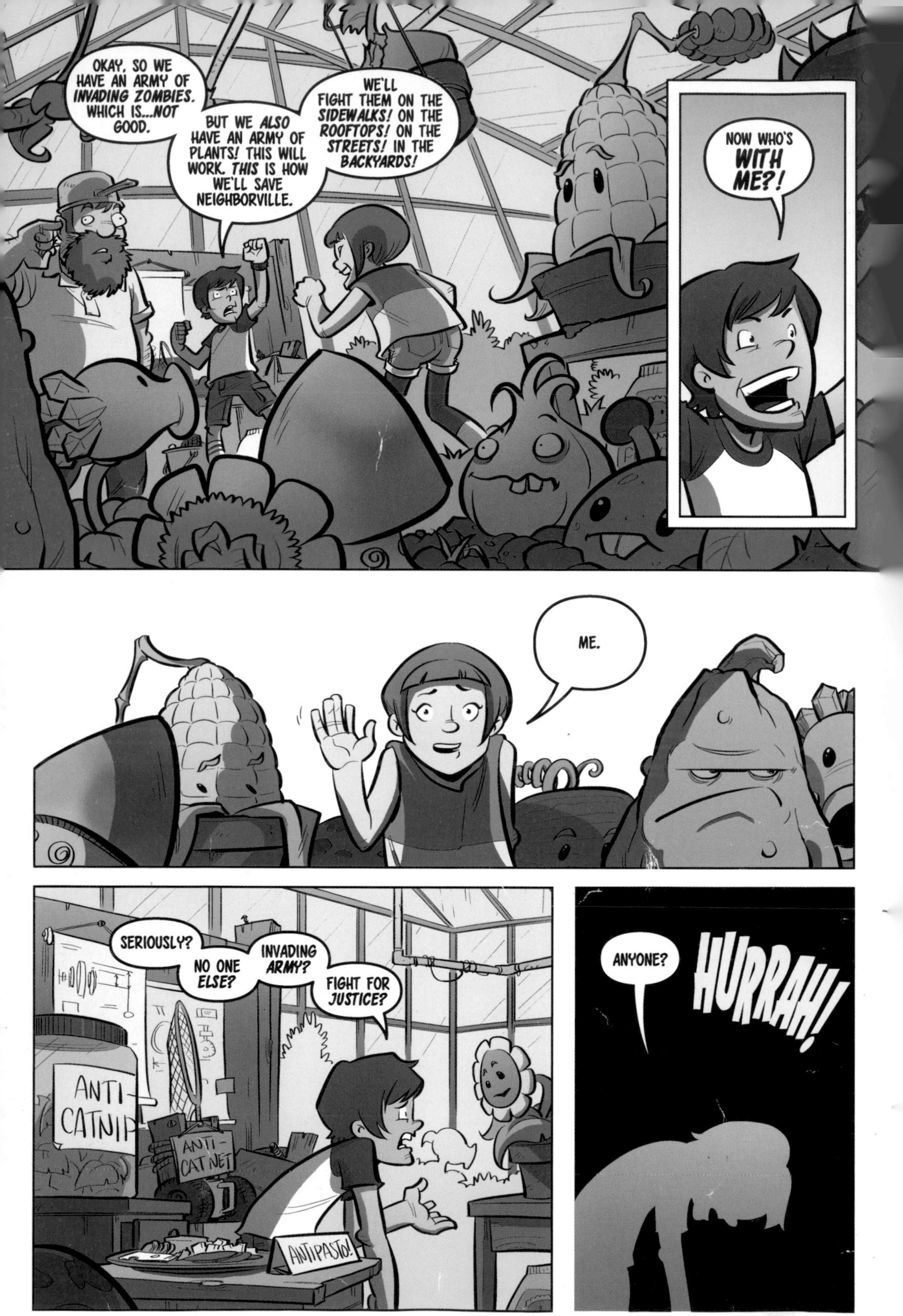
OKAY, SO WE HAVE AN ARMY OF INVADING ZOMBIES. WHICH IS...NOT GOOD.
BUT WE ALSO HAVE AN ARMY OF PLANTS! THIS WILL WORK. THIS IS HOW WE'LL SAVE NEIGHBORVILLE.
WE'LL FIGHT THEM ON THE SIDEWALKS! ON THE ROOFTOPS! ON THE STREETS! IN THE BACKYARDS!
NOW WHO'S WITH ME?!
ME.
SERIOUSLY?
NO ONE ELSE?
INVADING ARMY?
FIGHT FOR JUSTICE?
ANTI CATNIP
ANTI-CAT NET
ANTIPASTO!
ANYONE?
HURRAH!

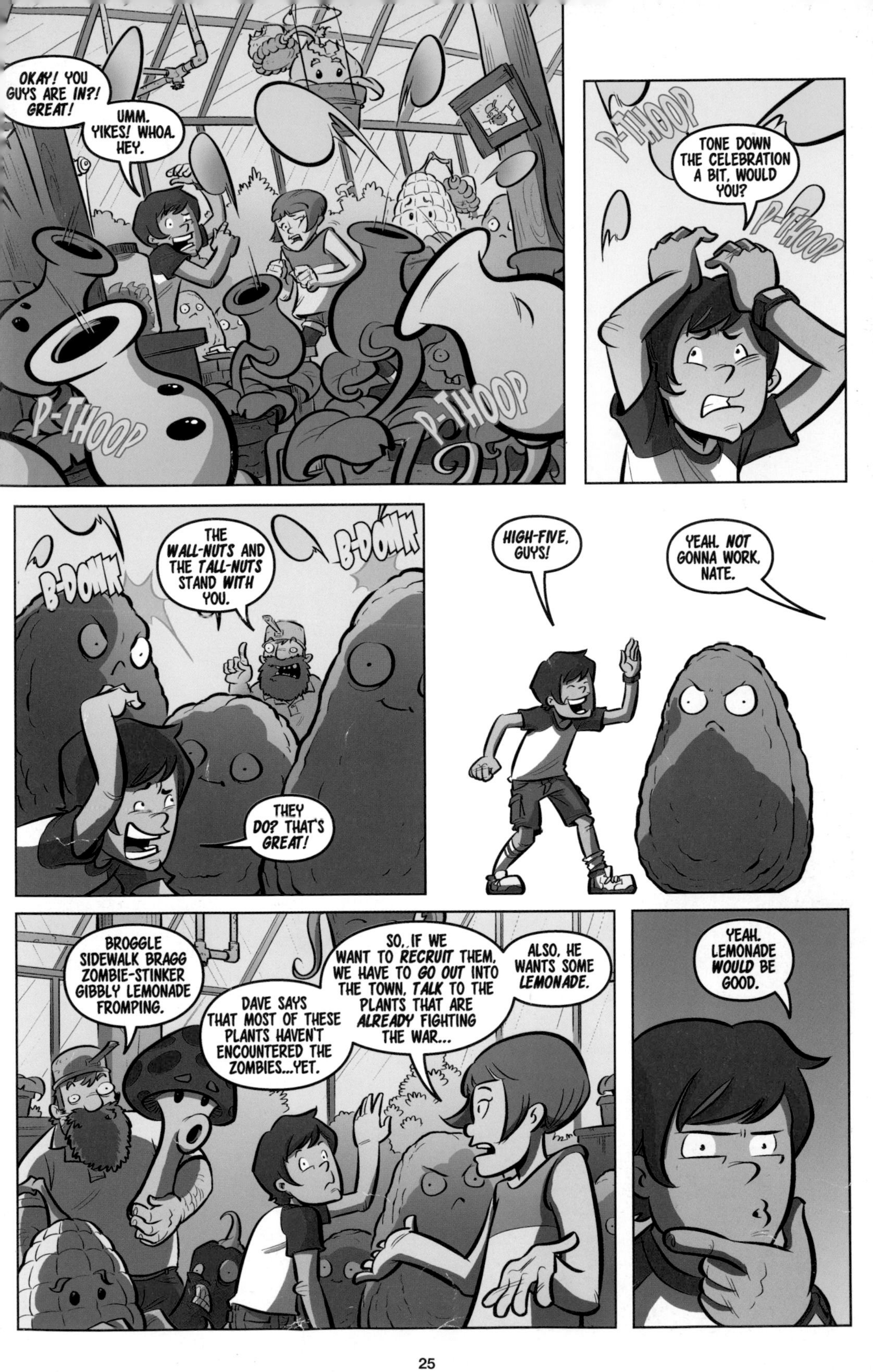
OKAY! YOU GUYS ARE IN?! GREAT!
UMM. YIKES! WHOA. HEY.
P-THOOP
P-THOOP
P-THOOP
TONE DOWN THE CELEBRATION A BIT, WOULD YOU?
P-THOOP
B-DONK
THE WALL-NUTS AND THE TALL-NUTS STAND WITH YOU.
B-DONK
THEY DO? THAT'S GREAT!
HIGH-FIVE, GUYS!
YEAH. NOT GONNA WORK, NATE.
BROGGLE SIDEWALK BRAGG ZOMBIE-STINKER GIBBLY LEMONADE FROMPING.
DAVE SAYS THAT MOST OF THESE PLANTS HAVEN'T ENCOUNTERED THE ZOMBIES...YET.
SO, IF WE WANT TO RECRUIT THEM, WE HAVE TO GO OUT INTO THE TOWN, TALK TO THE PLANTS THAT ARE ALREADY FIGHTING THE WAR...
ALSO, HE WANTS SOME LEMONADE.
YEAH. LEMONADE WOULD BE GOOD.

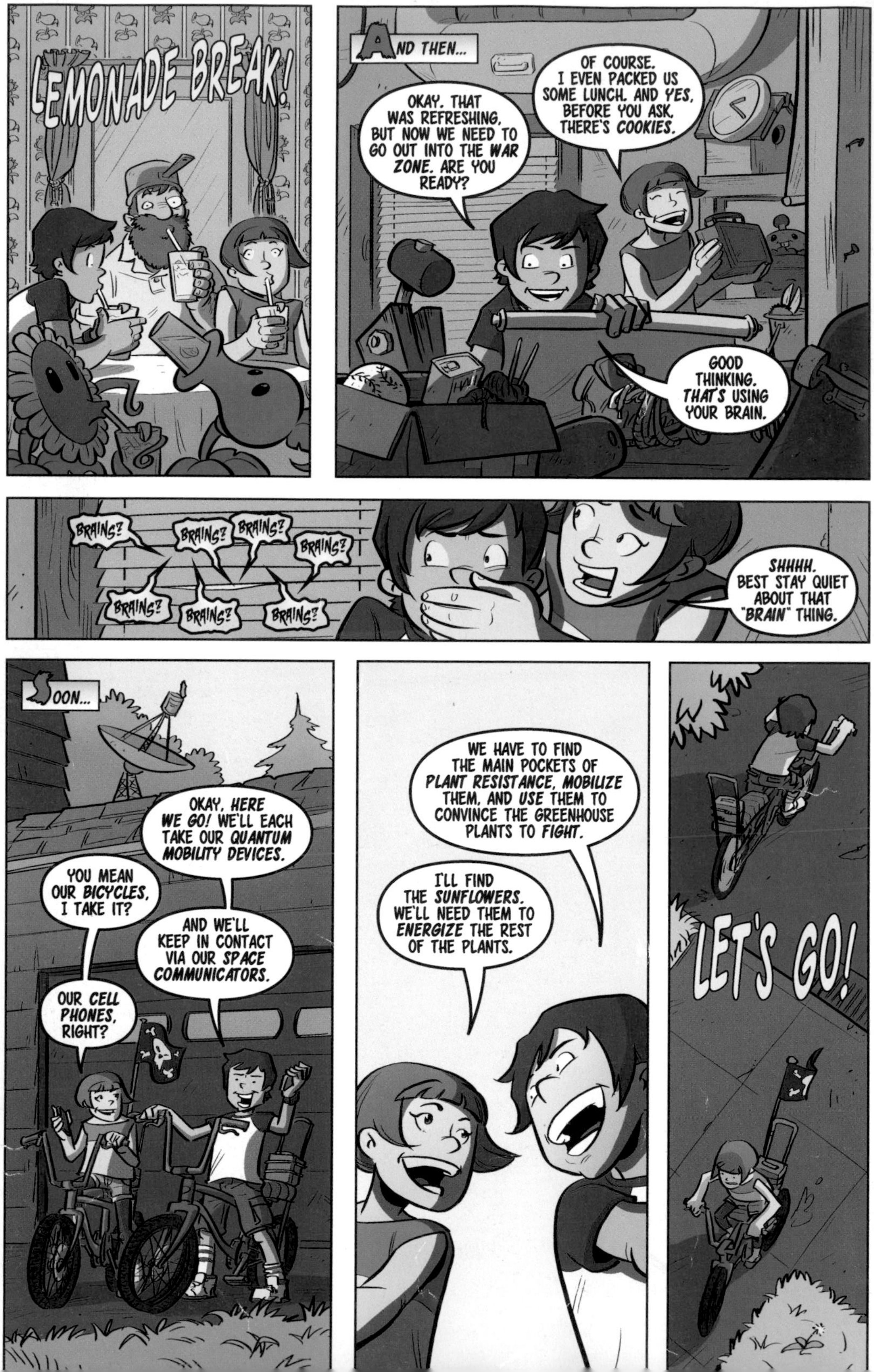
LEMONADE BREAK!
AND THEN...
OKAY. THAT WAS REFRESHING, BUT NOW WE NEED TO GO OUT INTO THE WAR ZONE. ARE YOU READY?
OF COURSE. I EVEN PACKED US SOME LUNCH. AND YES, BEFORE YOU ASK, THERE'S COOKIES.
GOOD THINKING. THAT'S USING YOUR BRAIN.
BRAINS?
BRAINS?
BRAINS?
BRAINS?
BRAINS?
BRAINS?
BRAINS?
SHHHH. BEST STAY QUIET ABOUT THAT "BRAIN" THING.
SOON...
OKAY, HERE WE GO! WE'LL EACH TAKE OUR QUANTUM MOBILITY DEVICES.
YOU MEAN OUR BICYCLES, I TAKE IT?
AND WE'LL KEEP IN CONTACT VIA OUR SPACE COMMUNICATORS.
OUR CELL PHONES, RIGHT?
WE HAVE TO FIND THE MAIN POCKETS OF PLANT RESISTANCE, MOBILIZE THEM, AND USE THEM TO CONVINCE THE GREENHOUSE PLANTS TO FIGHT.
I'LL FIND THE SUNFLOWERS. WE'LL NEED THEM TO ENERGIZE THE REST OF THE PLANTS.
LET'S GO!

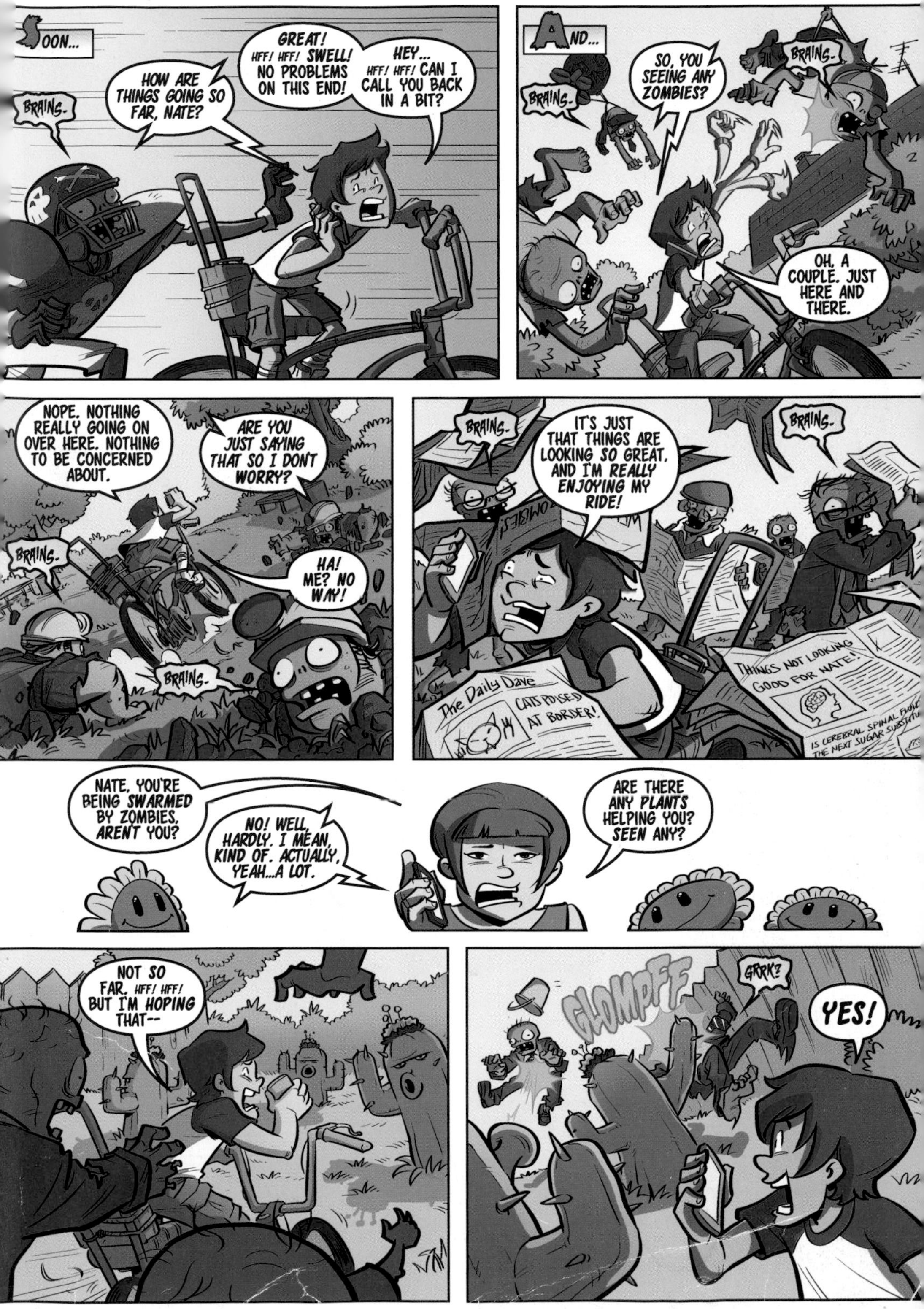
SOON...
BRAINS.
HOW ARE THINGS GOING SO FAR, NATE?
GREAT! HFF! HFF! SWELL! NO PROBLEMS ON THIS END!
HEY... HFF! HFF! CAN I CALL YOU BACK IN A BIT?
AND...
BRAINS.
SO, YOU SEEING ANY ZOMBIES?
BRAINS.
OH, A COUPLE. JUST HERE AND THERE.
NOPE. NOTHING REALLY GOING ON OVER HERE. NOTHING TO BE CONCERNED ABOUT.
ARE YOU JUST SAYING THAT SO I DON'T WORRY?
BRAINS.
HA! ME? NO WAY!
BRAINS.
BRAINS.
IT'S JUST THAT THINGS ARE LOOKING SO GREAT, AND I'M REALLY ENJOYING MY RIDE!
BRAINS.
The Daily Dave
CATS POISED AT BORDER!
THINGS NOT LOOKING GOOD FOR NATE!
NATE, YOU'RE BEING SWARMED BY ZOMBIES, AREN'T YOU?
NO! WELL, HARDLY. I MEAN, KIND OF. ACTUALLY, YEAH...A LOT.
ARE THERE ANY PLANTS HELPING YOU? SEEN ANY?
NOT SO FAR. HFF! HFF! BUT I'M HOPING THAT--
GLOMPFF
GRRK?
YES!

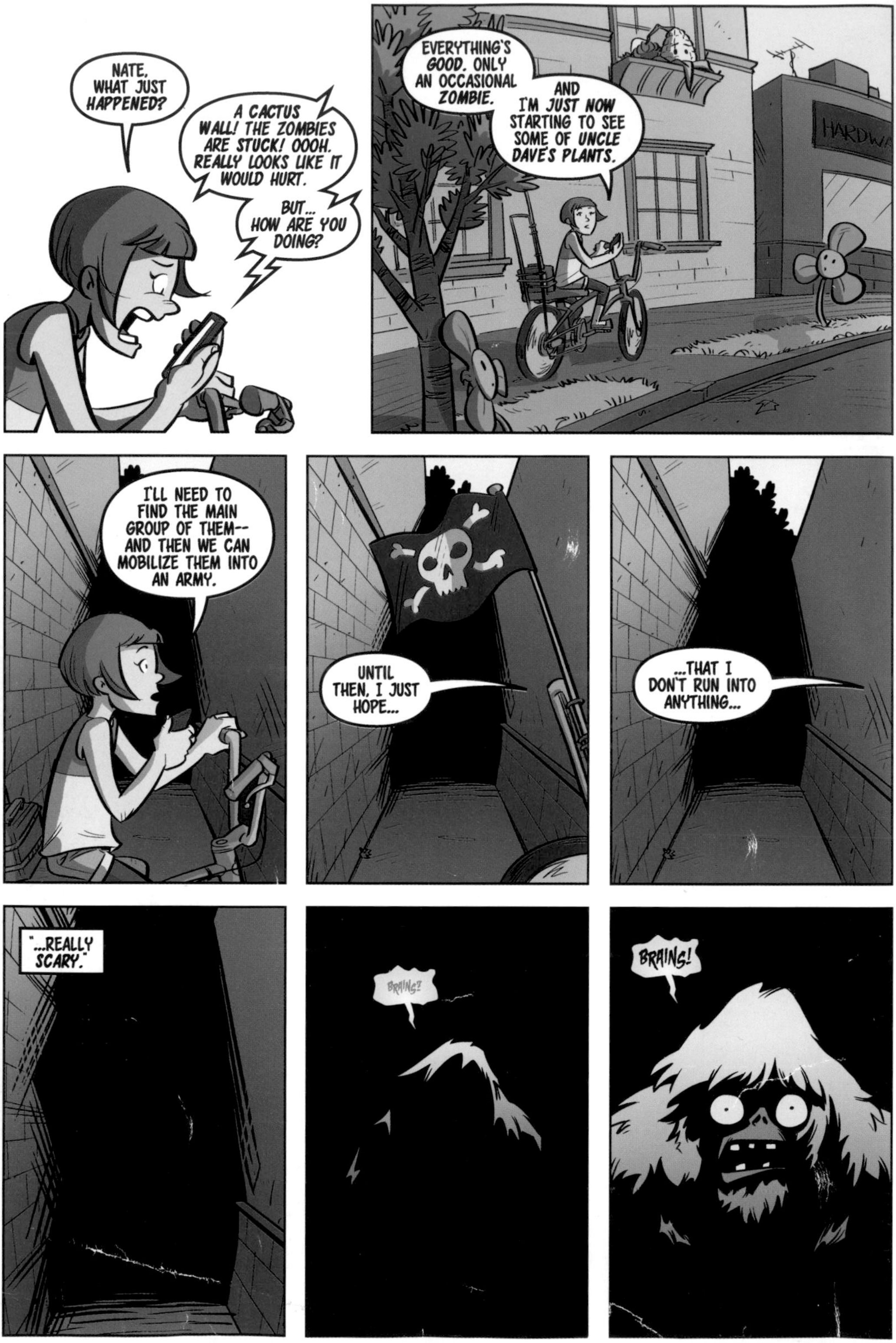
NATE, WHAT JUST HAPPENED?
A CACTUS WALL! THE ZOMBIES ARE STUCK! OOOH. REALLY LOOKS LIKE IT WOULD HURT.
BUT... HOW ARE YOU DOING?
EVERYTHING'S GOOD. ONLY AN OCCASIONAL ZOMBIE.
AND I'M JUST NOW STARTING TO SEE SOME OF UNCLE DAVE'S PLANTS.
HARDWA
I'LL NEED TO FIND THE MAIN GROUP OF THEM--AND THEN WE CAN MOBILIZE THEM INTO AN ARMY.
UNTIL THEN, I JUST HOPE...
...THAT I DON'T RUN INTO ANYTHING...
"...REALLY SCARY."
BRAINS?
BRAINS!

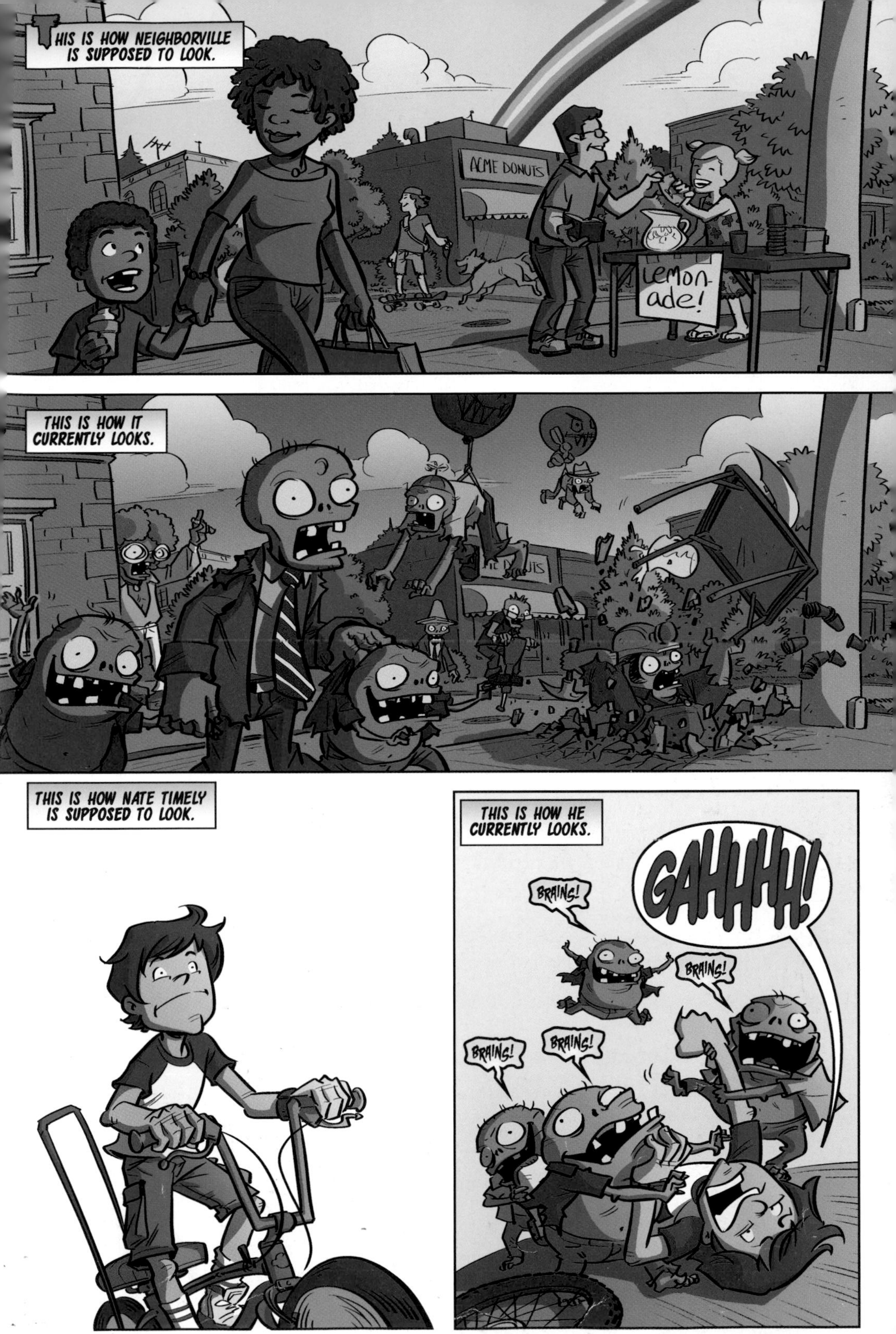
THIS IS HOW NEIGHBORVILLE IS SUPPOSED TO LOOK.
ACME DONUTS
lemon-ade!
THIS IS HOW IT CURRENTLY LOOKS.
THIS IS HOW NATE TIMELY IS SUPPOSED TO LOOK.
THIS IS HOW HE CURRENTLY LOOKS.
GAHHHH!
BRAINS!
BRAINS!
BRAINS!
BRAINS!

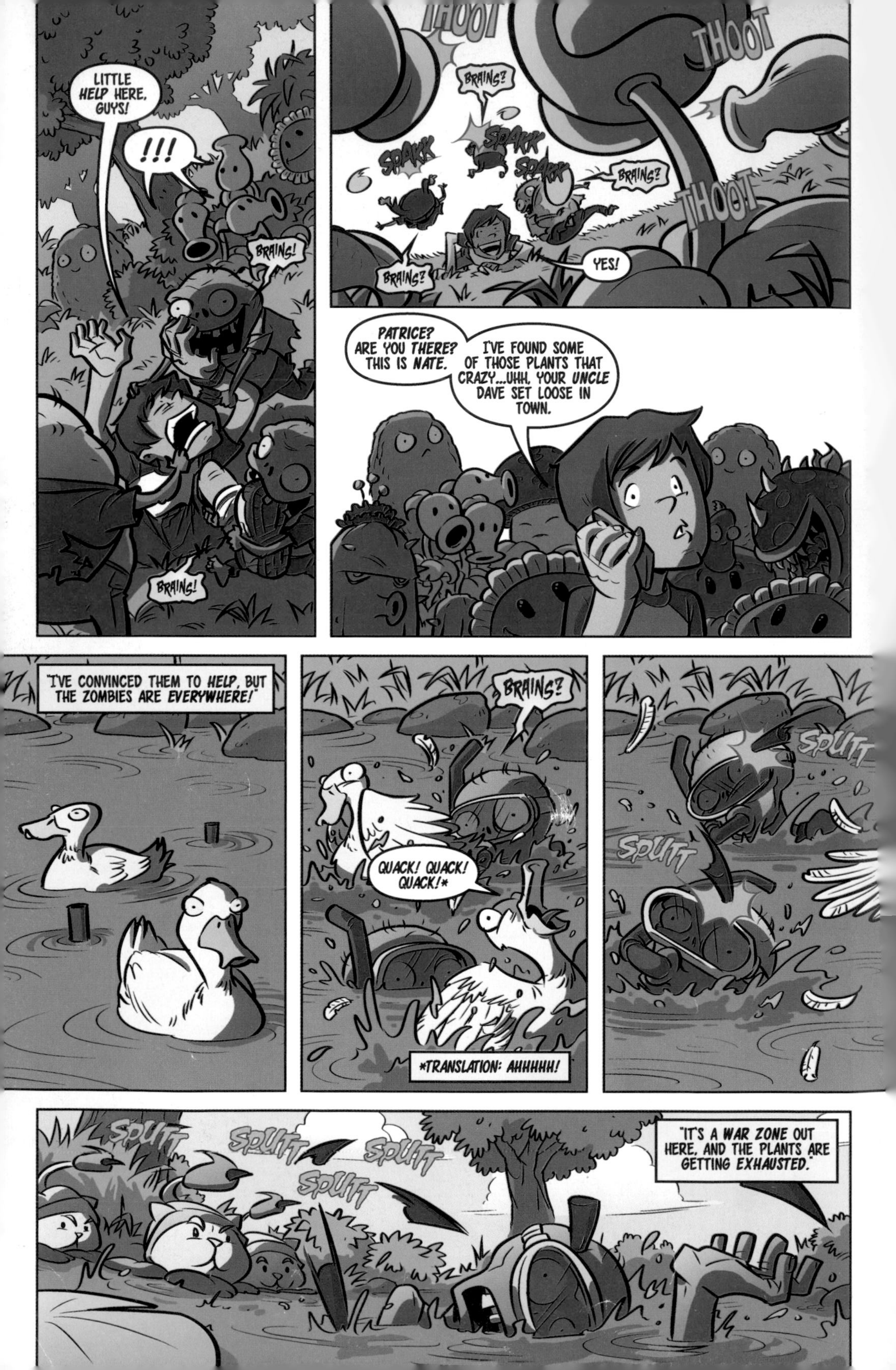
LITTLE HELP HERE, GUYS!
!!!
BRAINS!
BRAINS!
THOOT
THOOT
BRAINS?
SPAKK
SPAKK
SPAKK
BRAINS?
THOOT
BRAINS?
YES!
PATRICE? ARE YOU THERE? THIS IS NATE.
I'VE FOUND SOME OF THOSE PLANTS THAT CRAZY...UHH, YOUR UNCLE DAVE SET LOOSE IN TOWN.
"I'VE CONVINCED THEM TO HELP, BUT THE ZOMBIES ARE EVERYWHERE!"
BRAINS?
QUACK! QUACK! QUACK!*
*TRANSLATION: AHHHHH!
SPUTT
SPUTT
SPUTT
SPUTT
SPUTT
SPUTT
"IT'S A WAR ZONE OUT HERE, AND THE PLANTS ARE GETTING EXHAUSTED."

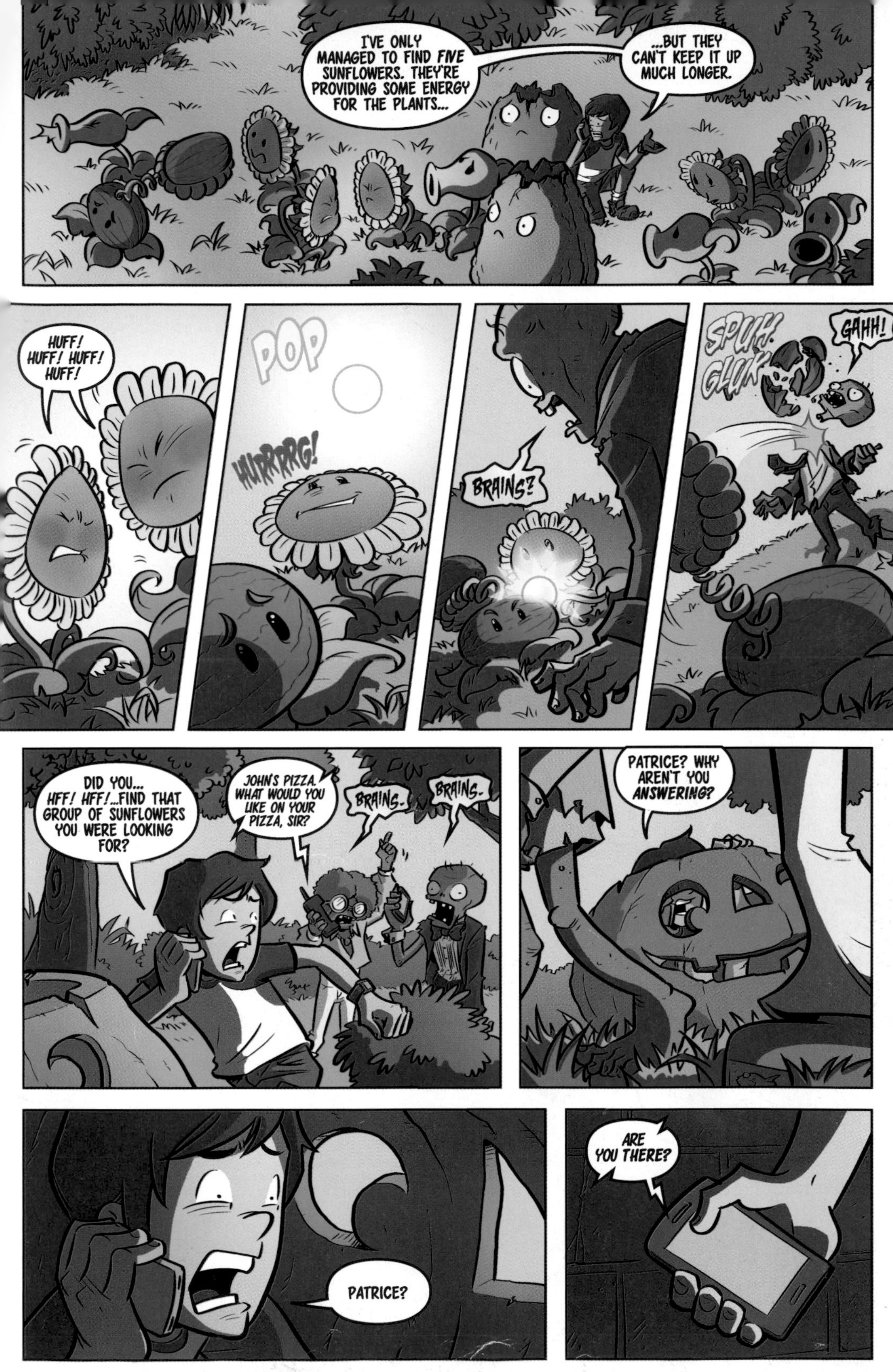

I'VE ONLY MANAGED TO FIND FIVE SUNFLOWERS. THEY'RE PROVIDING SOME ENERGY FOR THE PLANTS...
...BUT THEY CAN'T KEEP IT UP MUCH LONGER.
HUFF! HUFF! HUFF! HUFF!
POP
HURRRRG!
BRAINS?
SPUH. GLUK
GAHH!
DID YOU... HFF! HFF!...FIND THAT GROUP OF SUNFLOWERS YOU WERE LOOKING FOR?
JOHN'S PIZZA. WHAT WOULD YOU LIKE ON YOUR PIZZA, SIR?
BRAINS.
BRAINS.
PATRICE? WHY AREN'T YOU ANSWERING?
PATRICE?
ARE YOU THERE?

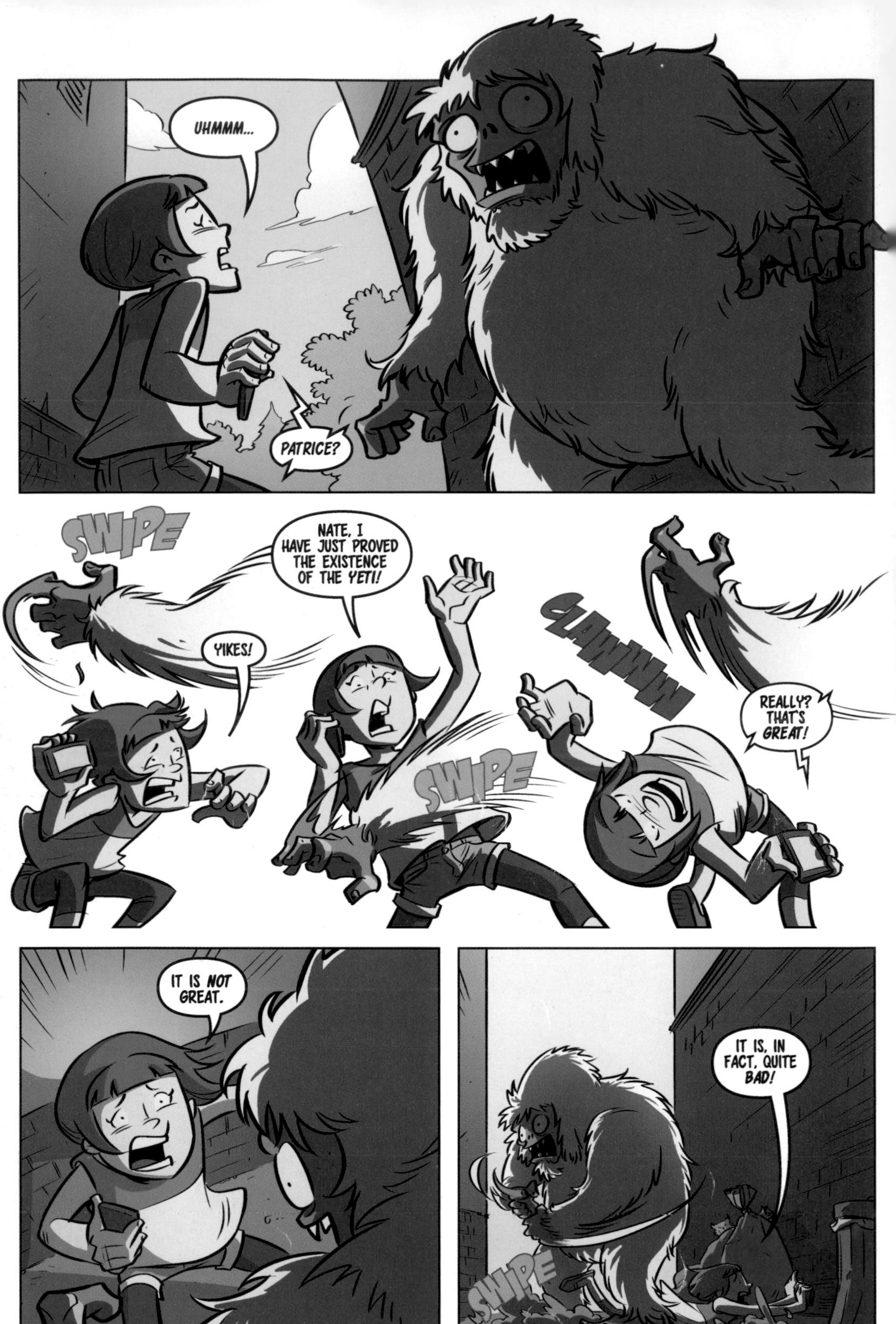
UHMMM...
PATRICE?
SWIPE
NATE, I HAVE JUST PROVED THE EXISTENCE OF THE YETI!
YIKES!
CLAWWW
REALLY? THAT'S GREAT!
SWIPE
IT IS NOT GREAT.
IT IS, IN FACT, QUITE BAD!
SWIPE

GOTTA RUN--THIS WAY!

OR NOT.

RWOWRR

SSSSTT

SKRASHHH

OKAY, THEN, THIS WAY!!

RAIN JUICE

POWWW!!

AMAZO THE CLOWN

OR...NOT.

RAIN JUICE

POWWW!!

AMAZO CLO

TRAPPED! SO MUCH FOR PLAN A.

I WAS HOPING TO AVOID MY PLAN B OF SCREAMING FOR...

...HELP?

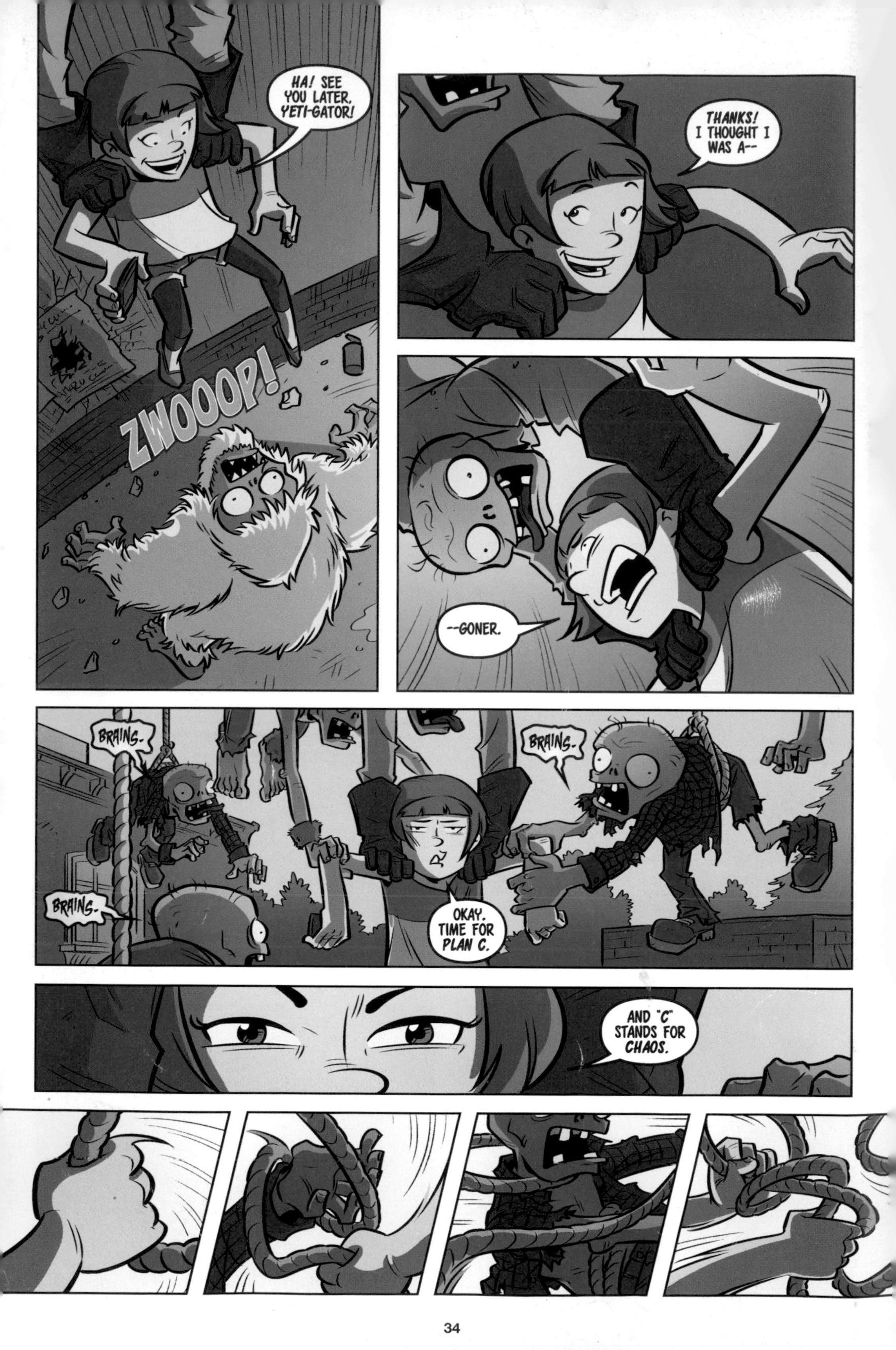
HA! SEE YOU LATER, YETI-GATOR!
ZWOOOP!
THANKS! I THOUGHT I WAS A--
--GONER.
BRAINS.
BRAINS.
BRAINS.
OKAY. TIME FOR PLAN C.
AND "C" STANDS FOR CHAOS.

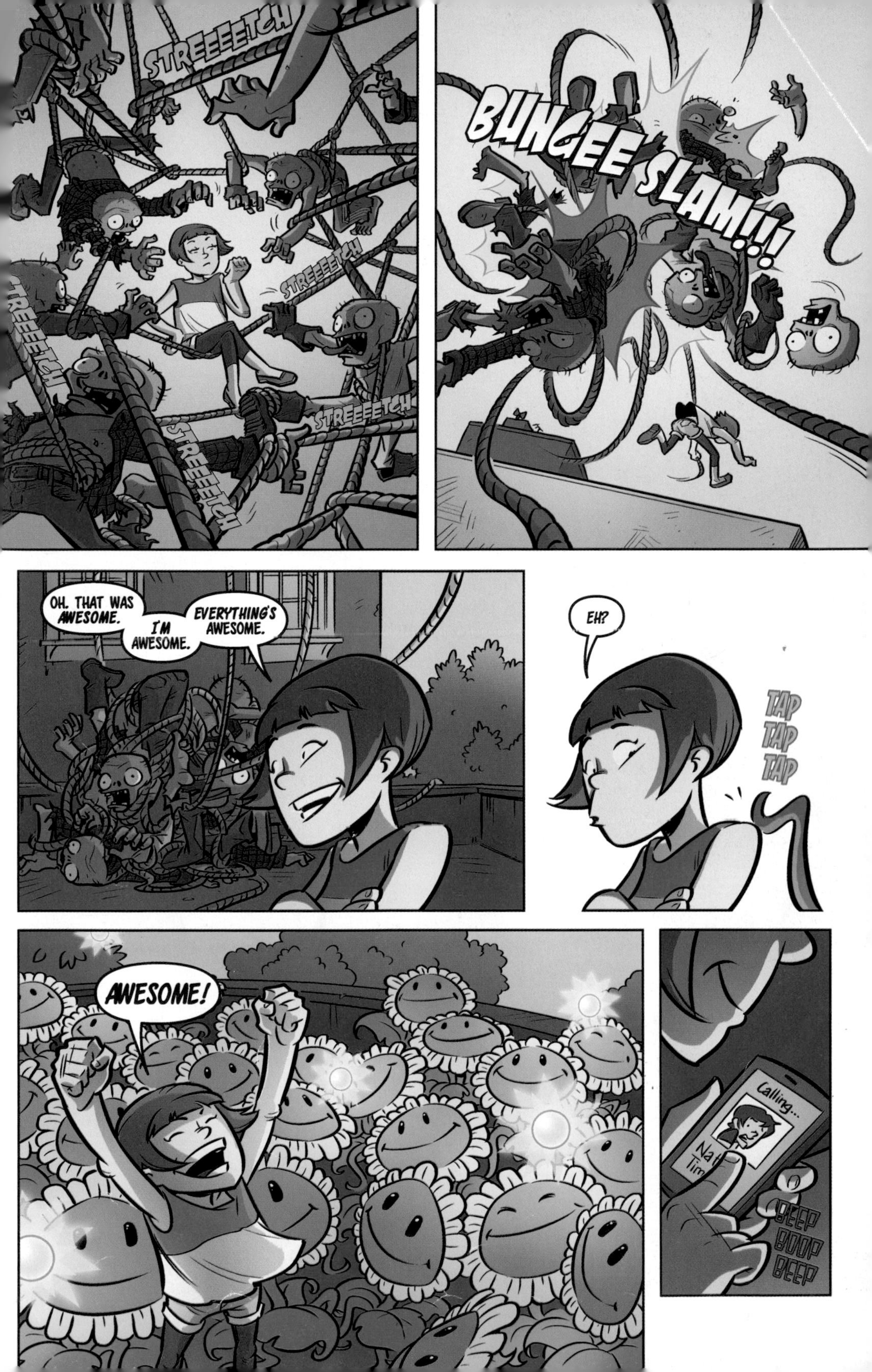
STREEEETCH
STREEEETCH
STREEEETCH
STREEEETCH
STREEEETCH
STREEEETCH
BUNGEE SLAM!!!
OH. THAT WAS AWESOME.
I'M AWESOME.
EVERYTHING'S AWESOME.
EH?
TAP TAP TAP
AWESOME!
Calling...
BEEP BOOP BEEP

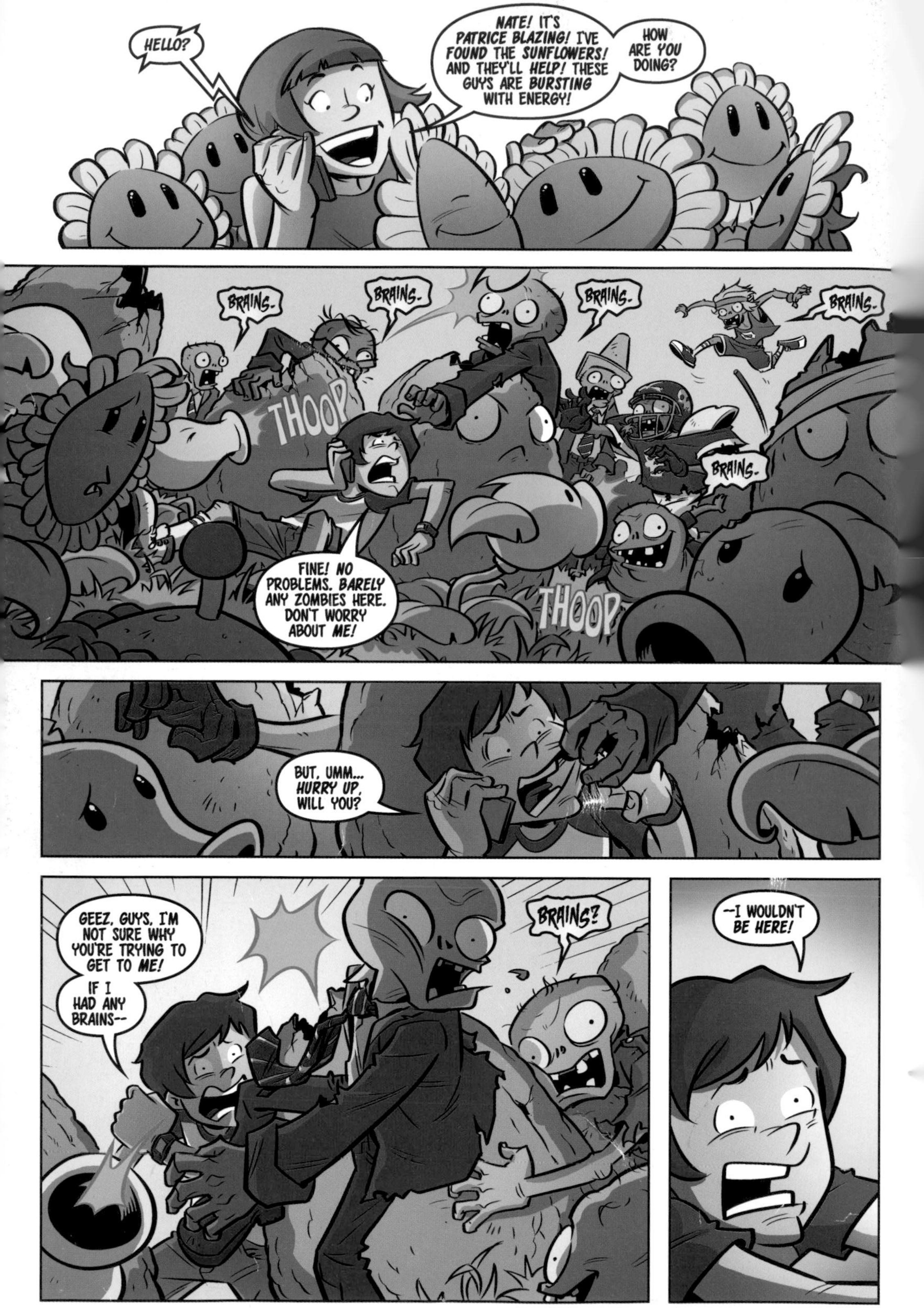
HELLO?
NATE! IT'S PATRICE BLAZING! I'VE FOUND THE SUNFLOWERS! AND THEY'LL HELP! THESE GUYS ARE BURSTING WITH ENERGY!
HOW ARE YOU DOING?
BRAINS.
BRAINS.
BRAINS.
BRAINS.
THOOP
BRAINS.
FINE! NO PROBLEMS. BARELY ANY ZOMBIES HERE. DON'T WORRY ABOUT ME!
THOOP
BUT, UMM... HURRY UP, WILL YOU?
GEEZ, GUYS, I'M NOT SURE WHY YOU'RE TRYING TO GET TO ME!
IF I HAD ANY BRAINS--
BRAINS?
--I WOULDN'T BE HERE!

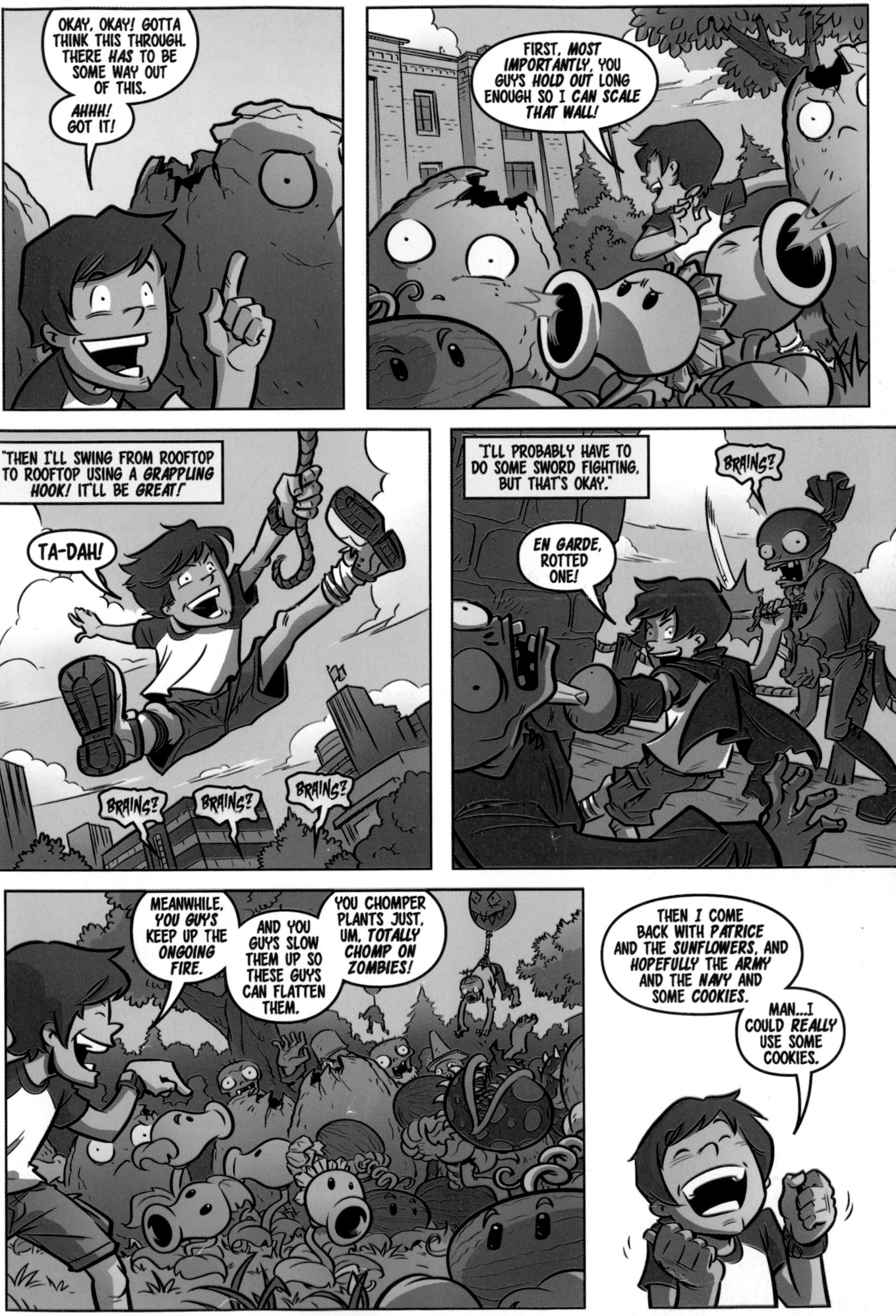
OKAY, OKAY! GOTTA THINK THIS THROUGH. THERE HAS TO BE SOME WAY OUT OF THIS.
AHHH! GOT IT!
FIRST, MOST IMPORTANTLY, YOU GUYS HOLD OUT LONG ENOUGH SO I CAN SCALE THAT WALL!
"THEN I'LL SWING FROM ROOFTOP TO ROOFTOP USING A GRAPPLING HOOK! IT'LL BE GREAT!"
TA-DAH!
BRAINS?
BRAINS?
BRAINS?
"I'LL PROBABLY HAVE TO DO SOME SWORD FIGHTING, BUT THAT'S OKAY."
BRAINS?
EN GARDE, ROTTED ONE!
MEANWHILE, YOU GUYS KEEP UP THE ONGOING FIRE.
AND YOU GUYS SLOW THEM UP SO THESE GUYS CAN FLATTEN THEM.
YOU CHOMPER PLANTS JUST, UM, TOTALLY CHOMP ON ZOMBIES!
THEN I COME BACK WITH PATRICE AND THE SUNFLOWERS, AND HOPEFULLY THE ARMY AND THE NAVY AND SOME COOKIES.
MAN...I COULD REALLY USE SOME COOKIES.

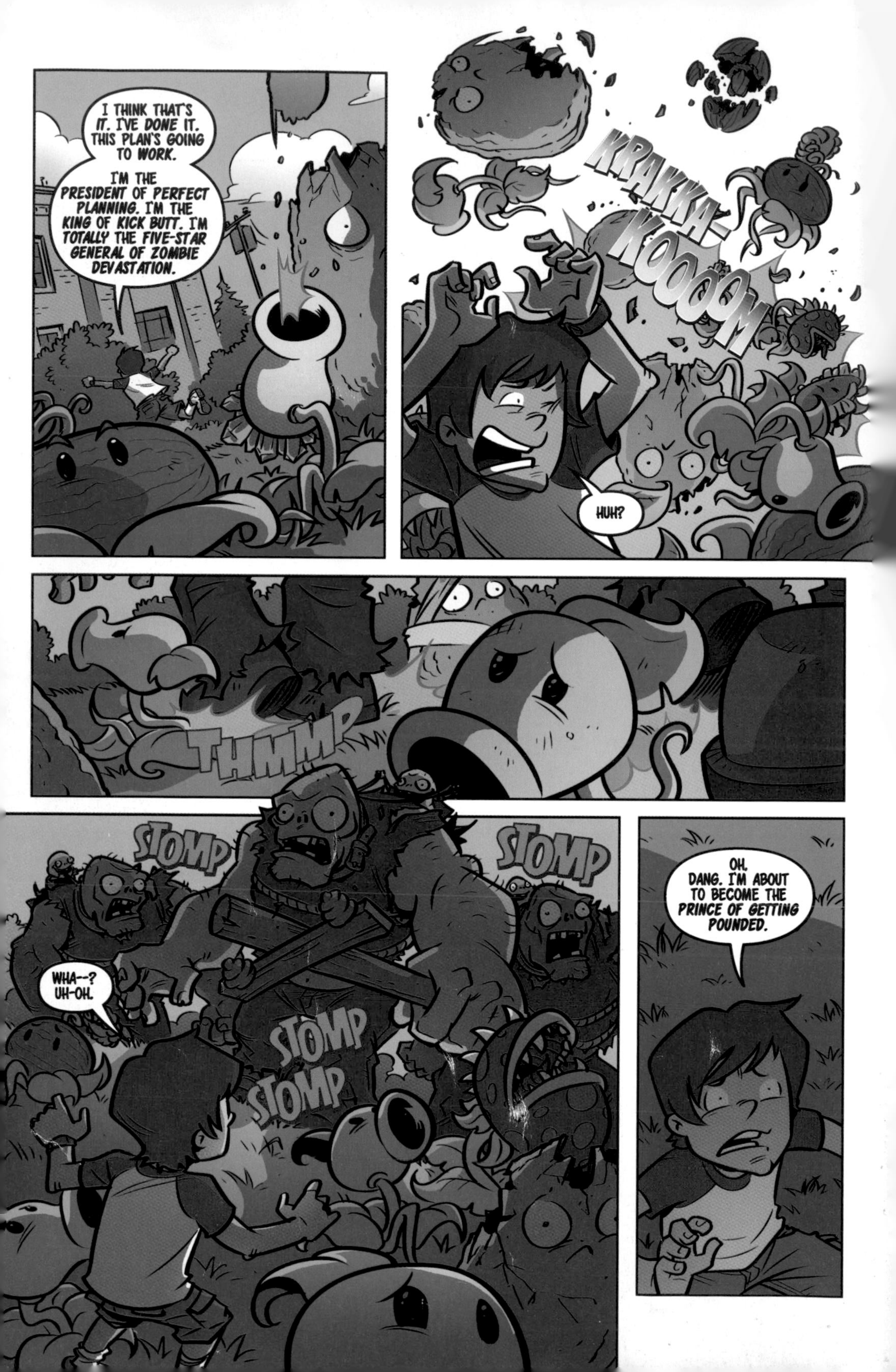
I THINK THAT'S IT. I'VE DONE IT. THIS PLAN'S GOING TO WORK.
I'M THE PRESIDENT OF PERFECT PLANNING. I'M THE KING OF KICK BUTT. I'M TOTALLY THE FIVE-STAR GENERAL OF ZOMBIE DEVASTATION.
KRAKKA-KOOOOM
HUH?
THMMP
STOMP
STOMP
STOMP
STOMP
WHA--? UH-OH.
OH, DANG. I'M ABOUT TO BECOME THE PRINCE OF GETTING POUNDED.

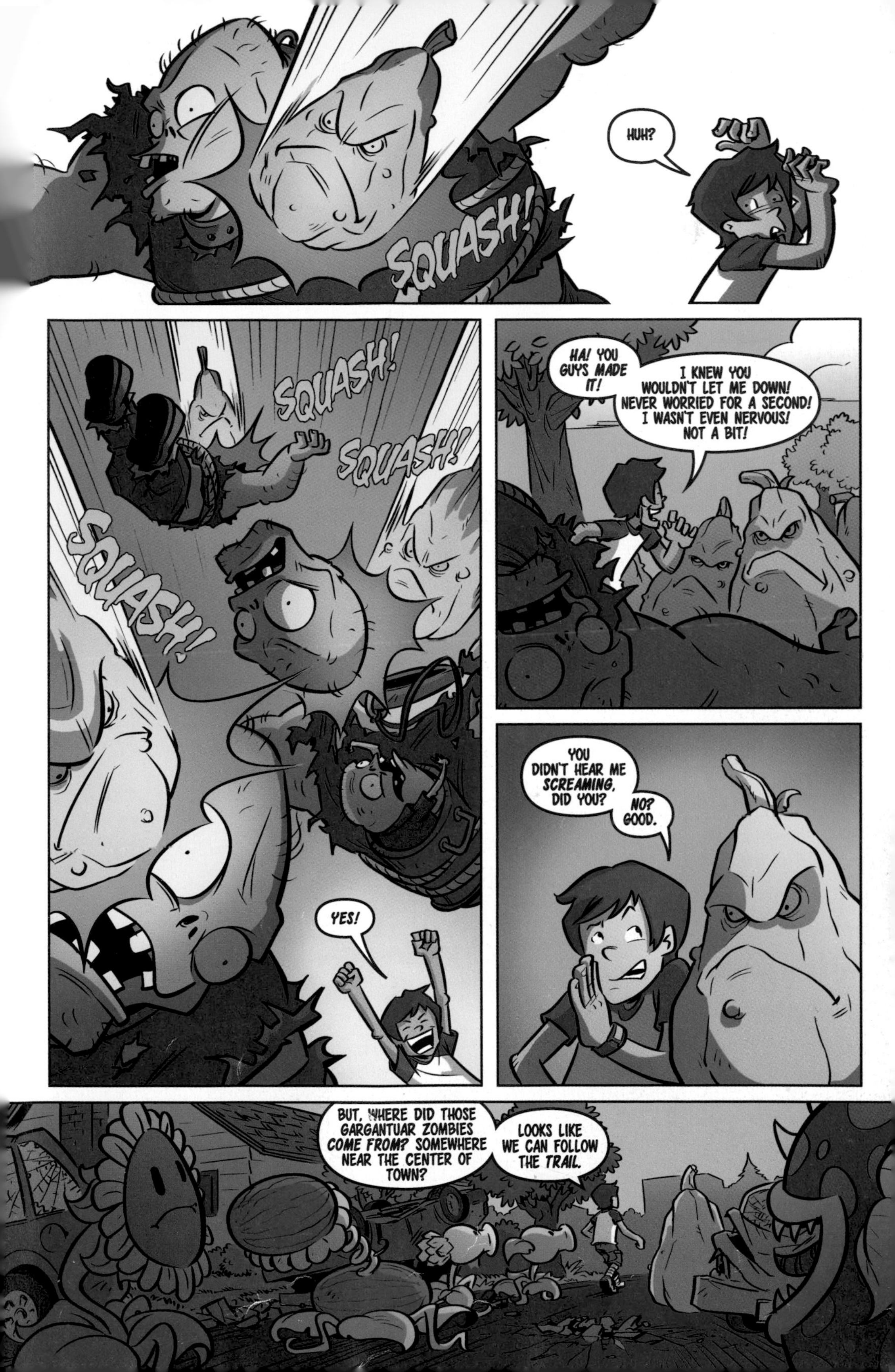
SQUASH!
HUH?
SQUASH!
SQUASH!
SQUASH!
YES!
HA! YOU GUYS MADE IT!
I KNEW YOU WOULDN'T LET ME DOWN! NEVER WORRIED FOR A SECOND! I WASN'T EVEN NERVOUS! NOT A BIT!
YOU DIDN'T HEAR ME SCREAMING, DID YOU?
NO? GOOD.
BUT, WHERE DID THOSE GARGANTUAR ZOMBIES COME FROM? SOMEWHERE NEAR THE CENTER OF TOWN?
LOOKS LIKE WE CAN FOLLOW THE TRAIL.

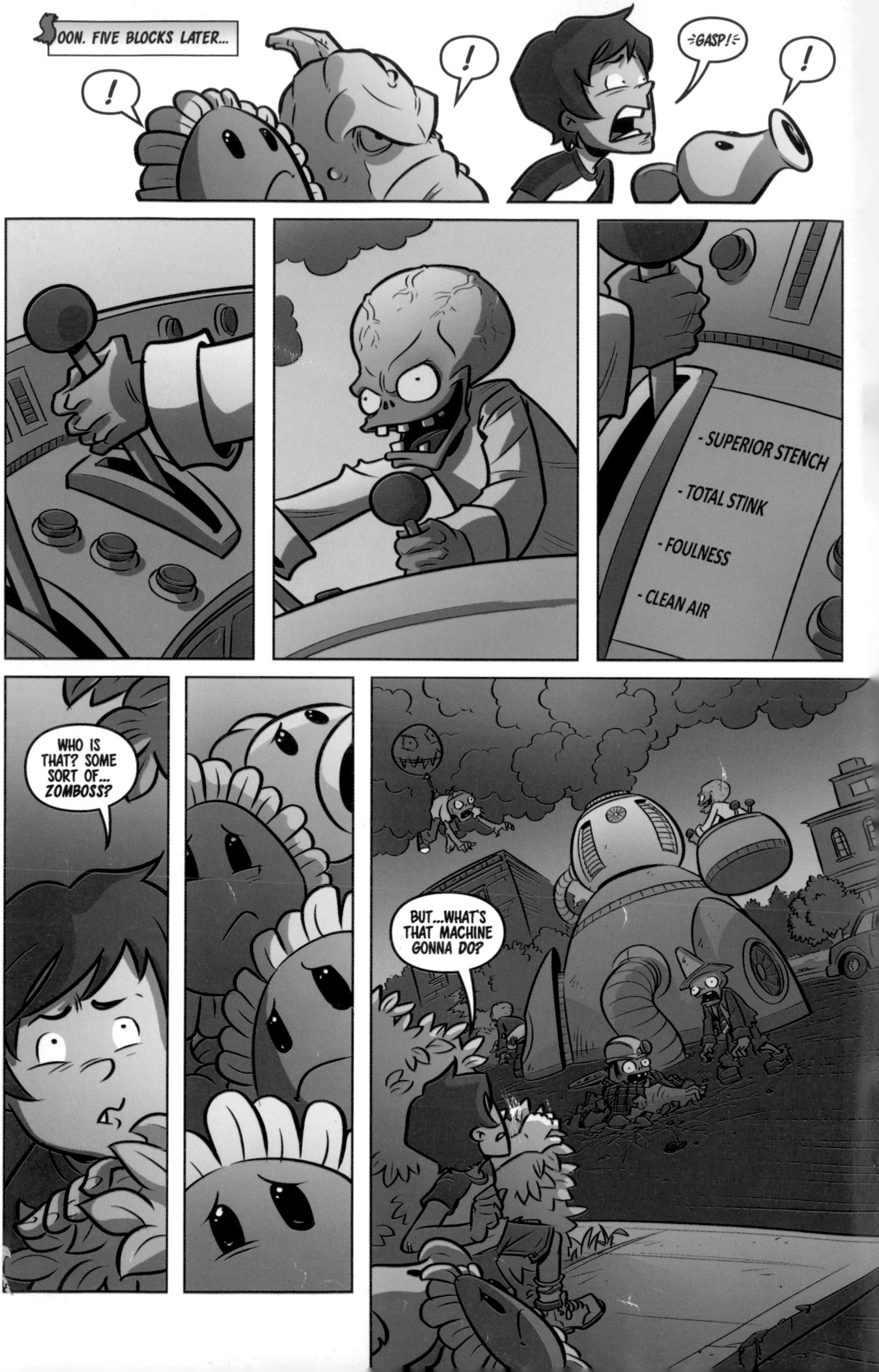
SOON. FIVE BLOCKS LATER...
!
!
GASP!
!
- SUPERIOR STENCH
- TOTAL STINK
- FOULNESS
- CLEAN AIR
WHO IS THAT? SOME SORT OF... ZOMBOSS?
BUT...WHAT'S THAT MACHINE GONNA DO?

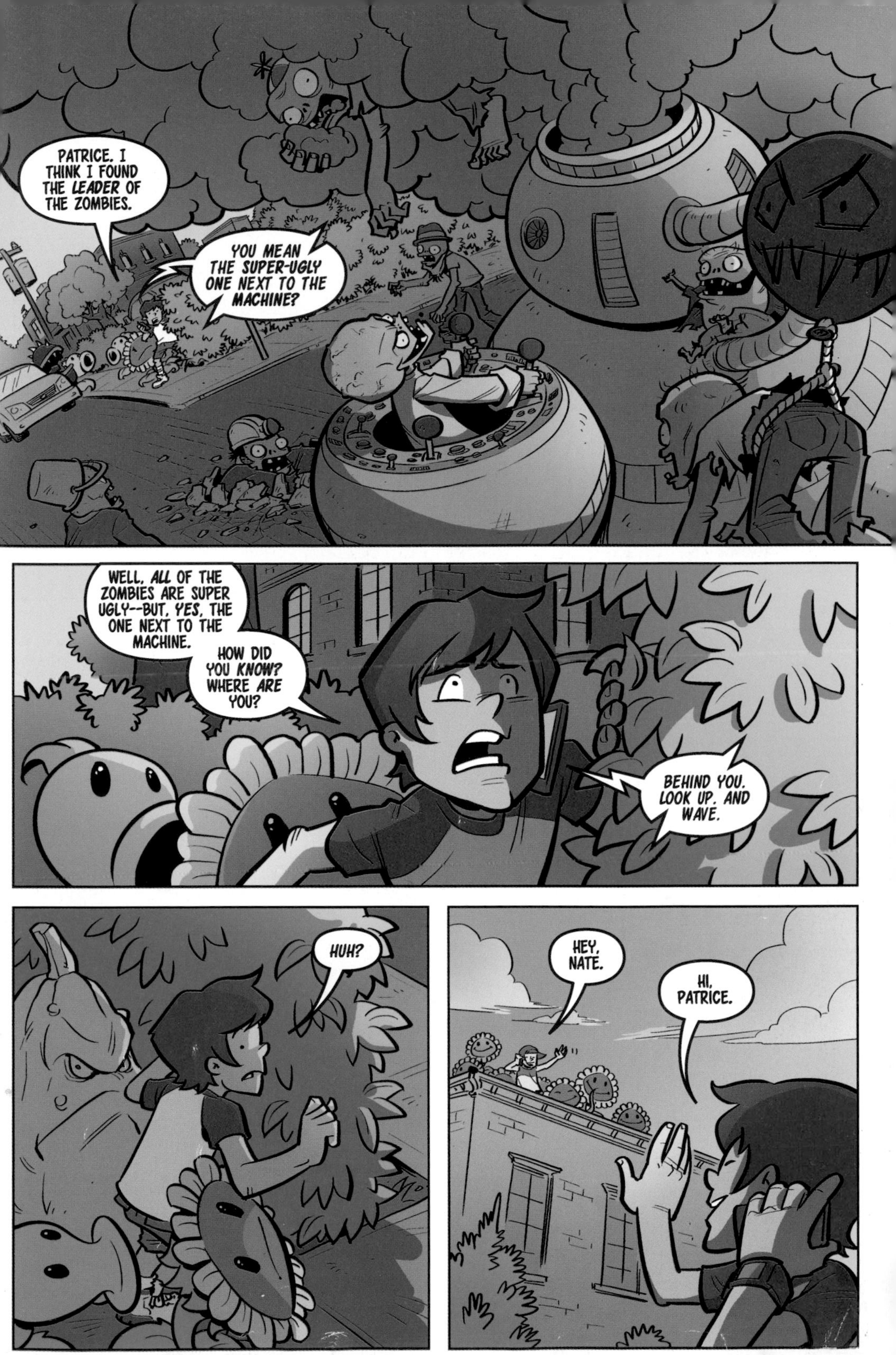
PATRICE. I THINK I FOUND THE *LEADER* OF THE ZOMBIES.
YOU MEAN THE SUPER-UGLY ONE NEXT TO THE MACHINE?
WELL, *ALL* OF THE ZOMBIES ARE SUPER UGLY--BUT, *YES*, THE ONE NEXT TO THE MACHINE.
HOW DID YOU *KNOW*? WHERE *ARE* YOU?
BEHIND YOU. LOOK UP. AND WAVE.
HUH?
HEY, NATE.
HI, PATRICE.

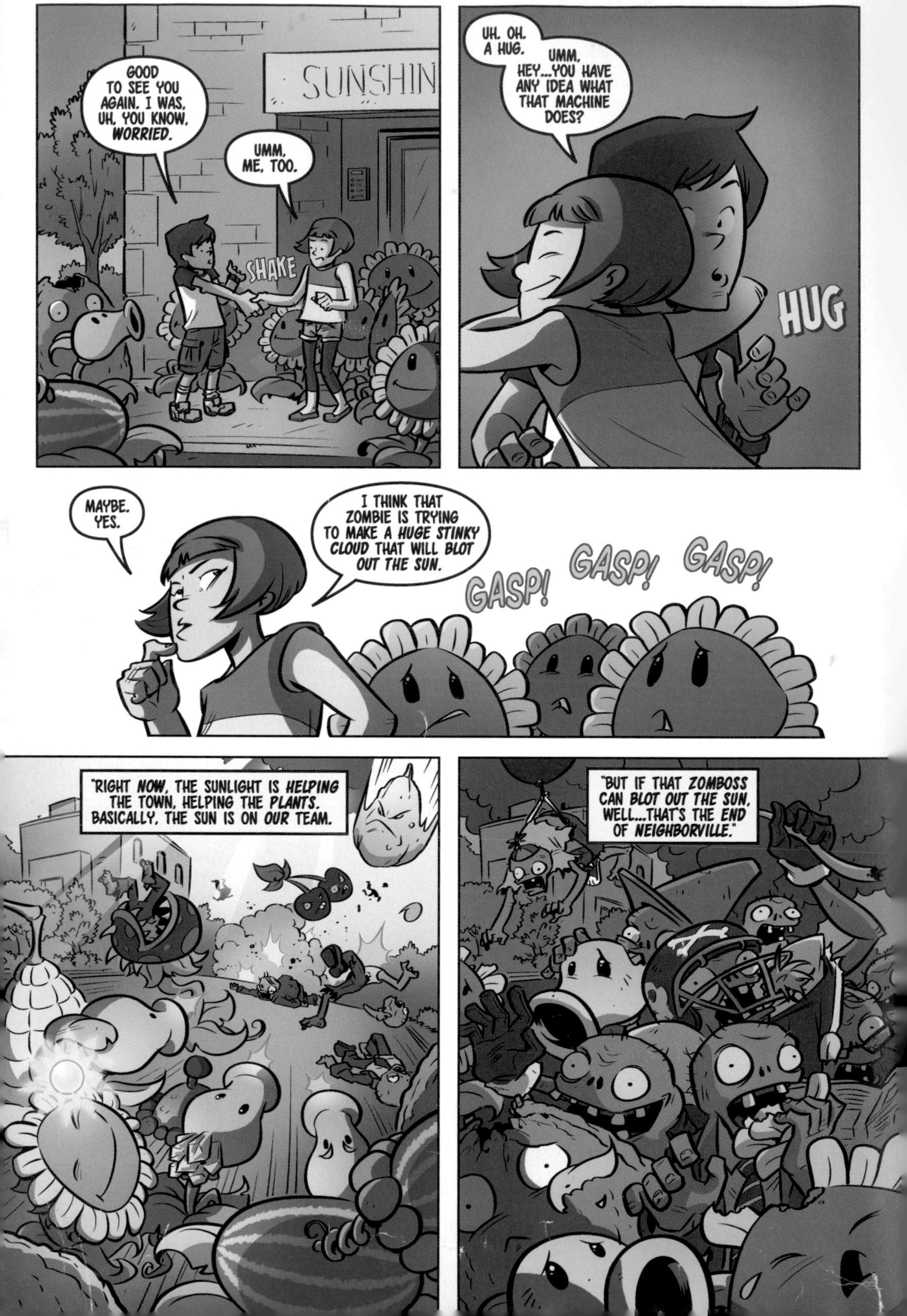
SUNSHIN
GOOD TO SEE YOU AGAIN. I WAS, UH, YOU KNOW, *WORRIED*.
UMM, ME, TOO.
SHAKE
UH. OH. A HUG.
UMM, HEY...YOU HAVE ANY IDEA WHAT THAT MACHINE DOES?
HUG
MAYBE. YES.
I THINK THAT ZOMBIE IS TRYING TO MAKE A *HUGE STINKY CLOUD* THAT WILL *BLOT OUT THE SUN*.
GASP!
GASP!
GASP!
"RIGHT *NOW*, THE SUNLIGHT IS *HELPING* THE TOWN, HELPING THE *PLANTS*. BASICALLY, THE SUN IS ON *OUR* TEAM.
"BUT IF THAT *ZOMBOSS* CAN *BLOT OUT THE SUN*, WELL...THAT'S THE END OF *NEIGHBORVILLE*."

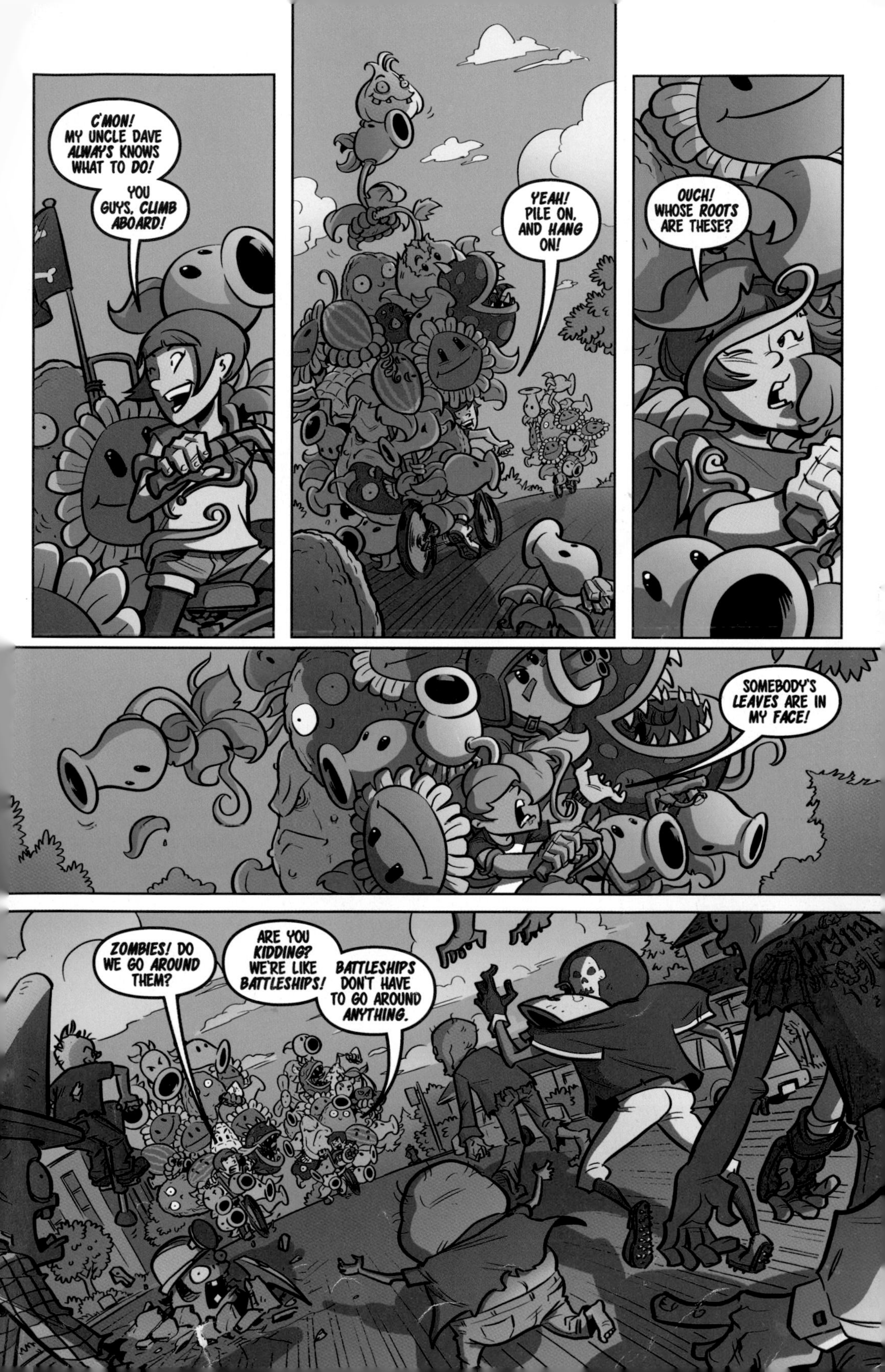
C'MON! MY UNCLE DAVE ALWAYS KNOWS WHAT TO DO!
YOU GUYS, CLIMB ABOARD!
YEAH! PILE ON, AND HANG ON!
OUCH! WHOSE ROOTS ARE THESE?
SOMEBODY'S LEAVES ARE IN MY FACE!
ZOMBIES! DO WE GO AROUND THEM?
ARE YOU KIDDING? WE'RE LIKE BATTLESHIPS!
BATTLESHIPS DON'T HAVE TO GO AROUND ANYTHING.

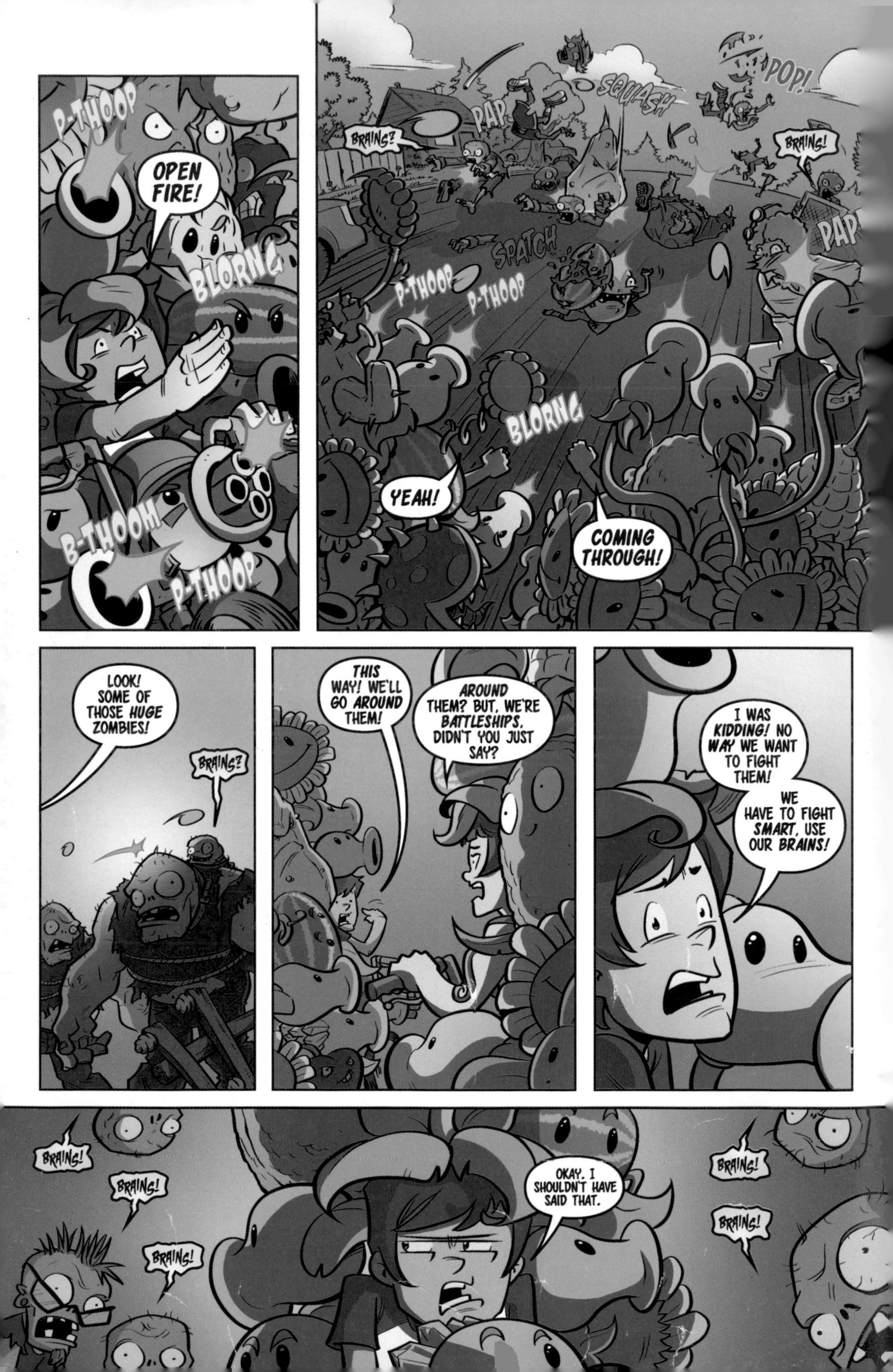
P-THOOP
OPEN FIRE!
BLORNG
B-THOOM
P-THOOP
POP!
SQUASH
PAP
BRAINS?
BRAINS!
PAP
SPATCH
P-THOOP
P-THOOP
BLORNG
YEAH!
COMING THROUGH!
LOOK! SOME OF THOSE HUGE ZOMBIES!
BRAINS?
THIS WAY! WE'LL GO AROUND THEM!
AROUND THEM? BUT, WE'RE BATTLESHIPS, DIDN'T YOU JUST SAY?
I WAS KIDDING! NO WAY WE WANT TO FIGHT THEM!
WE HAVE TO FIGHT SMART, USE OUR BRAINS!
BRAINS!
BRAINS!
BRAINS!
OKAY. I SHOULDN'T HAVE SAID THAT.
BRAINS!
BRAINS!

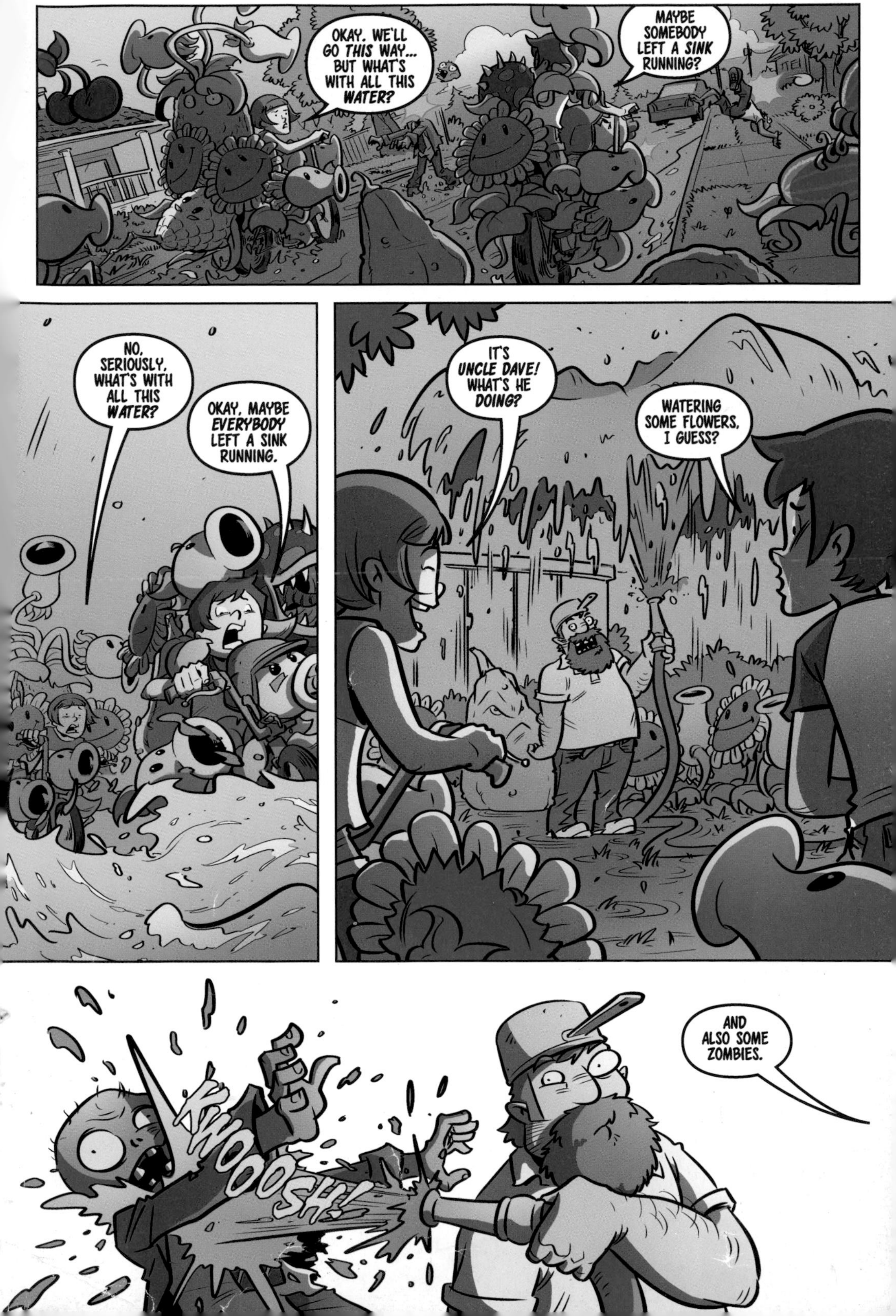
OKAY. WE'LL GO THIS WAY... BUT WHAT'S WITH ALL THIS WATER?
MAYBE SOMEBODY LEFT A SINK RUNNING?
NO, SERIOUSLY, WHAT'S WITH ALL THIS WATER?
OKAY, MAYBE EVERYBODY LEFT A SINK RUNNING.
IT'S UNCLE DAVE! WHAT'S HE DOING?
WATERING SOME FLOWERS, I GUESS?
KWOOOSH!
AND ALSO SOME ZOMBIES.

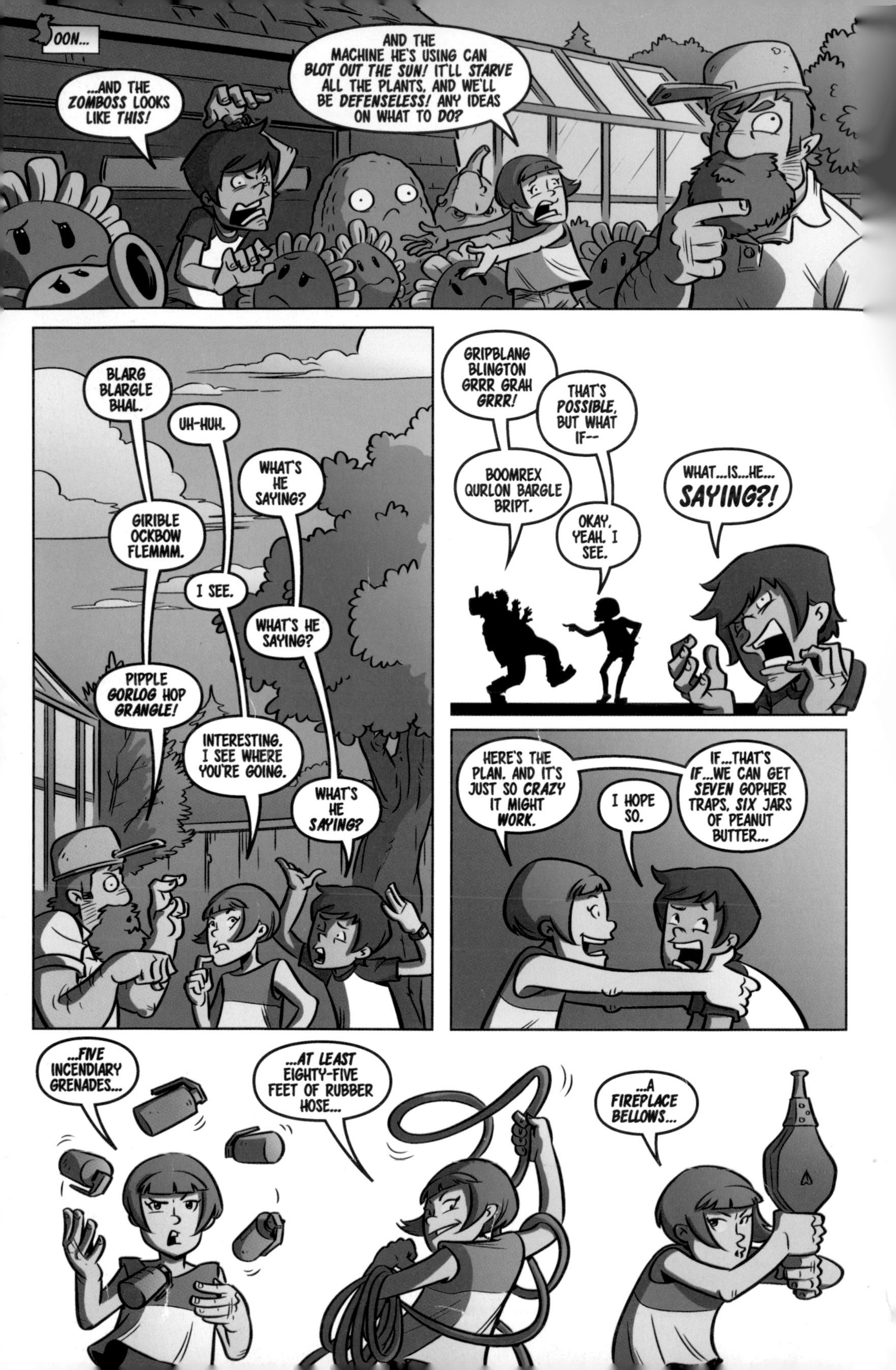
SOON...
...AND THE ZOMBOSS LOOKS LIKE THIS!
AND THE MACHINE HE'S USING CAN BLOT OUT THE SUN! IT'LL STARVE ALL THE PLANTS, AND WE'LL BE DEFENSELESS! ANY IDEAS ON WHAT TO DO?
BLARG BLARGLE BHAL.
UH-HUH.
WHAT'S HE SAYING?
GIRIBLE OCKBOW FLEMMM.
I SEE.
WHAT'S HE SAYING?
PIPPLE GORLOG HOP GRANGLE!
INTERESTING. I SEE WHERE YOU'RE GOING.
WHAT'S HE SAYING?
GRIPBLANG BLINGTON GRRR GRAH GRRR!
THAT'S POSSIBLE, BUT WHAT IF--
BOOMREX QURLON BARGLE BRIPT.
OKAY, YEAH. I SEE.
WHAT...IS...HE... SAYING?!
HERE'S THE PLAN. AND IT'S JUST SO CRAZY IT MIGHT WORK.
I HOPE SO.
IF...THAT'S IF...WE CAN GET SEVEN GOPHER TRAPS, SIX JARS OF PEANUT BUTTER...
...FIVE INCENDIARY GRENADES...
...AT LEAST EIGHTY-FIVE FEET OF RUBBER HOSE...
...A FIREPLACE BELLOWS...

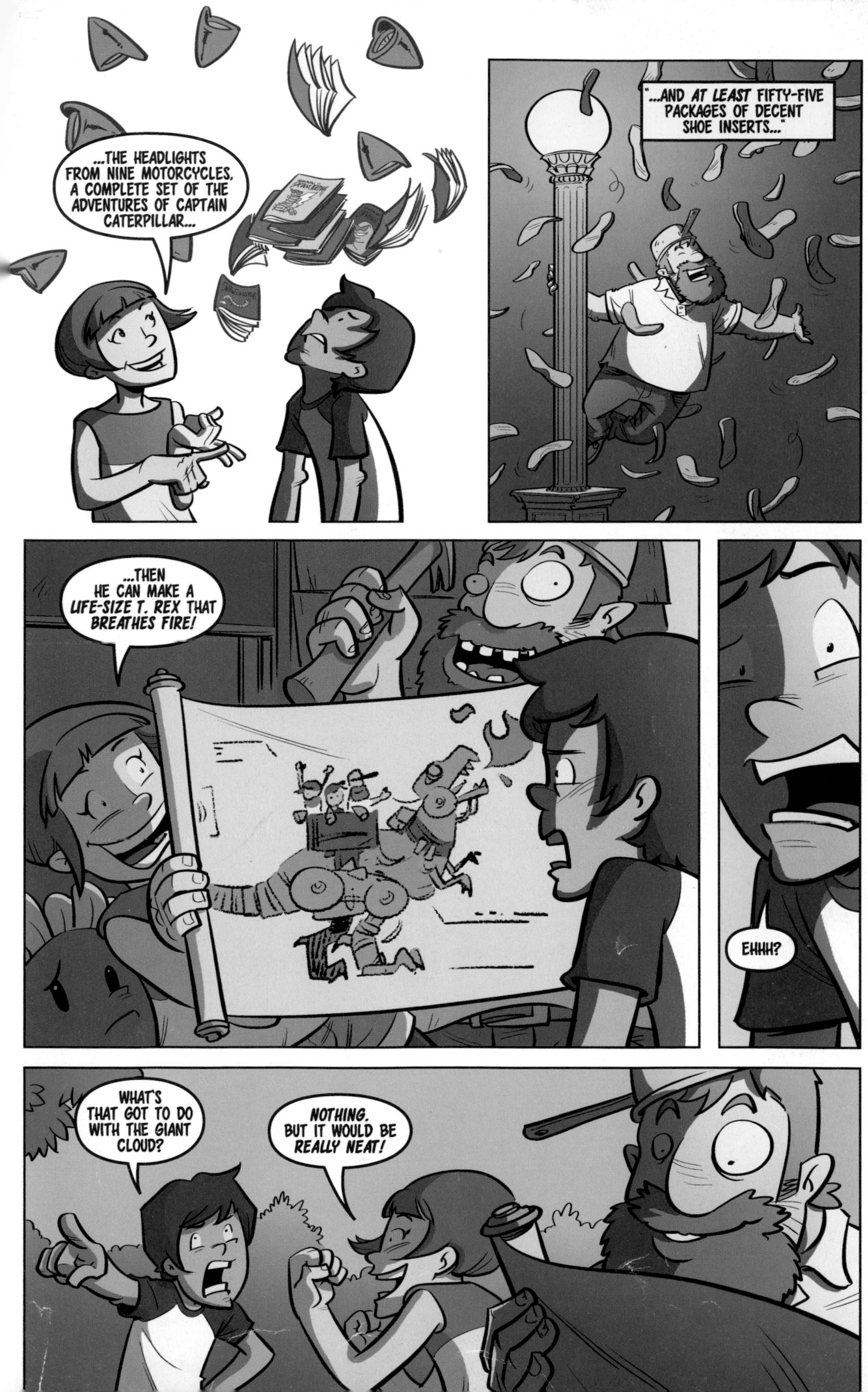
...THE HEADLIGHTS FROM NINE MOTORCYCLES, A COMPLETE SET OF THE ADVENTURES OF CAPTAIN CATERPILLAR...
"...AND AT LEAST FIFTY-FIVE PACKAGES OF DECENT SHOE INSERTS..."
...THEN HE CAN MAKE A LIFE-SIZE T. REX THAT BREATHES FIRE!
EHHH?
WHAT'S THAT GOT TO DO WITH THE GIANT CLOUD?
NOTHING. BUT IT WOULD BE REALLY NEAT!

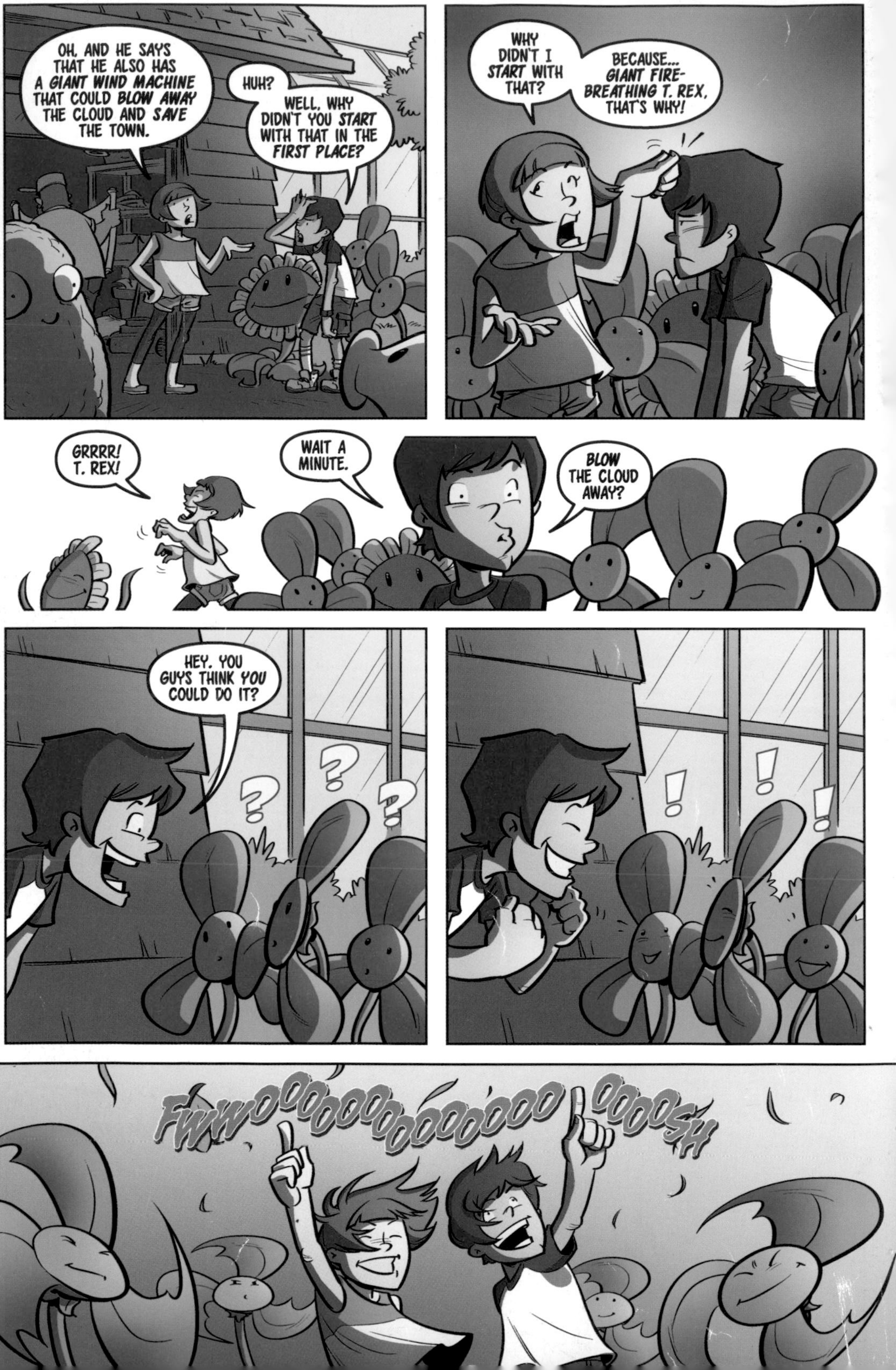
OH, AND HE SAYS THAT HE ALSO HAS A GIANT WIND MACHINE THAT COULD BLOW AWAY THE CLOUD AND SAVE THE TOWN.
HUH?
WELL, WHY DIDN'T YOU START WITH THAT IN THE FIRST PLACE?
WHY DIDN'T I START WITH THAT?
BECAUSE... GIANT FIRE-BREATHING T. REX, THAT'S WHY!
GRRRR! T. REX!
WAIT A MINUTE.
BLOW THE CLOUD AWAY?
HEY. YOU GUYS THINK YOU COULD DO IT?
FWWOOOOOOOOOOOOOOOOOOOSH

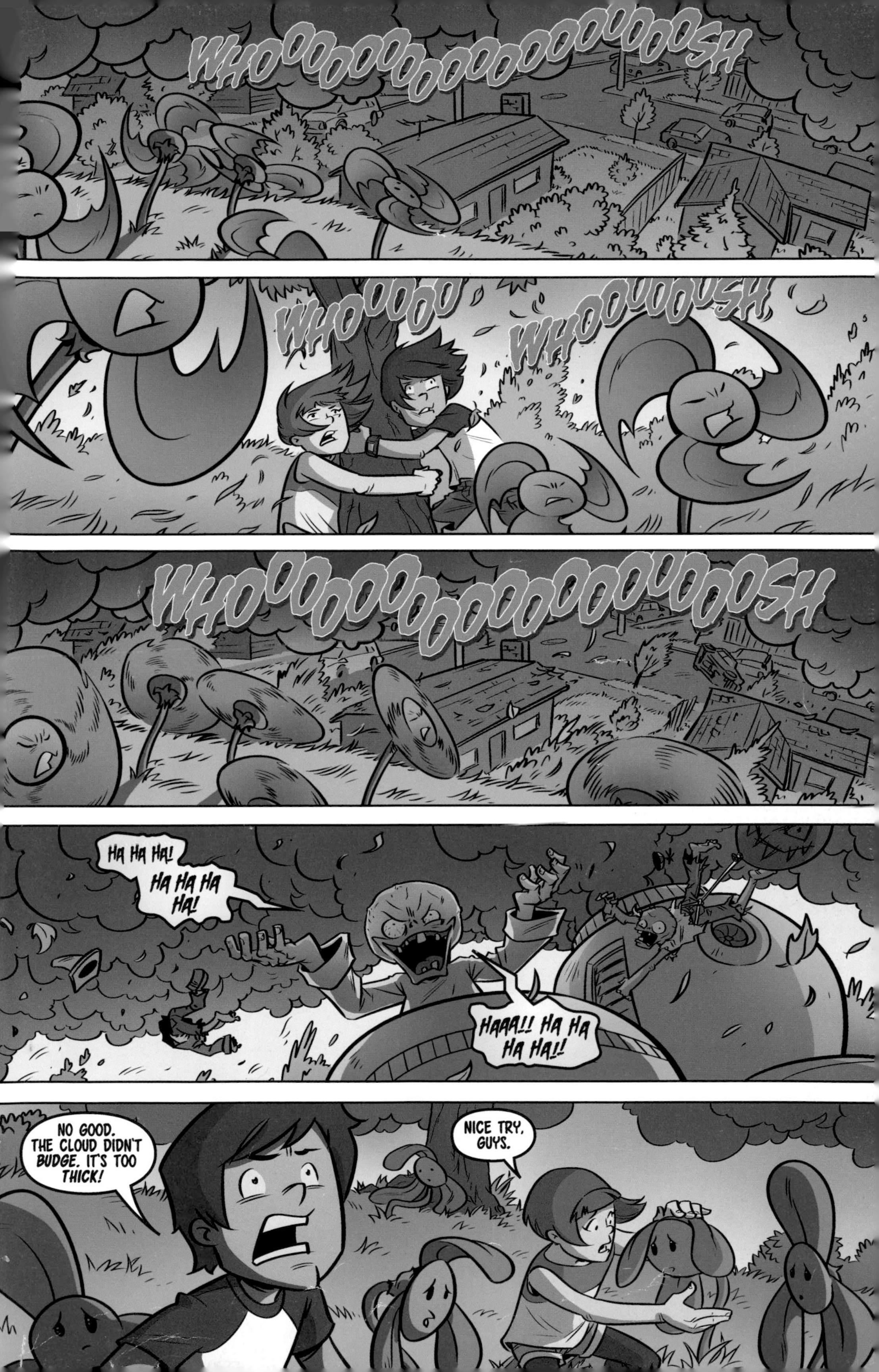
WHOOOOOOOOOOOOOOOOOOSH
WHOOOOOO
WHOOOOOOOSH
WHOOOOOOOOOOOOOOOOOOOOSH
HA HA HA!
HA HA HA HA!
HAAA!! HA HA HA HA!!
NO GOOD. THE CLOUD DIDN'T BUDGE. IT'S TOO THICK!
NICE TRY, GUYS.

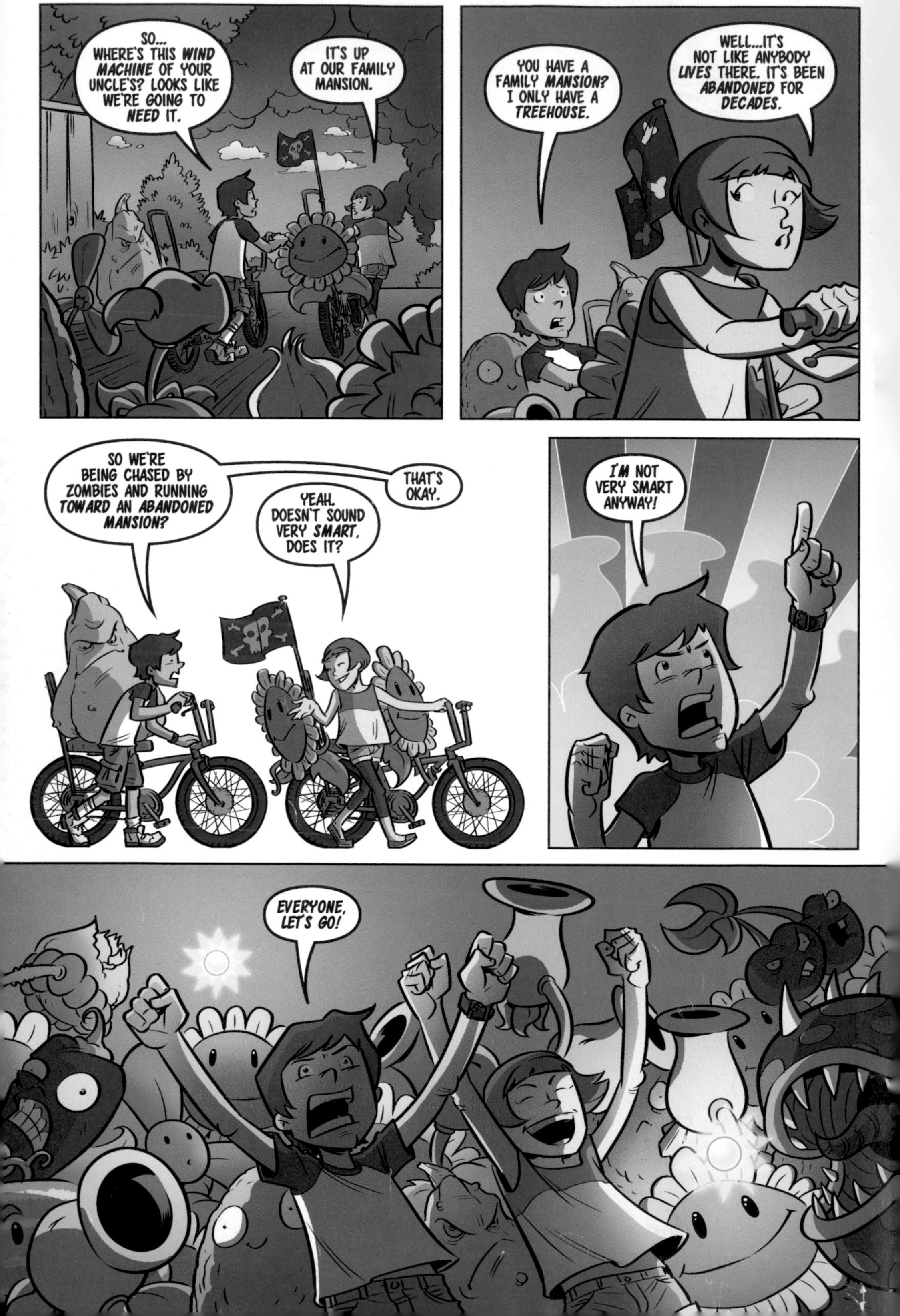

SO... WHERE'S THIS WIND MACHINE OF YOUR UNCLE'S? LOOKS LIKE WE'RE GOING TO NEED IT.
IT'S UP AT OUR FAMILY MANSION.
YOU HAVE A FAMILY MANSION? I ONLY HAVE A TREEHOUSE.
WELL...IT'S NOT LIKE ANYBODY LIVES THERE. IT'S BEEN ABANDONED FOR DECADES.
SO WE'RE BEING CHASED BY ZOMBIES AND RUNNING TOWARD AN ABANDONED MANSION?
YEAH. DOESN'T SOUND VERY SMART, DOES IT?
THAT'S OKAY.
I'M NOT VERY SMART ANYWAY!
EVERYONE, LET'S GO!

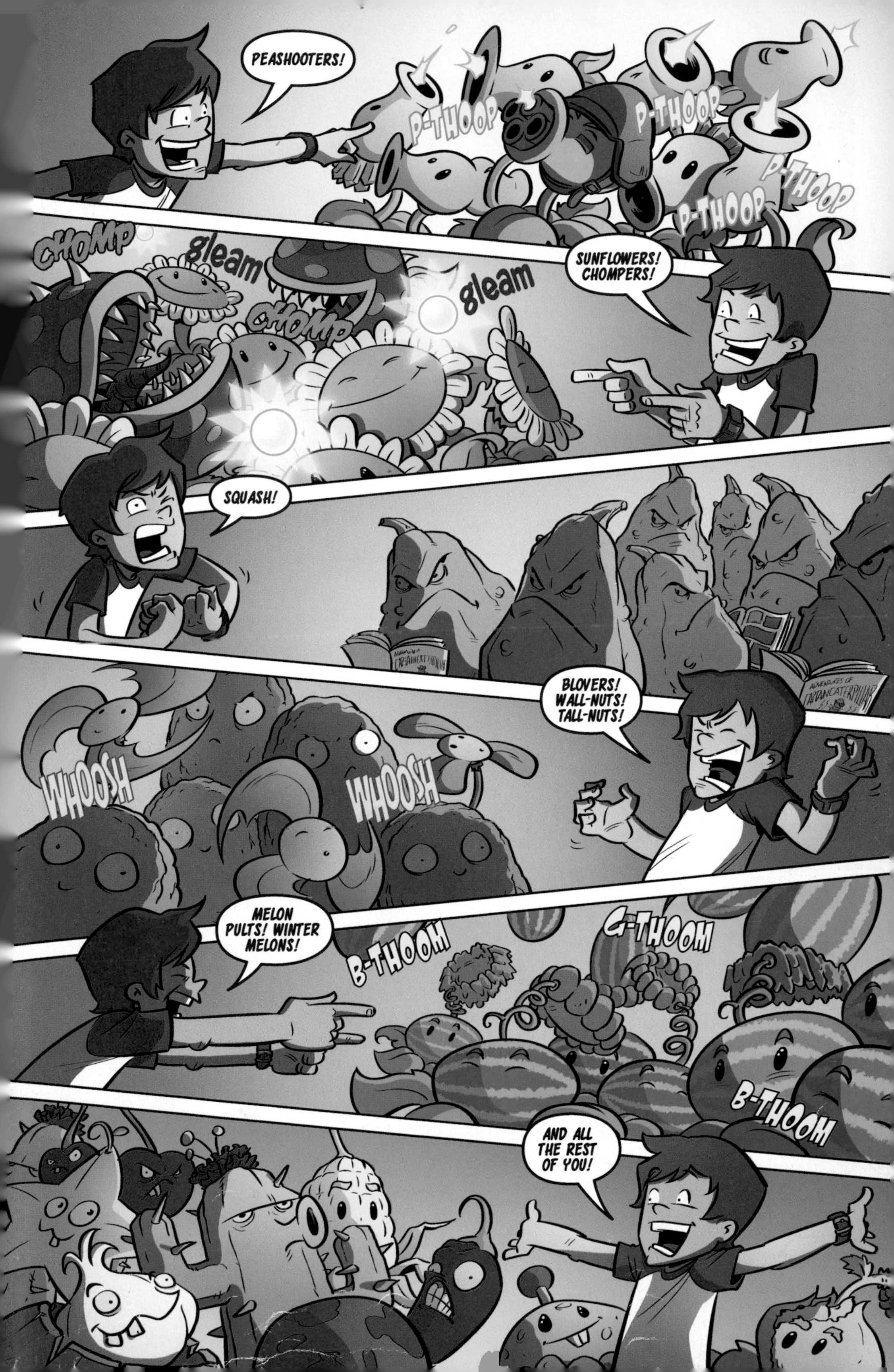
PEASHOOTERS!
P-THOOP
P-THOOP
P-THOOP
P-THOOP
CHOMP
gleam
CHOMP
gleam
SUNFLOWERS! CHOMPERS!
SQUASH!
BLOVERS! WALL-NUTS! TALL-NUTS!
WHOOSH
WHOOSH
MELON PULTS! WINTER MELONS!
B-THOOM
G-THOOM
B-THOOM
AND ALL THE REST OF YOU!

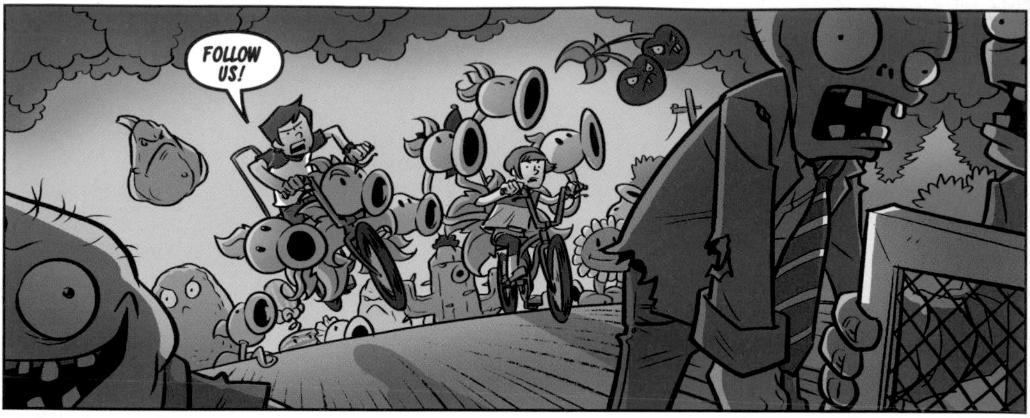
FOLLOW US!

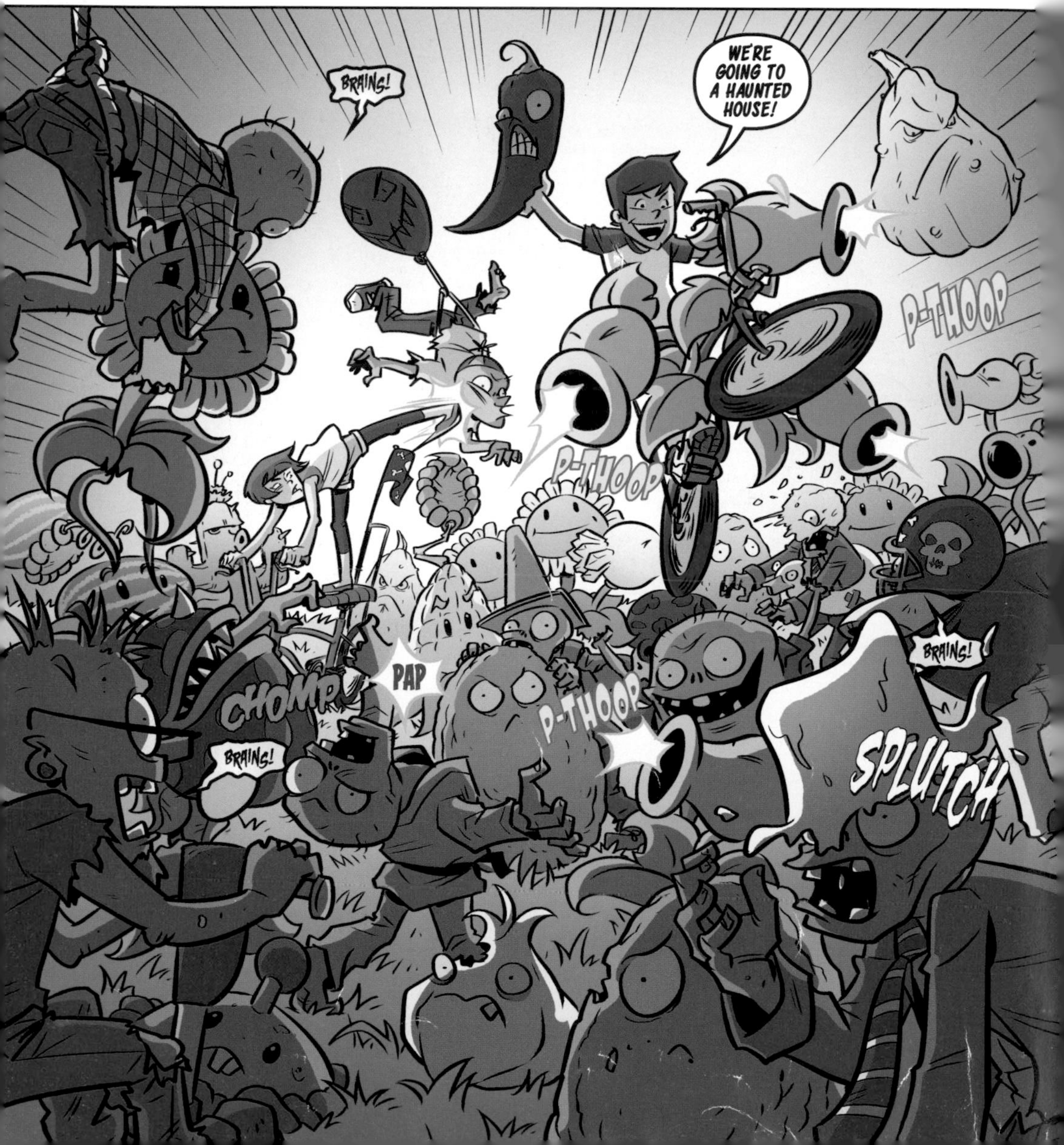
BRAINS!
WE'RE GOING TO A HAUNTED HOUSE!
P-THOOP
P-THOOP
CHOMP
PAP
P-THOOP
BRAINS!
BRAINS!
SPLUTCH

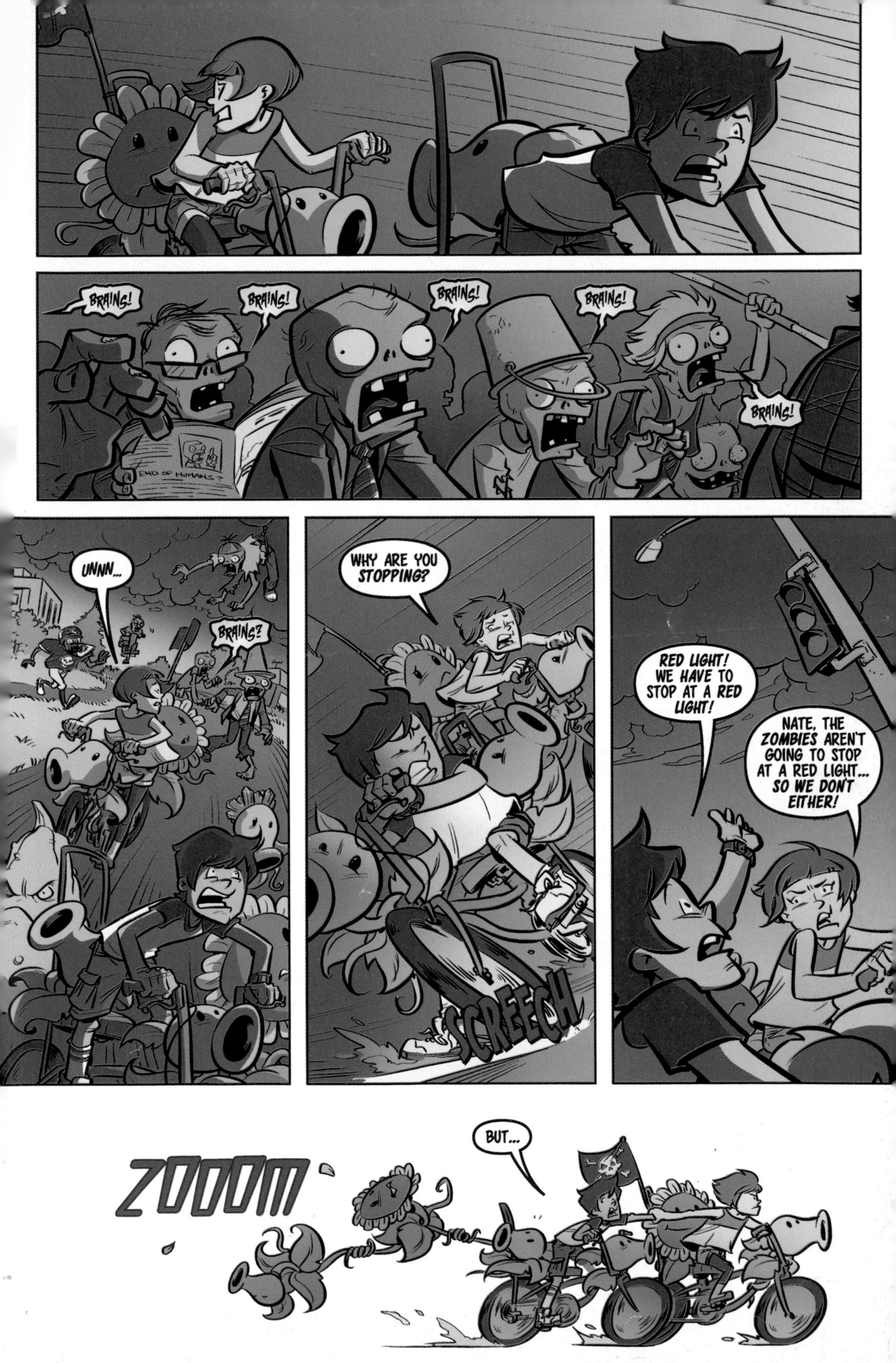
BRAINS!
BRAINS!
BRAINS!
BRAINS!
BRAINS!
END OF HUMANS?
UNNN...
BRAINS?
WHY ARE YOU STOPPING?
SCREECH
RED LIGHT! WE HAVE TO STOP AT A RED LIGHT!
NATE, THE ZOMBIES AREN'T GOING TO STOP AT A RED LIGHT... SO WE DON'T EITHER!
ZOOOM
BUT...

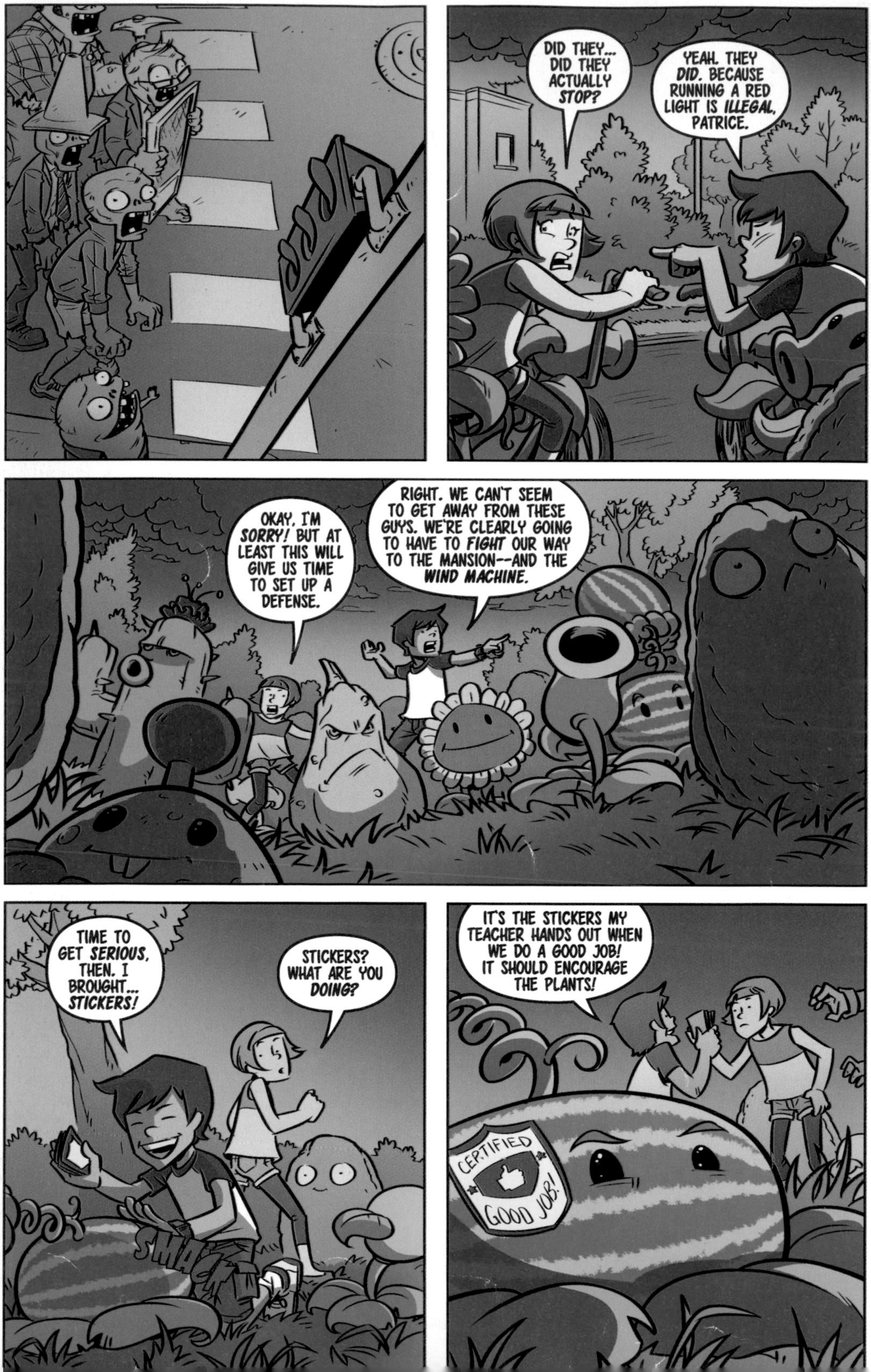

DID THEY... DID THEY ACTUALLY STOP?
YEAH. THEY DID. BECAUSE RUNNING A RED LIGHT IS ILLEGAL, PATRICE.
OKAY, I'M SORRY! BUT AT LEAST THIS WILL GIVE US TIME TO SET UP A DEFENSE.
RIGHT. WE CAN'T SEEM TO GET AWAY FROM THESE GUYS. WE'RE CLEARLY GOING TO HAVE TO FIGHT OUR WAY TO THE MANSION--AND THE WIND MACHINE.
TIME TO GET SERIOUS, THEN. I BROUGHT... STICKERS!
STICKERS? WHAT ARE YOU DOING?
IT'S THE STICKERS MY TEACHER HANDS OUT WHEN WE DO A GOOD JOB! IT SHOULD ENCOURAGE THE PLANTS!
CERTIFIED
GOOD JOB!

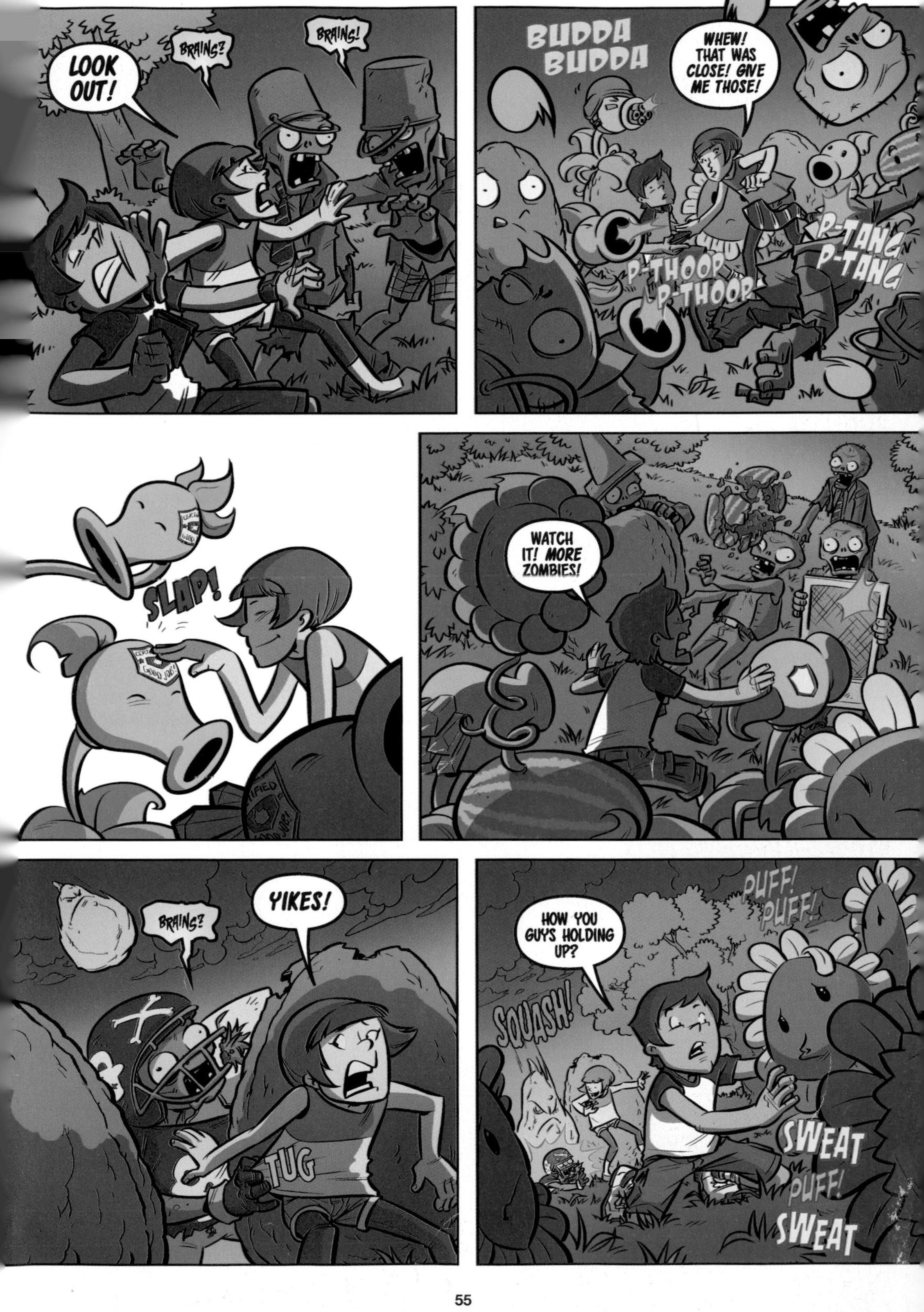

LOOK OUT!
BRAINS?
BRAINS!
BUDDA BUDDA
WHEW! THAT WAS CLOSE! GIVE ME THOSE!
P-THOOP P-THOOP
P-TANG P-TANG
SLAP!
WATCH IT! MORE ZOMBIES!
BRAINS?
YIKES!
TUG
HOW YOU GUYS HOLDING UP?
PUFF! PUFF!
SQUASH!
SWEAT
PUFF!
SWEAT

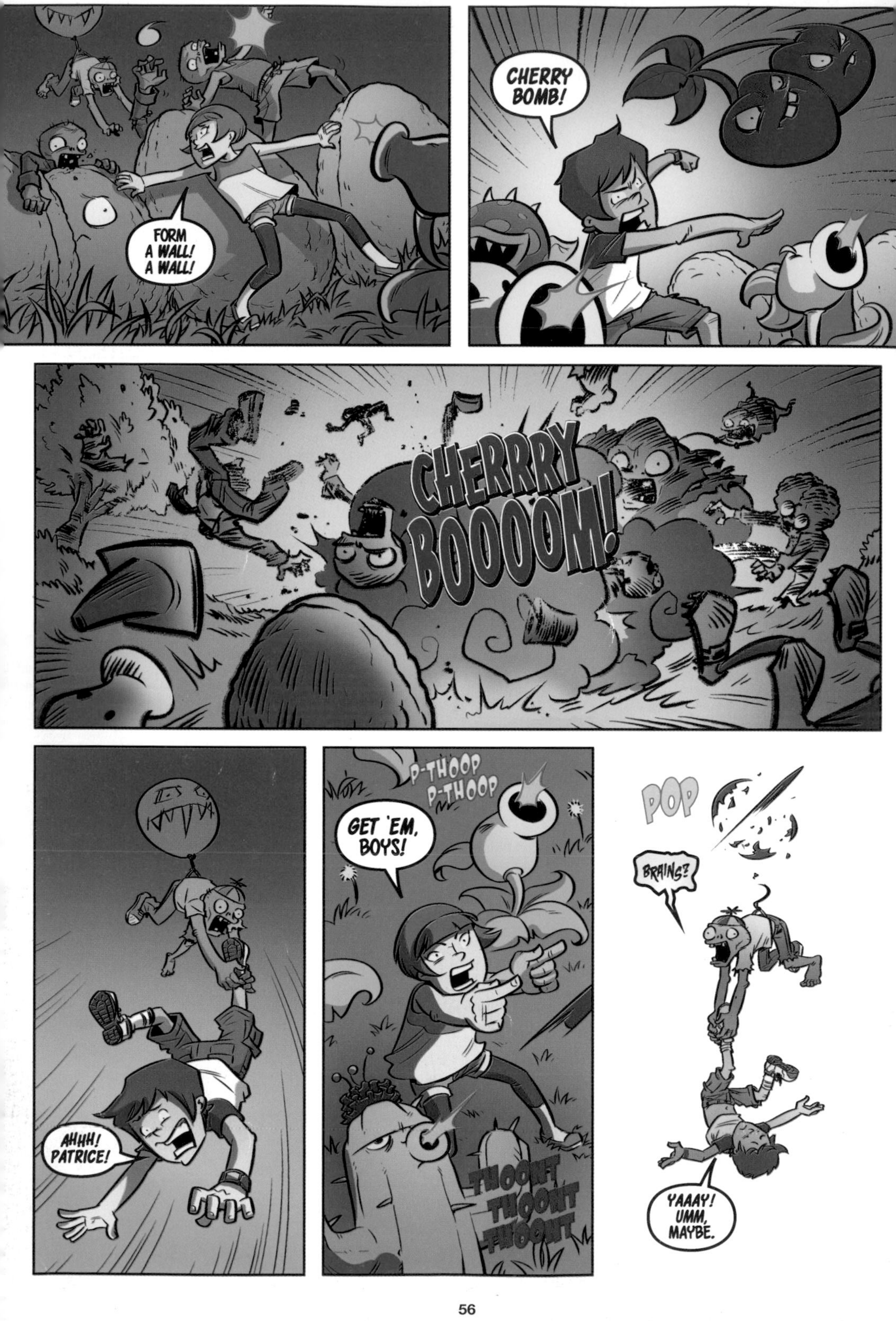
FORM A WALL! A WALL!
CHERRY BOMB!
CHERRRY BOOOOM!
AHHH! PATRICE!
P-THOOP P-THOOP
GET 'EM, BOYS!
THOONT THOONT THOONT
POP
BRAINS?
YAAAY! UMM, MAYBE.

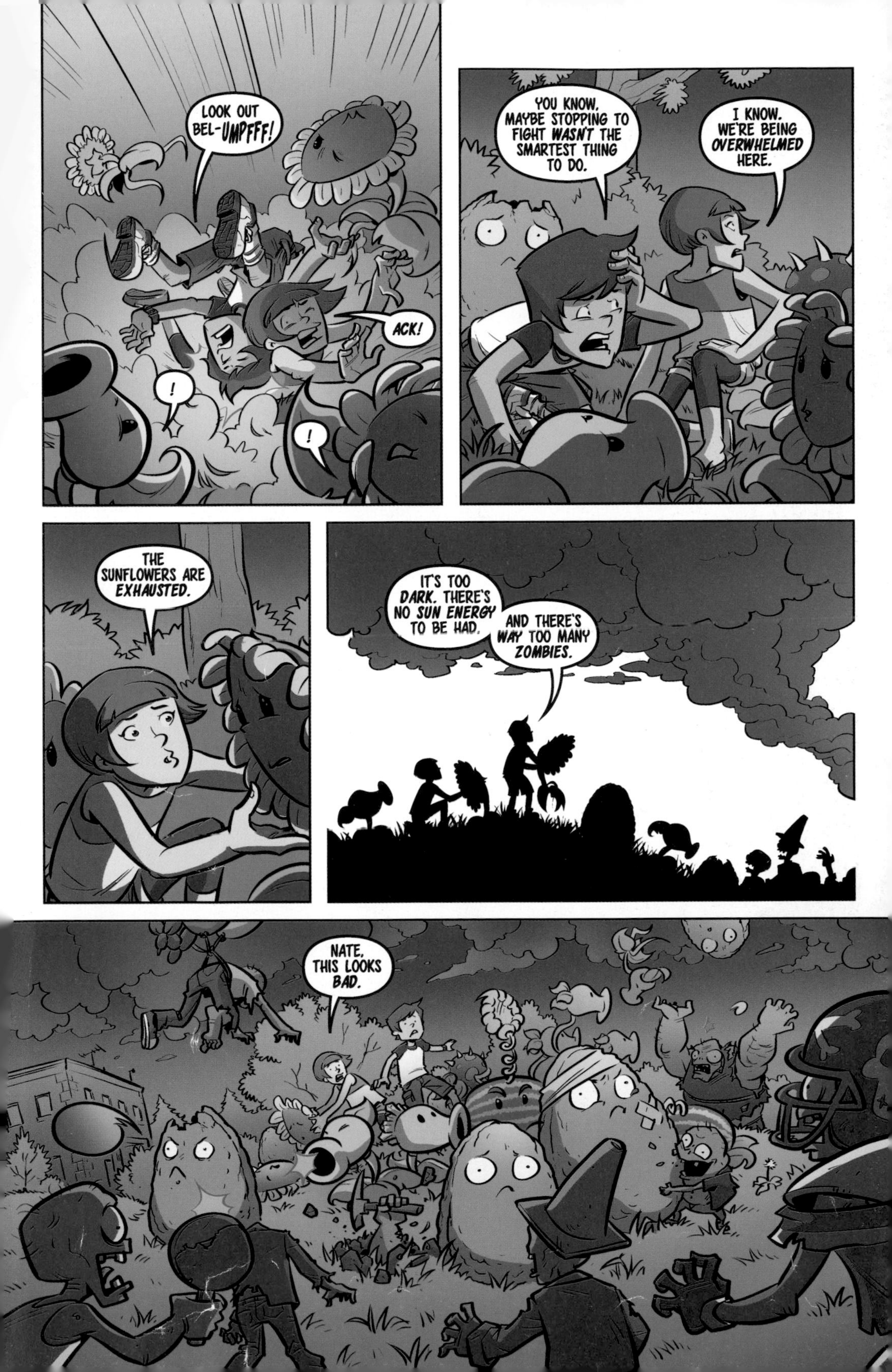
LOOK OUT BEL-UMPFFF!
ACK!
!
!
YOU KNOW, MAYBE STOPPING TO FIGHT WASN'T THE SMARTEST THING TO DO.
I KNOW. WE'RE BEING OVERWHELMED HERE.
THE SUNFLOWERS ARE EXHAUSTED.
IT'S TOO DARK. THERE'S NO SUN ENERGY TO BE HAD.
AND THERE'S WAY TOO MANY ZOMBIES.
NATE, THIS LOOKS BAD.

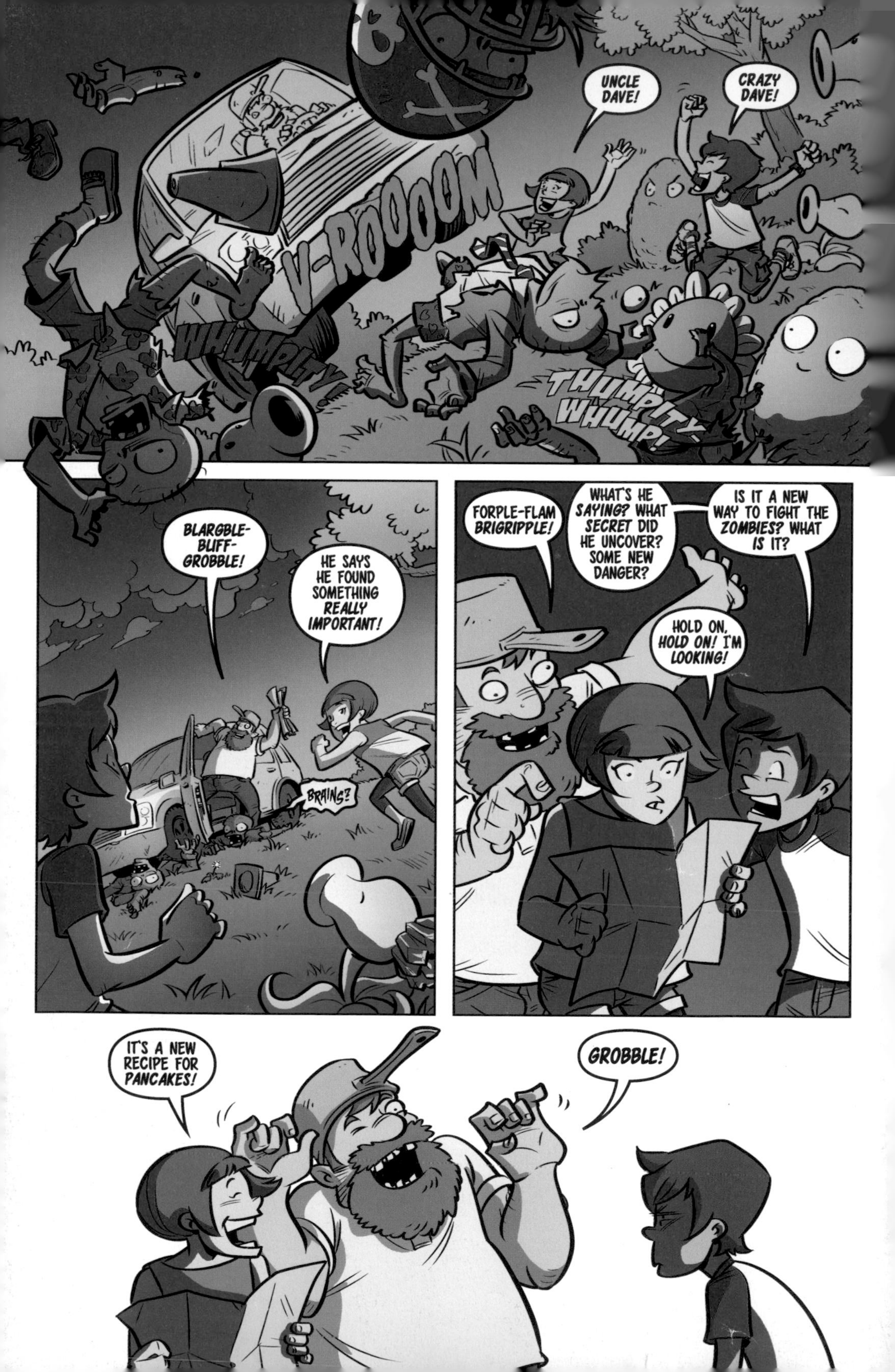

UNCLE DAVE!
CRAZY DAVE!
V-ROOOOM
WHUMPITY!
THUMPITY-WHUMP!
BLARGBLE-BUFF-GROBBLE!
HE SAYS HE FOUND SOMETHING REALLY IMPORTANT!
BRAINS?
FORPLE-FLAM BRIGRIPPLE!
WHAT'S HE SAYING? WHAT SECRET DID HE UNCOVER? SOME NEW DANGER?
IS IT A NEW WAY TO FIGHT THE ZOMBIES? WHAT IS IT?
HOLD ON, HOLD ON! I'M LOOKING!
IT'S A NEW RECIPE FOR PANCAKES!
GROBBLE!

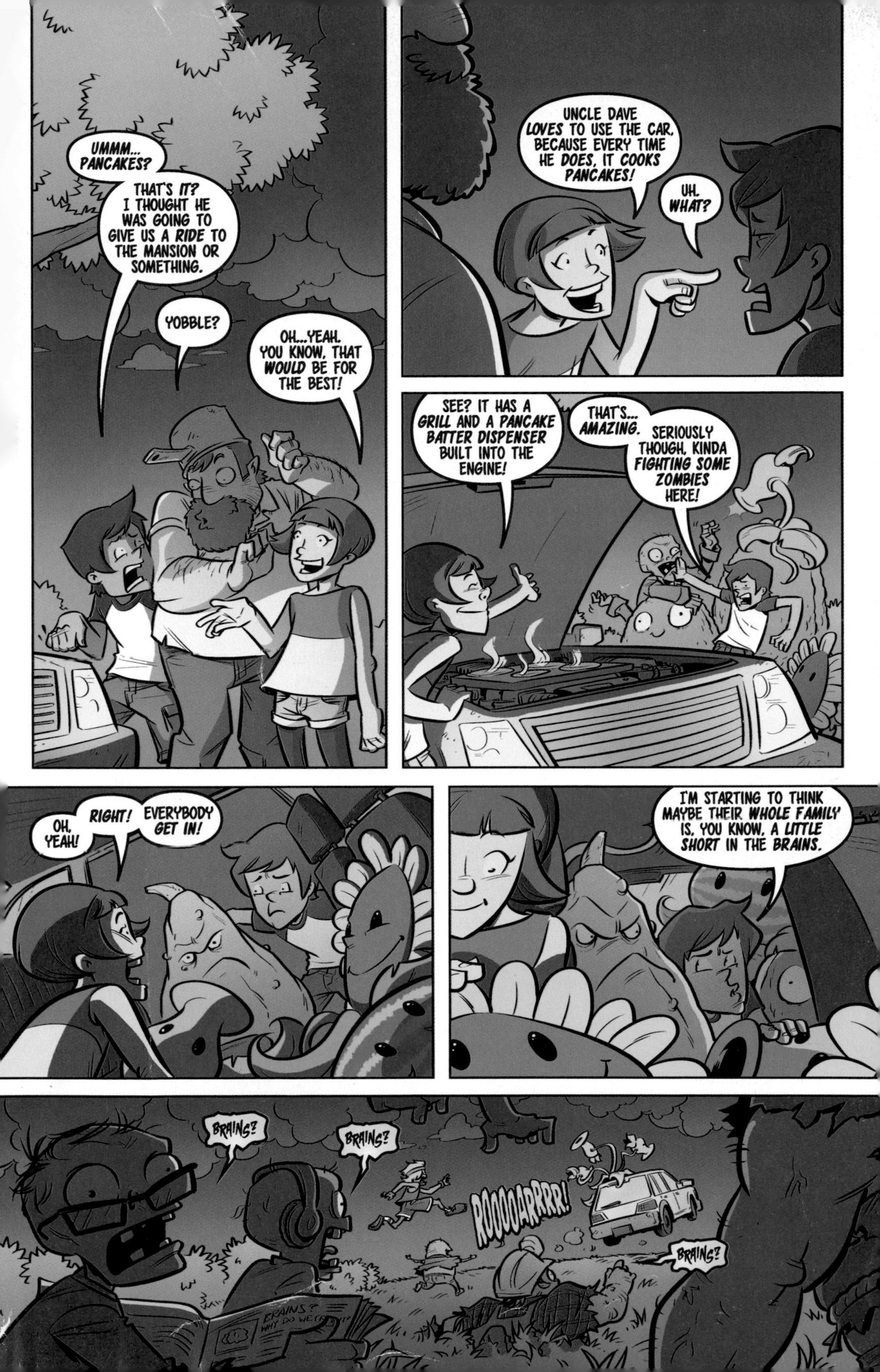

UMMM... PANCAKES?
THAT'S IT? I THOUGHT HE WAS GOING TO GIVE US A RIDE TO THE MANSION OR SOMETHING.
YOBBLE?
OH...YEAH. YOU KNOW, THAT WOULD BE FOR THE BEST!
UNCLE DAVE LOVES TO USE THE CAR, BECAUSE EVERY TIME HE DOES, IT COOKS PANCAKES!
UH. WHAT?
SEE? IT HAS A GRILL AND A PANCAKE BATTER DISPENSER BUILT INTO THE ENGINE!
THAT'S... AMAZING.
SERIOUSLY THOUGH, KINDA FIGHTING SOME ZOMBIES HERE!
OH, YEAH!
RIGHT!
EVERYBODY GET IN!
I'M STARTING TO THINK MAYBE THEIR WHOLE FAMILY IS, YOU KNOW, A LITTLE SHORT IN THE BRAINS.
BRAINS?
BRAINS?
ROOOOARRRR!
BRAINS?

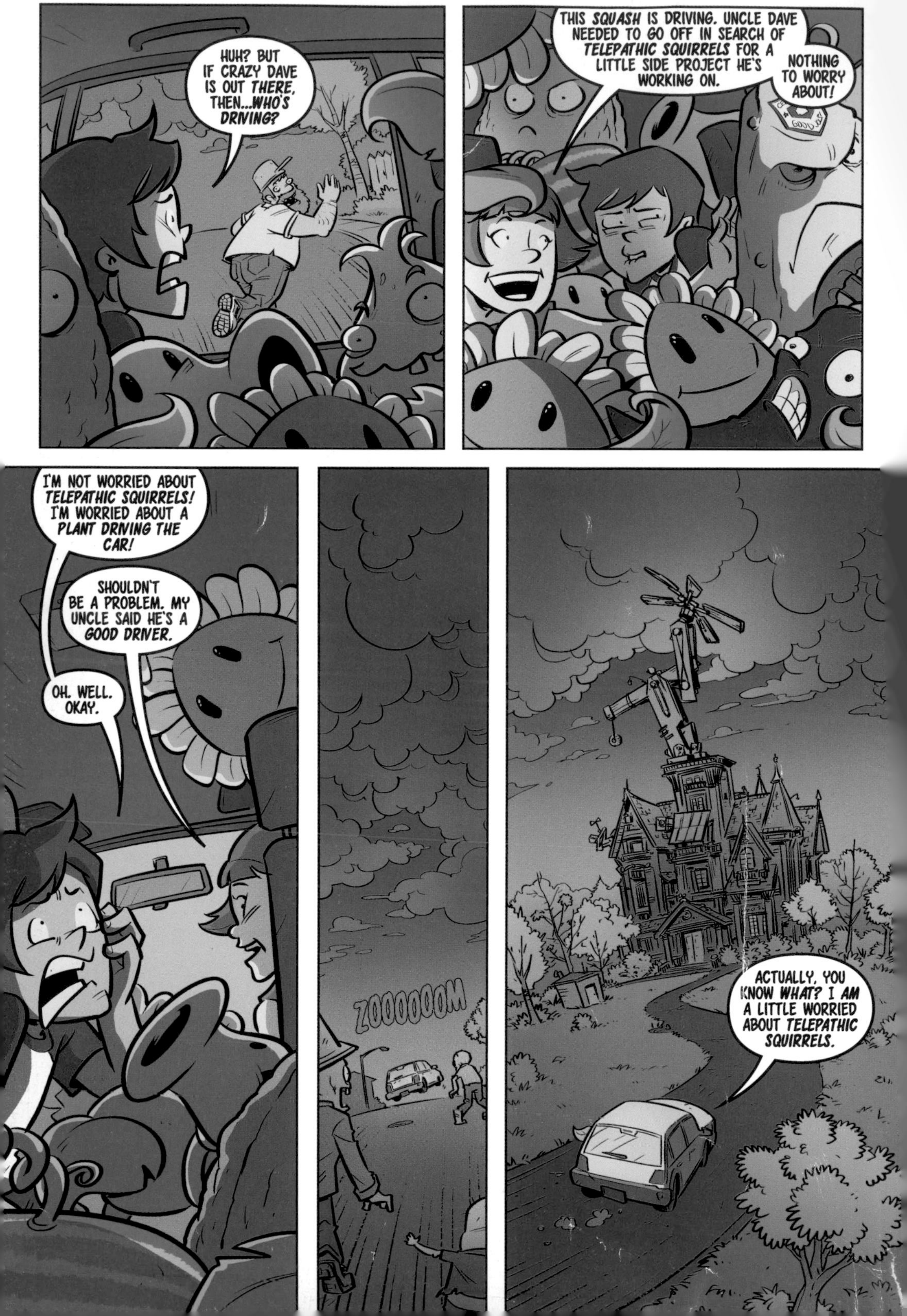
HUH? BUT IF CRAZY DAVE IS OUT THERE, THEN...WHO'S DRIVING?
THIS SQUASH IS DRIVING. UNCLE DAVE NEEDED TO GO OFF IN SEARCH OF TELEPATHIC SQUIRRELS FOR A LITTLE SIDE PROJECT HE'S WORKING ON.
NOTHING TO WORRY ABOUT!
I'M NOT WORRIED ABOUT TELEPATHIC SQUIRRELS! I'M WORRIED ABOUT A PLANT DRIVING THE CAR!
SHOULDN'T BE A PROBLEM. MY UNCLE SAID HE'S A GOOD DRIVER.
OH. WELL. OKAY.
ZOOOOOOM
ACTUALLY, YOU KNOW WHAT? I AM A LITTLE WORRIED ABOUT TELEPATHIC SQUIRRELS.

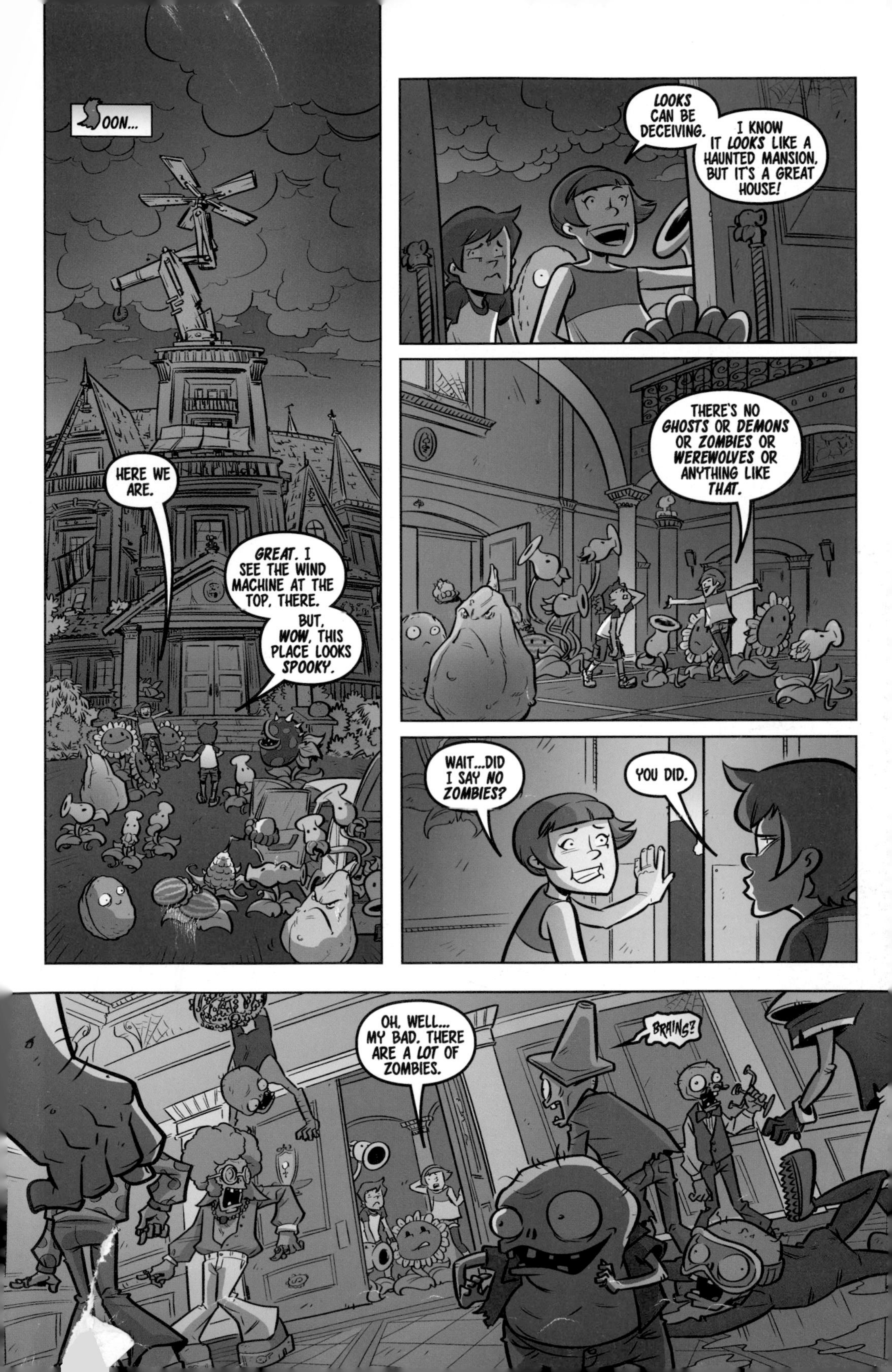
SOON...
HERE WE ARE.
GREAT. I SEE THE WIND MACHINE AT THE TOP, THERE.
BUT, WOW, THIS PLACE LOOKS SPOOKY.
LOOKS CAN BE DECEIVING.
I KNOW IT LOOKS LIKE A HAUNTED MANSION, BUT IT'S A GREAT HOUSE!
THERE'S NO GHOSTS OR DEMONS OR ZOMBIES OR WEREWOLVES OR ANYTHING LIKE THAT.
WAIT...DID I SAY NO ZOMBIES?
YOU DID.
OH, WELL... MY BAD. THERE ARE A LOT OF ZOMBIES.
BRAINS?

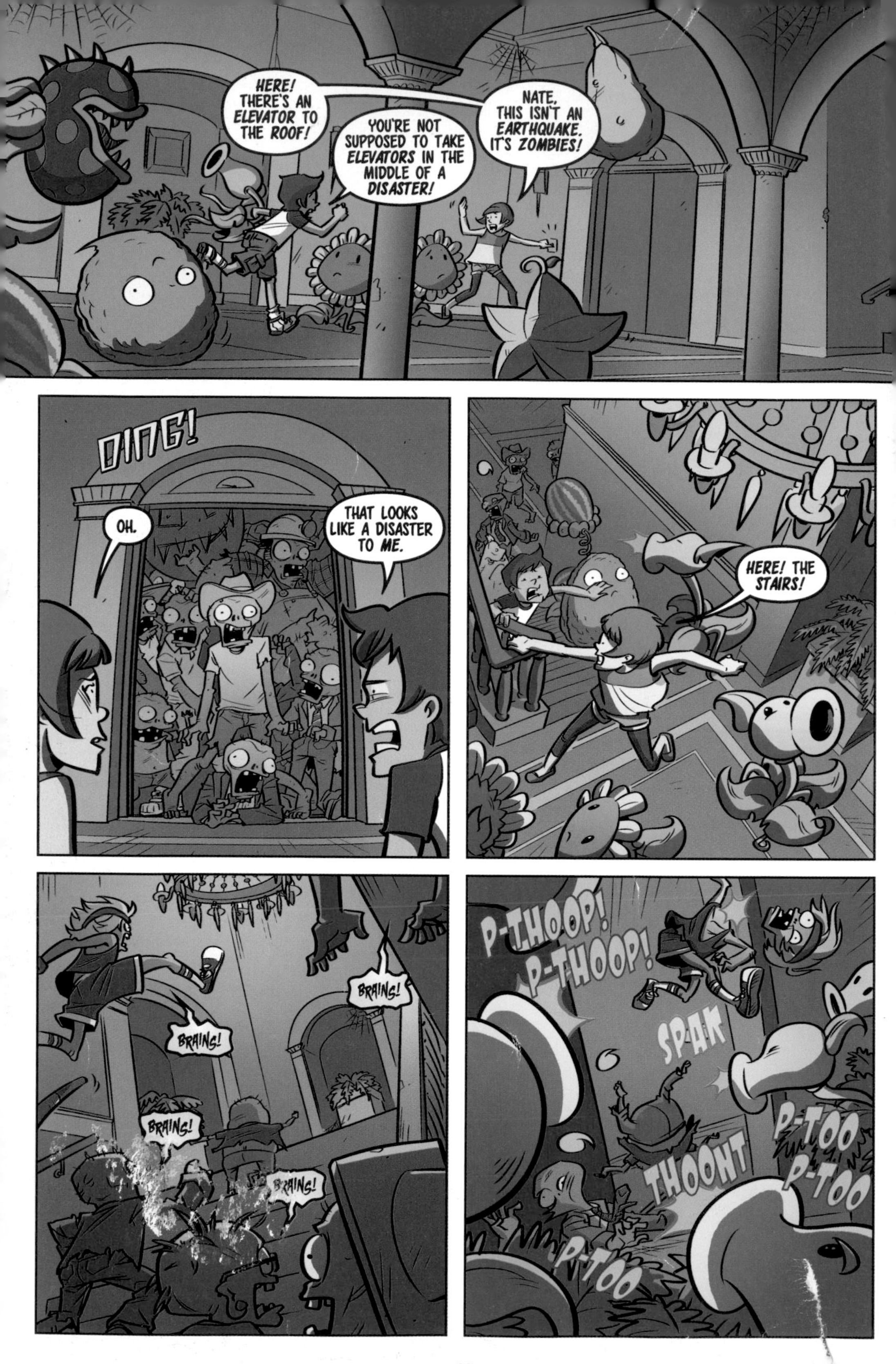
HERE! THERE'S AN ELEVATOR TO THE ROOF!
YOU'RE NOT SUPPOSED TO TAKE ELEVATORS IN THE MIDDLE OF A DISASTER!
NATE, THIS ISN'T AN EARTHQUAKE. IT'S ZOMBIES!
DING!
OH.
THAT LOOKS LIKE A DISASTER TO ME.
HERE! THE STAIRS!
BRAINS!
BRAINS!
BRAINS!
BRAINS!
P-THOOP! P-THOOP!
SPAK
THOONT
P-TOO P-TOO
P-TOO

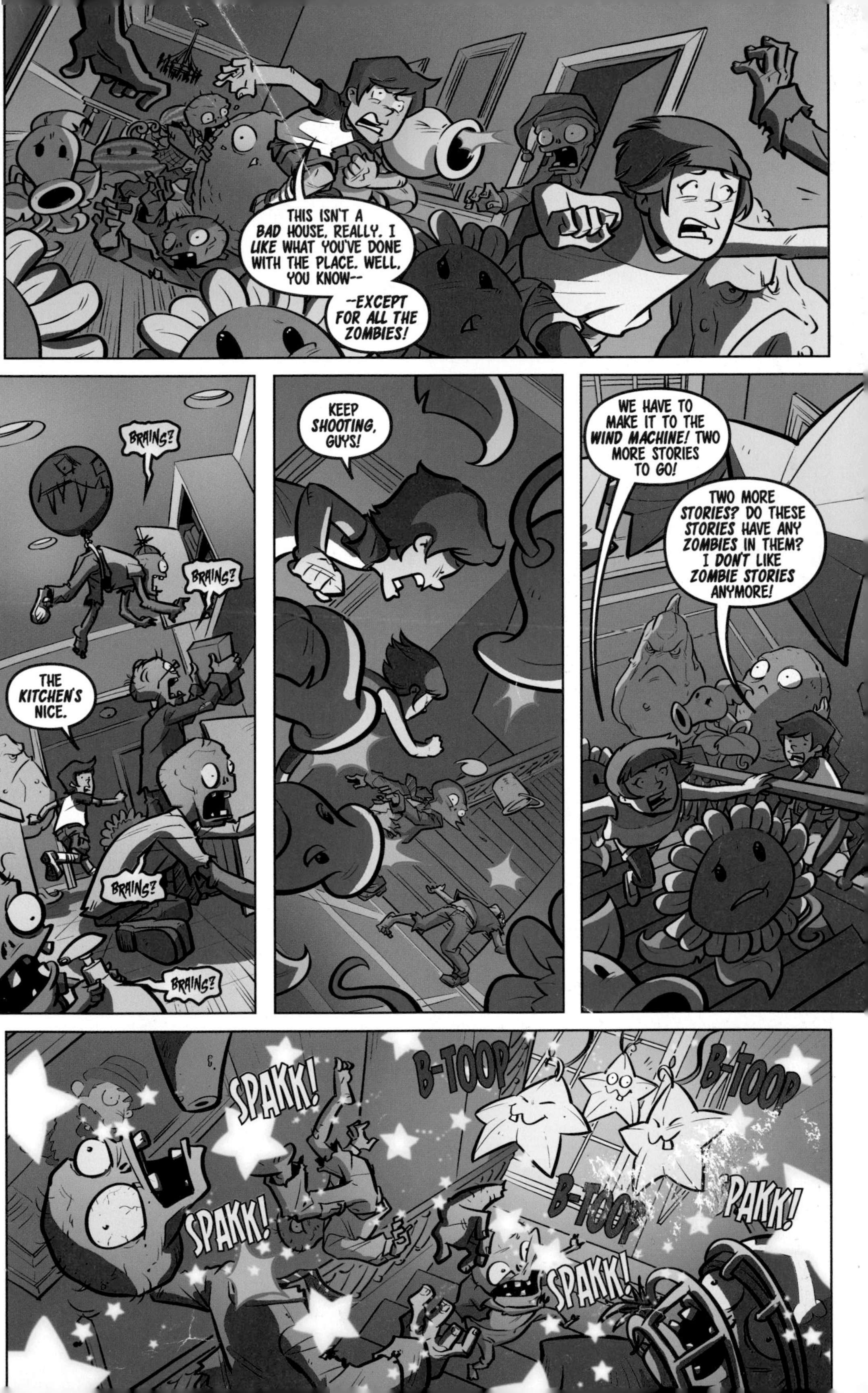
THIS ISN'T A BAD HOUSE, REALLY. I LIKE WHAT YOU'VE DONE WITH THE PLACE. WELL, YOU KNOW--
--EXCEPT FOR ALL THE ZOMBIES!
BRAINS?
BRAINS?
THE KITCHEN'S NICE.
BRAINS?
BRAINS?
KEEP SHOOTING, GUYS!
WE HAVE TO MAKE IT TO THE WIND MACHINE! TWO MORE STORIES TO GO!
TWO MORE STORIES? DO THESE STORIES HAVE ANY ZOMBIES IN THEM? I DON'T LIKE ZOMBIE STORIES ANYMORE!
SPAKK!
B-TOOP
B-TOOP
SPAKK!
B-TOOP
PAKK!
SPAKK!

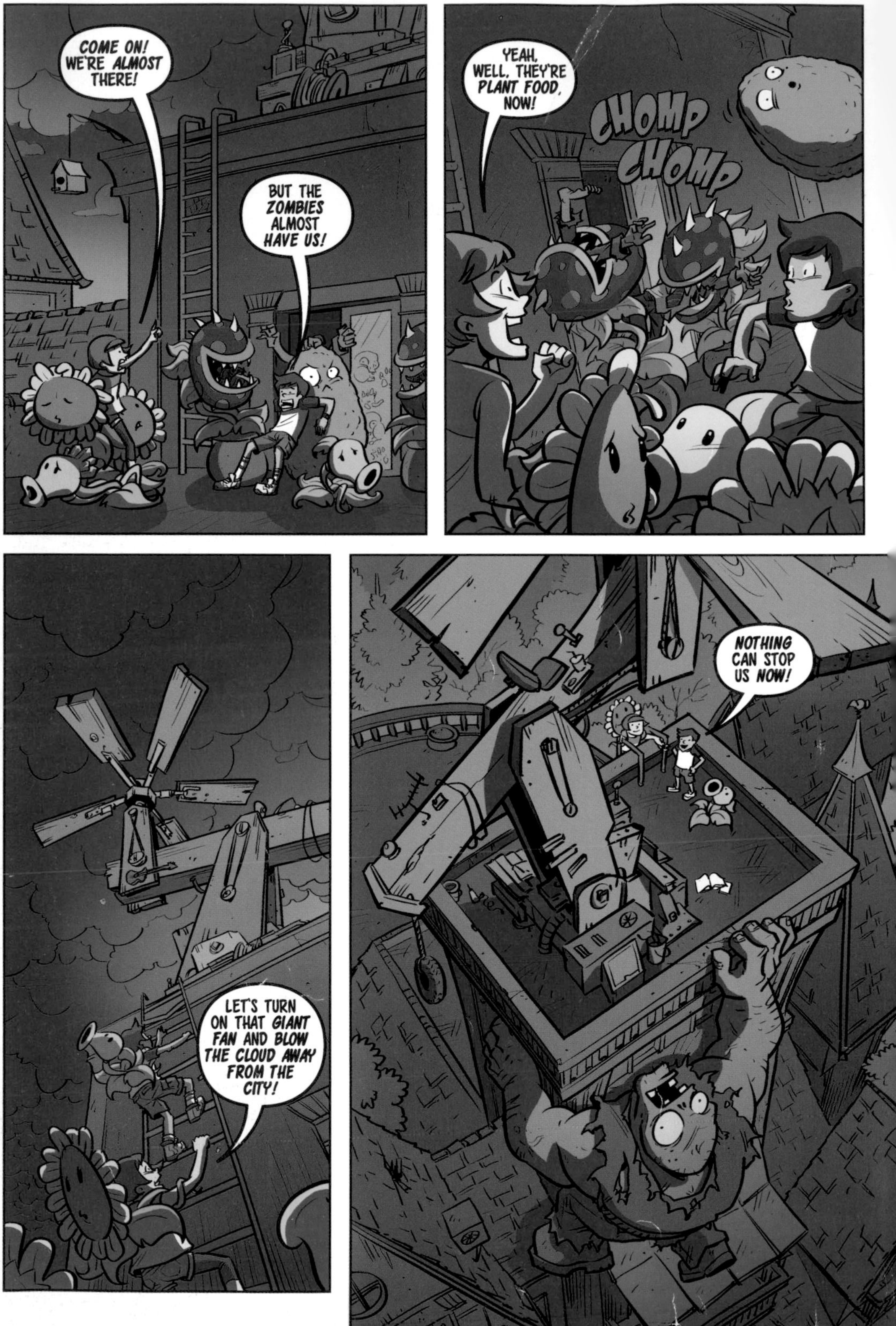
COME ON! WE'RE *ALMOST* THERE!
BUT THE *ZOMBIES* ALMOST *HAVE US!*
YEAH, WELL, THEY'RE *PLANT FOOD*, NOW!
CHOMP
CHOMP
LET'S TURN ON THAT *GIANT FAN* AND *BLOW THE CLOUD AWAY FROM THE CITY!*
NOTHING CAN STOP US *NOW!*

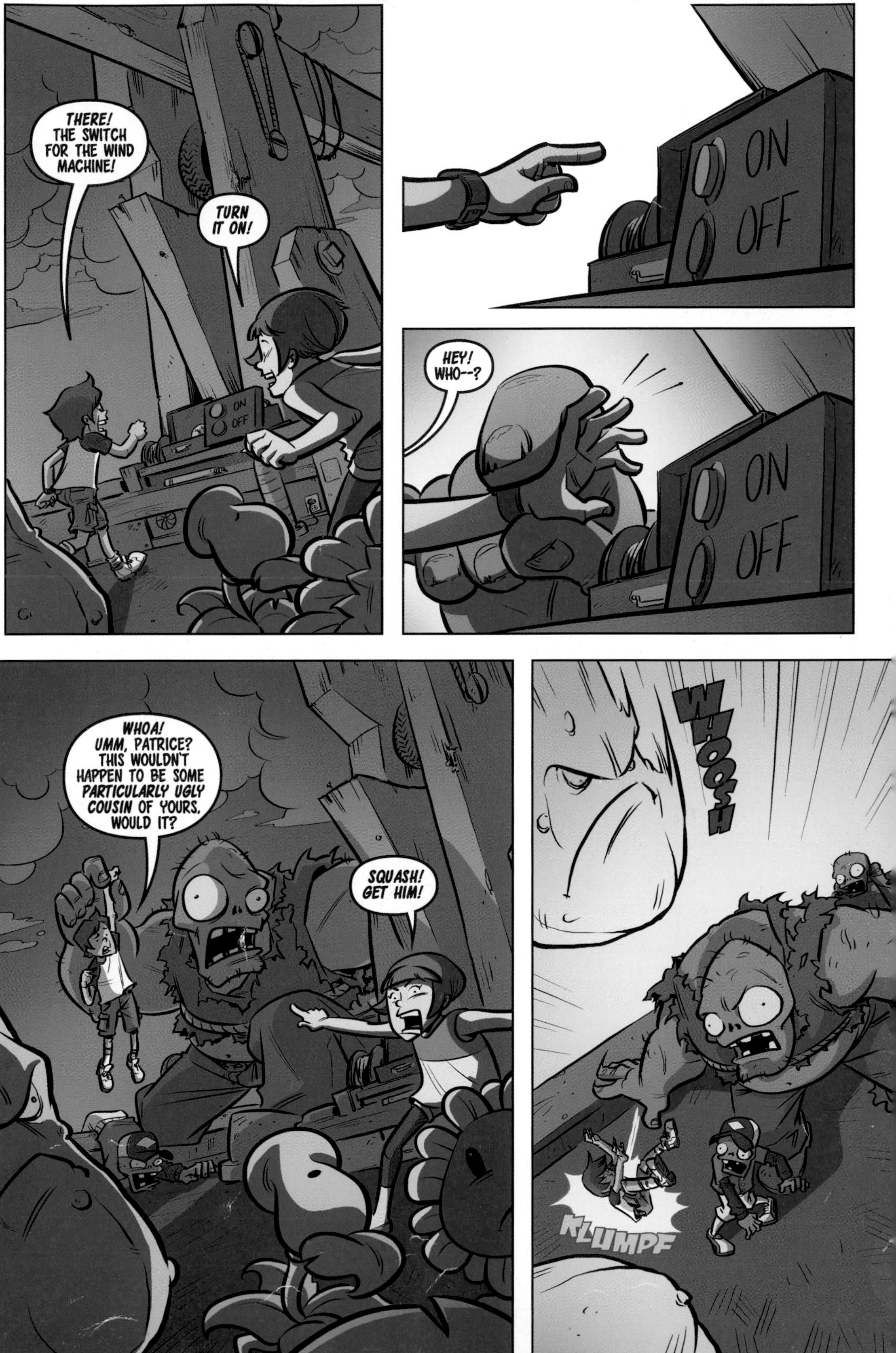
THERE! THE SWITCH FOR THE WIND MACHINE!
TURN IT ON!
ON
OFF
ON
OFF
HEY! WHO--?
ON
OFF
WHOA! UMM, PATRICE? THIS WOULDN'T HAPPEN TO BE SOME PARTICULARLY UGLY COUSIN OF YOURS, WOULD IT?
SQUASH! GET HIM!
WHOOSH
KLUMPF

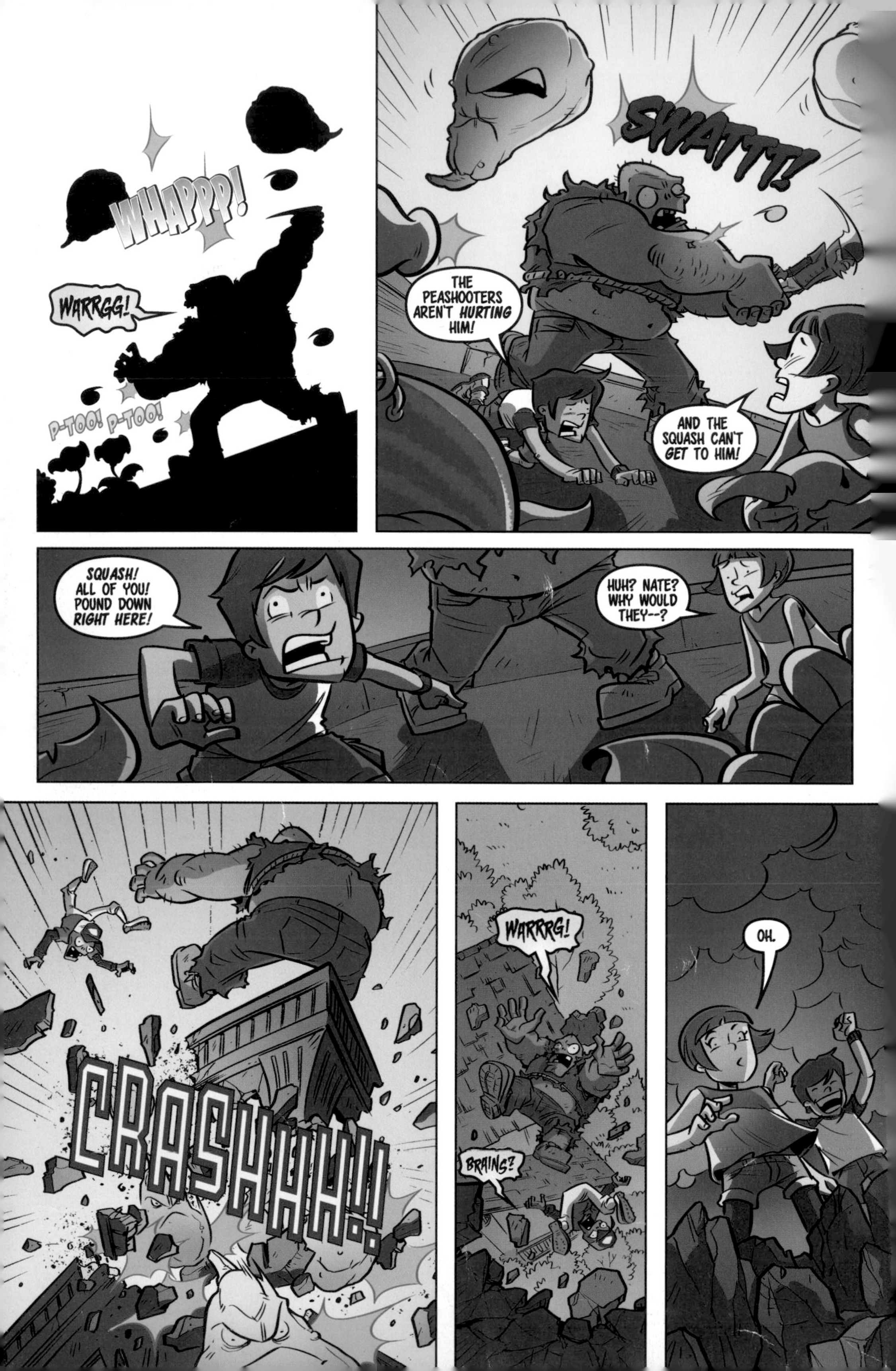
WHAPPP!
WARRGG!
P-TOO! P-TOO!
SWATTT!
THE PEASHOOTERS AREN'T HURTING HIM!
AND THE SQUASH CAN'T GET TO HIM!
SQUASH! ALL OF YOU! POUND DOWN RIGHT HERE!
HUH? NATE? WHY WOULD THEY--?
CRASHHH!!
WARRRG!
BRAINS?
OH.

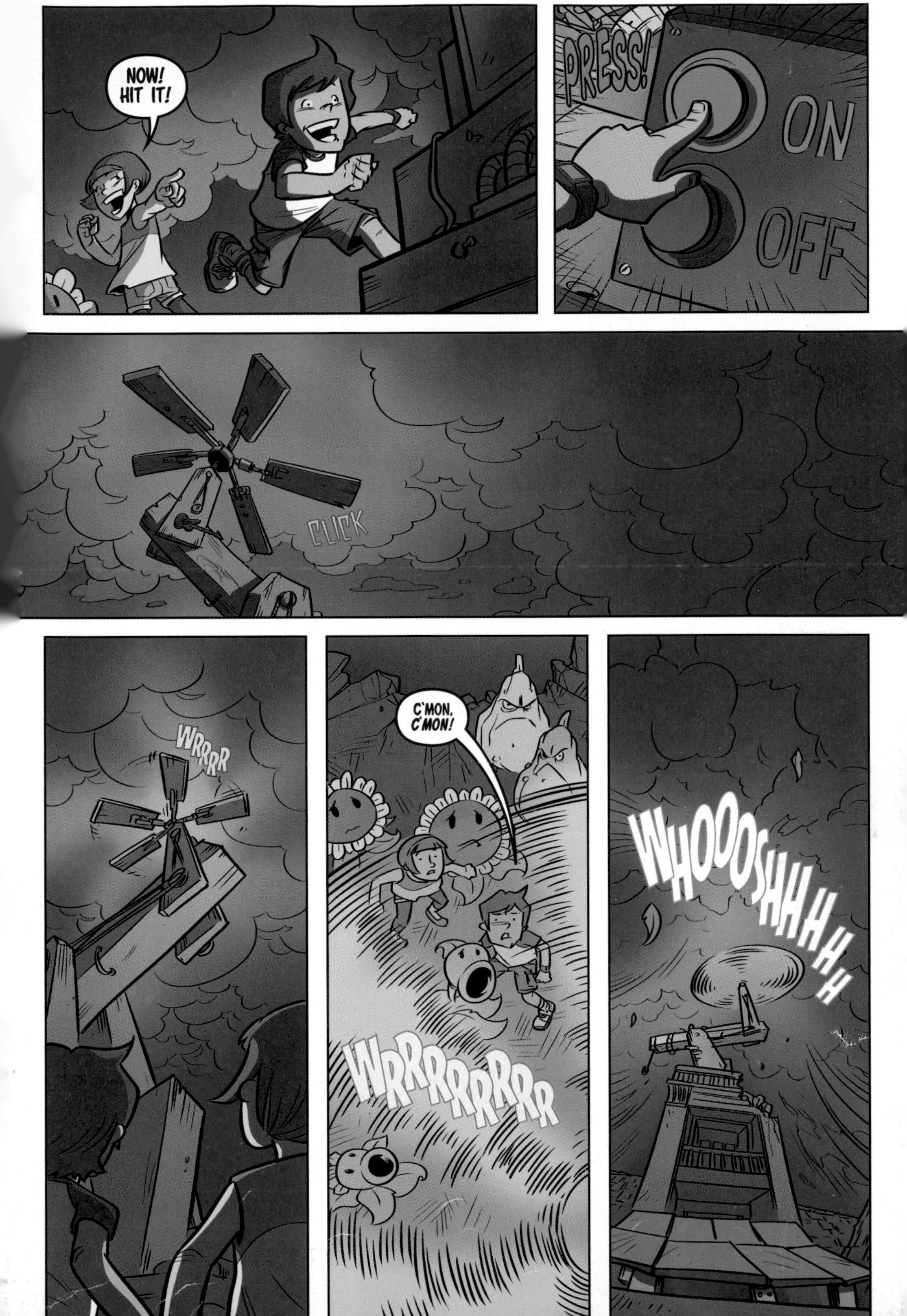
NOW! HIT IT!
PRESS!
ON
OFF
CLICK
WRRRR
C'MON, C'MON!
WRRRRRRRRR
WHOOOSHHHHHH

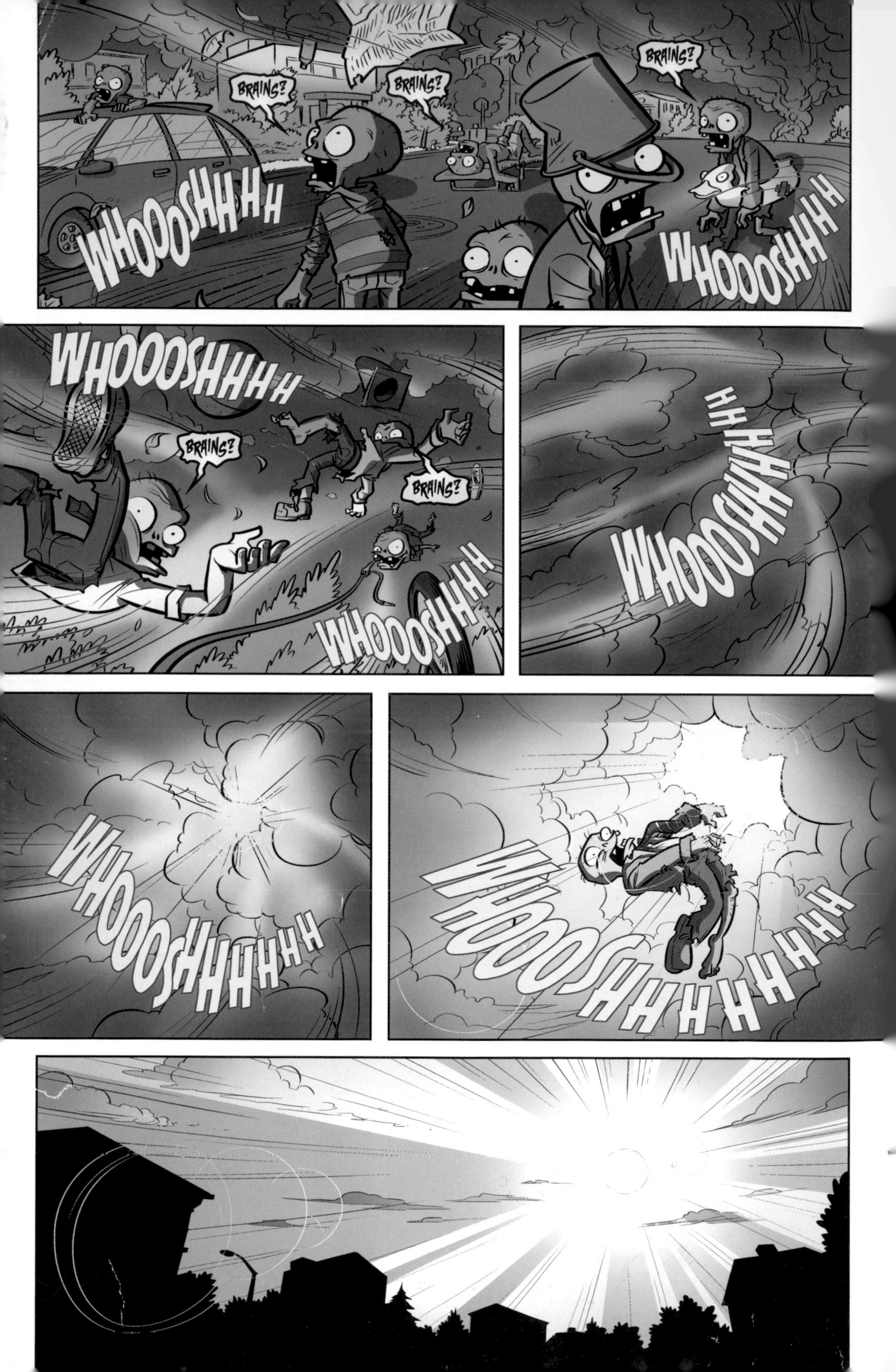
BRAINS?
BRAINS?
BRAINS?
WHOOOSHHHH
WHOOOSHHH
WHOOOSHHHH
BRAINS?
BRAINS?
WHOOOSHHH
WHOOOSHHHHH
WHOOOSHHHHHH
WHOOOSHHHHHHHHHH

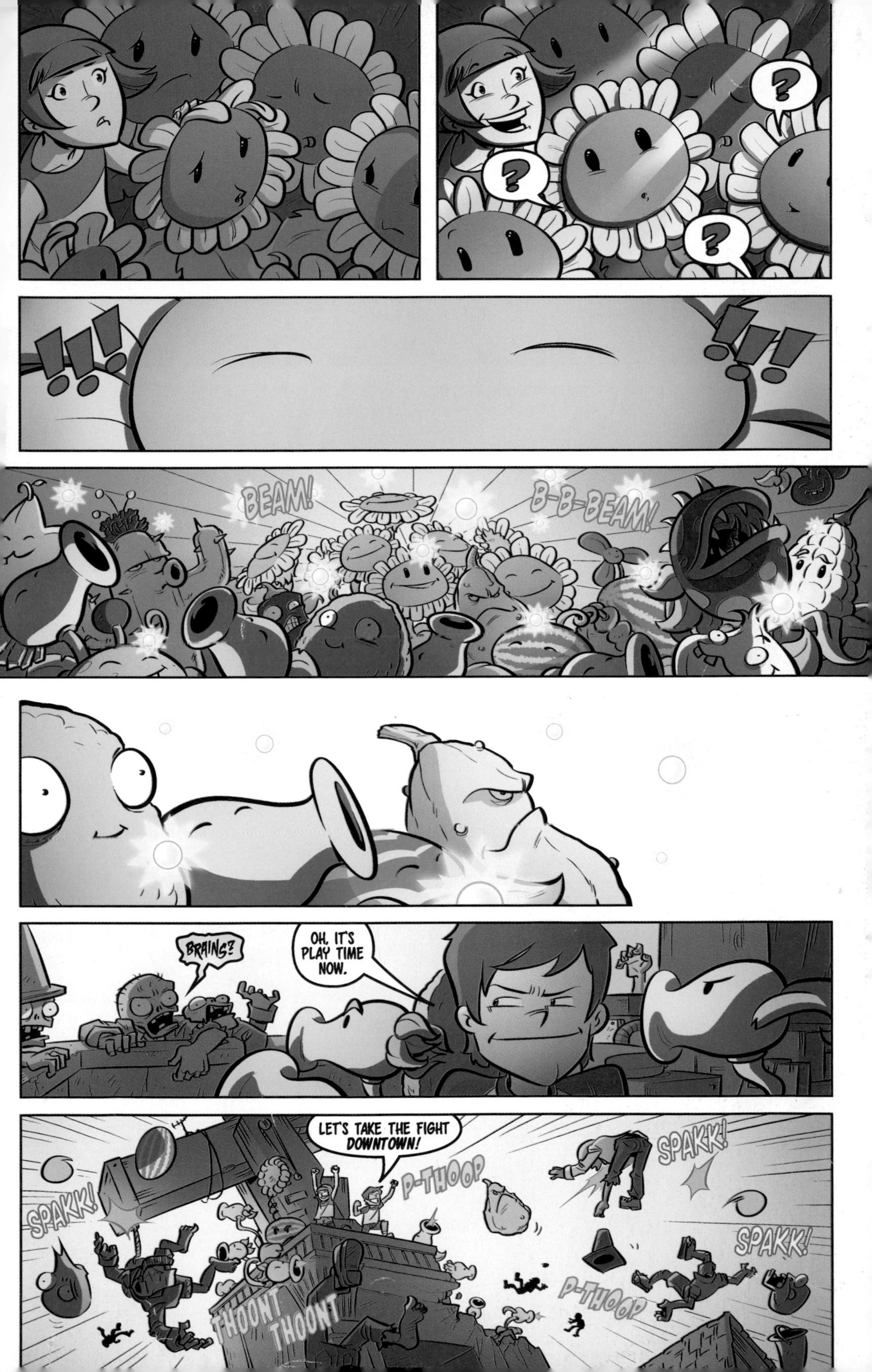
?
?
?
!!!
!!!
BEAM!
B-B-BEAM!
BRAINS?
OH, IT'S PLAY TIME NOW.
LET'S TAKE THE FIGHT DOWNTOWN!
P-THOOP
SPAKK!
SPAKK!
SPAKK!
P-THOOP
THOONT
THOONT

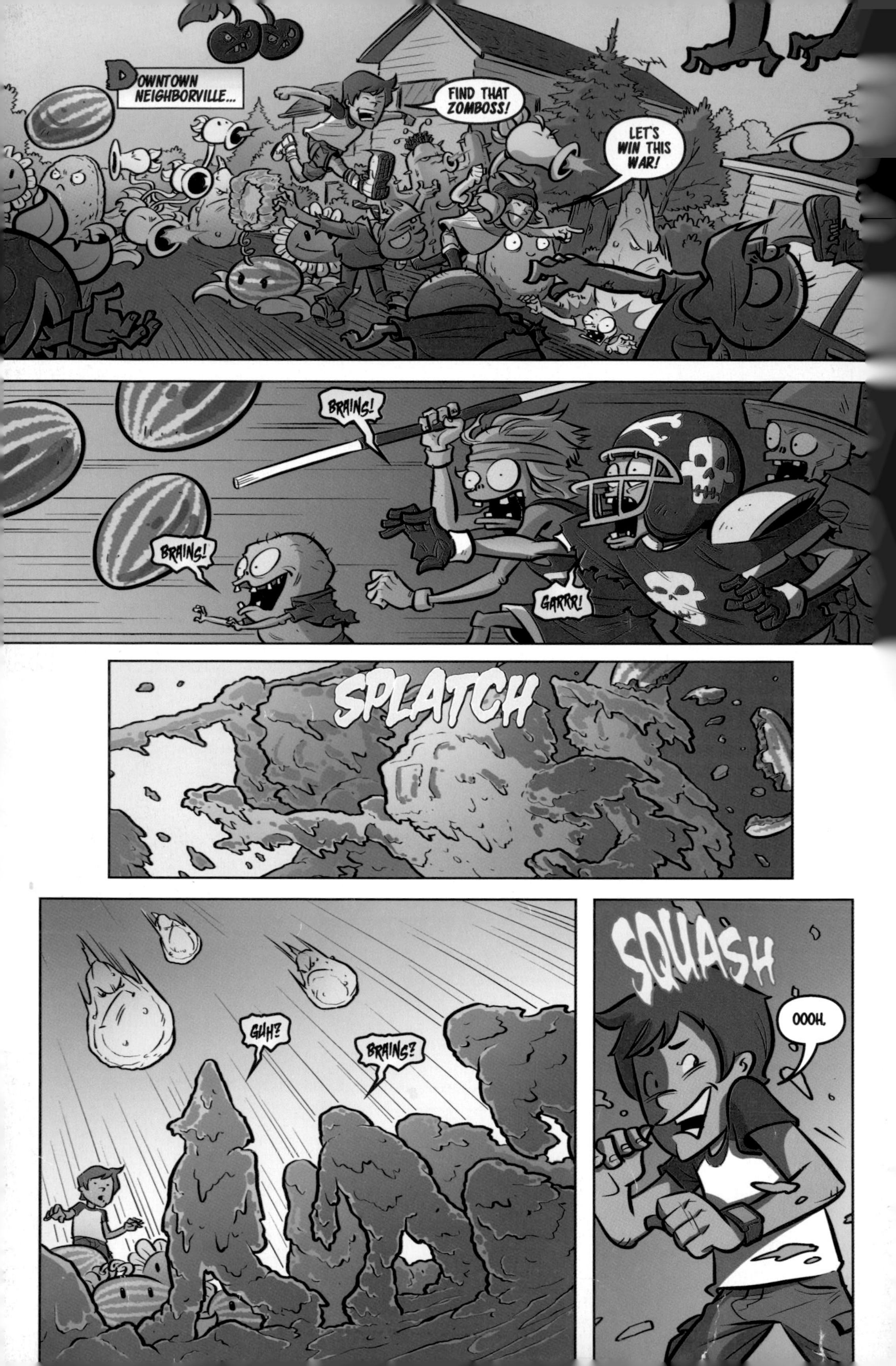

DOWNTOWN NEIGHBORVILLE...
FIND THAT ZOMBOSS!
LET'S WIN THIS WAR!
BRAINS!
BRAINS!
GARRR!
SPLATCH
GUH?
BRAINS?
SQUASH
OOOH.

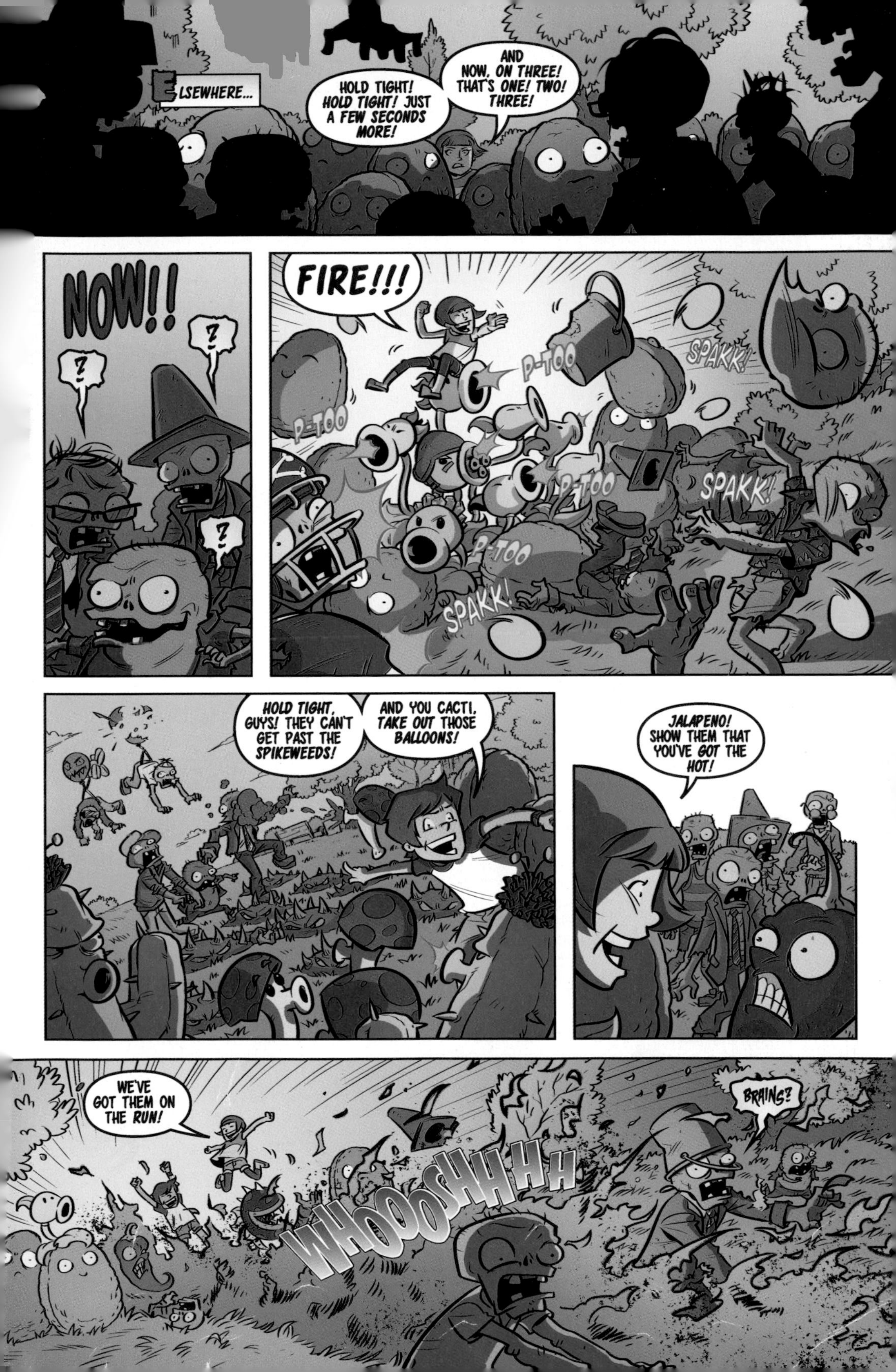
ELSEWHERE...
HOLD TIGHT! HOLD TIGHT! JUST A FEW SECONDS MORE!
AND NOW, ON THREE! THAT'S ONE! TWO! THREE!
NOW!!
?
?
?
FIRE!!!
P-TOO
P-TOO
P-TOO
P-TOO
SPAKK!
SPAKK!
SPAKK!
HOLD TIGHT, GUYS! THEY CAN'T GET PAST THE SPIKEWEEDS!
AND YOU CACTI, TAKE OUT THOSE BALLOONS!
JALAPENO! SHOW THEM THAT YOU'VE GOT THE HOT!
WE'VE GOT THEM ON THE RUN!
BRAINS?
WHOOOOSHHHHH

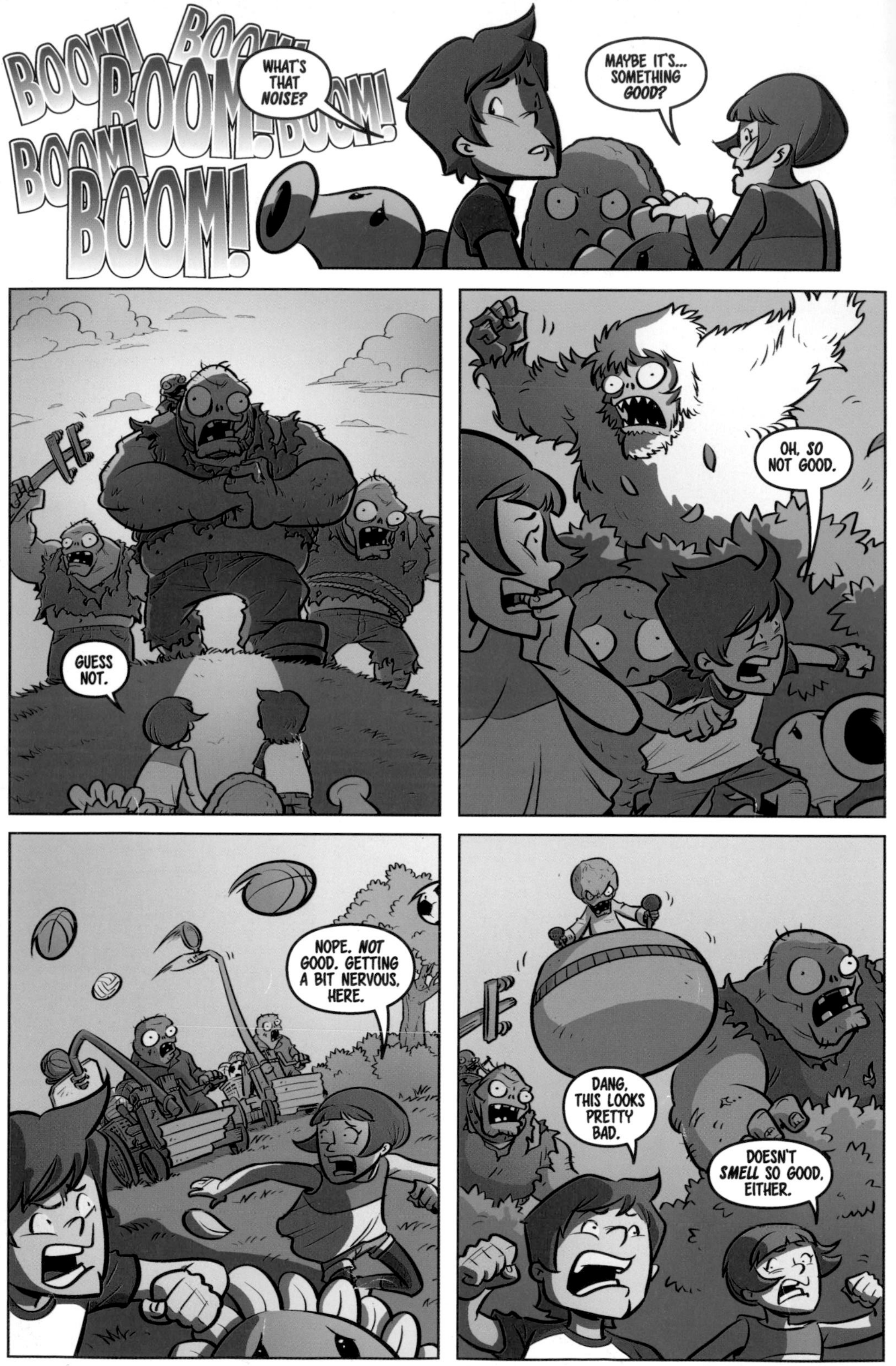
BOOM! BOOM! BOOM! BOOM! BOOM! BOOM!
WHAT'S THAT *NOISE?*
MAYBE IT'S... SOMETHING *GOOD?*
GUESS NOT.
OH, *SO* NOT GOOD.
NOPE. *NOT* GOOD. GETTING A BIT NERVOUS, HERE.
DANG, THIS LOOKS PRETTY BAD.
DOESN'T *SMELL* SO GOOD, EITHER.

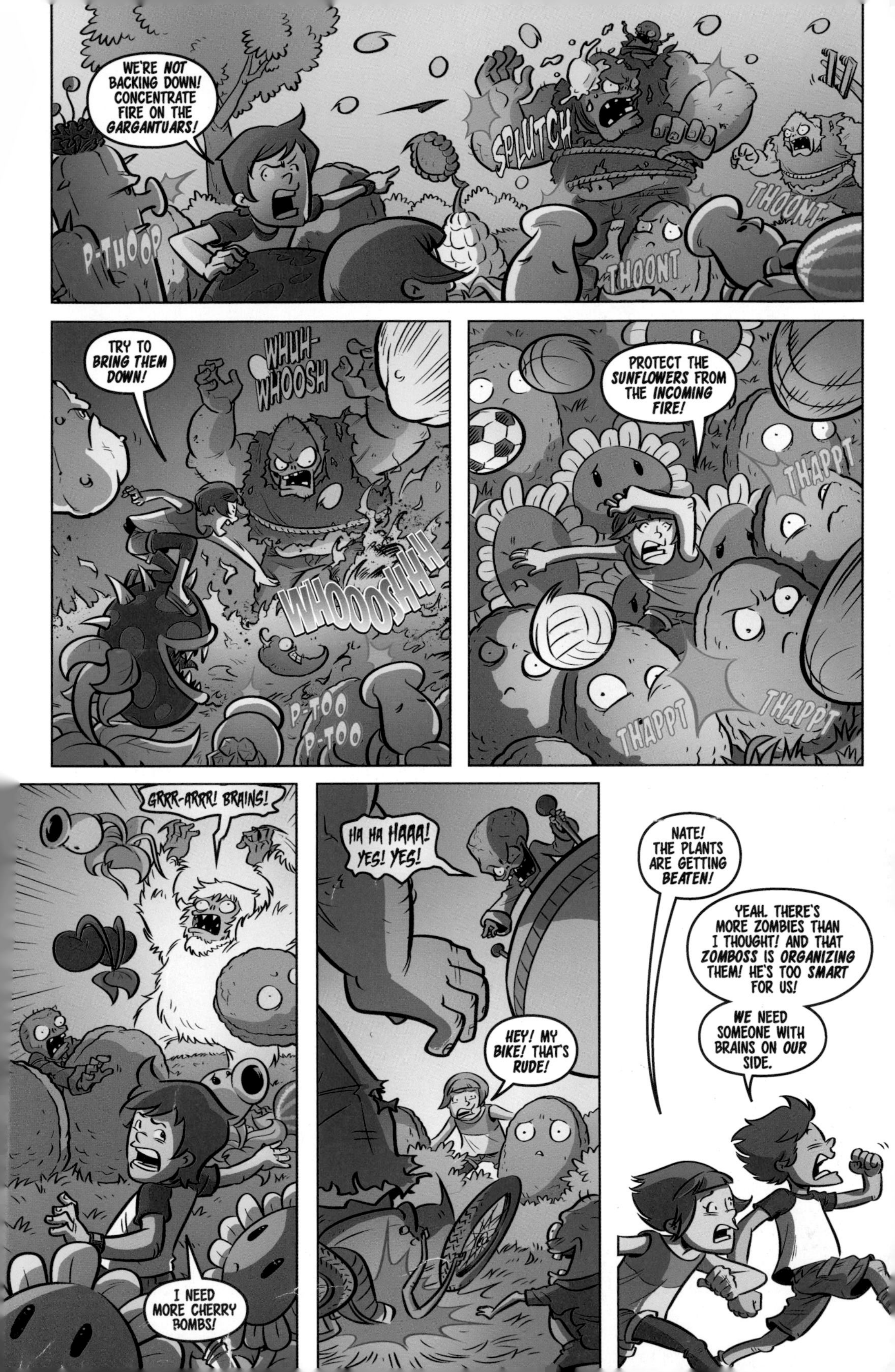
WE'RE NOT BACKING DOWN! CONCENTRATE FIRE ON THE GARGANTUARS!
SPLUTCH
P-THOOP
THOONT
THOONT
TRY TO BRING THEM DOWN!
WHUH-WHOOSH
WHOOOSHHH
P-TOO P-TOO
PROTECT THE SUNFLOWERS FROM THE INCOMING FIRE!
THAPPT
THAPPT
THAPPT
GRRR-ARRR! BRAINS!
I NEED MORE CHERRY BOMBS!
HA HA HAAA! YES! YES!
HEY! MY BIKE! THAT'S RUDE!
NATE! THE PLANTS ARE GETTING BEATEN!
YEAH. THERE'S MORE ZOMBIES THAN I THOUGHT! AND THAT ZOMBOSS IS ORGANIZING THEM! HE'S TOO SMART FOR US!
WE NEED SOMEONE WITH BRAINS ON OUR SIDE.

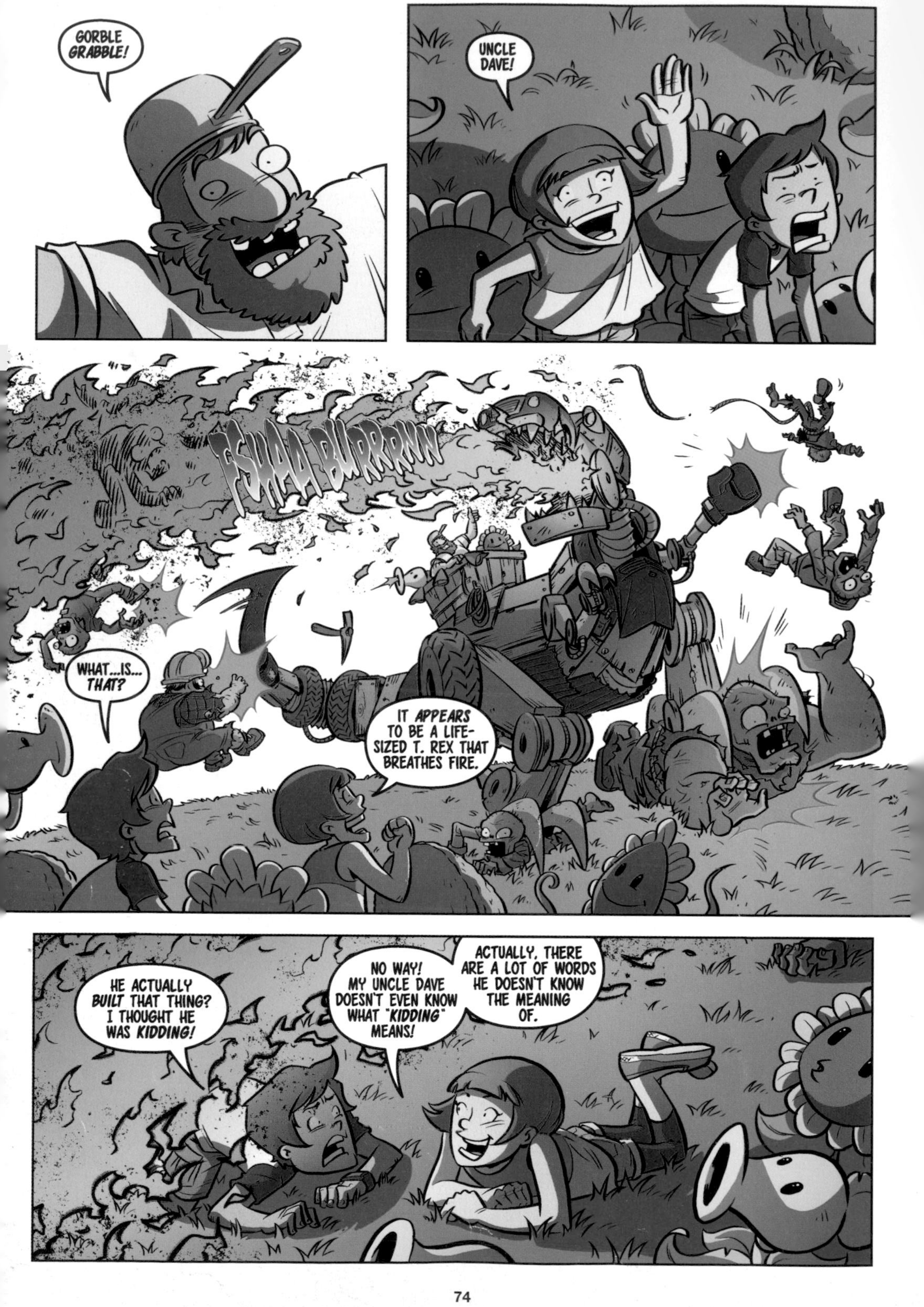
GORBLE GRABBLE!
UNCLE DAVE!
FSHAA BURRRNN
WHAT...IS... THAT?
IT APPEARS TO BE A LIFE-SIZED T. REX THAT BREATHES FIRE.
HE ACTUALLY BUILT THAT THING? I THOUGHT HE WAS KIDDING!
NO WAY! MY UNCLE DAVE DOESN'T EVEN KNOW WHAT "KIDDING" MEANS!
ACTUALLY, THERE ARE A LOT OF WORDS HE DOESN'T KNOW THE MEANING OF.

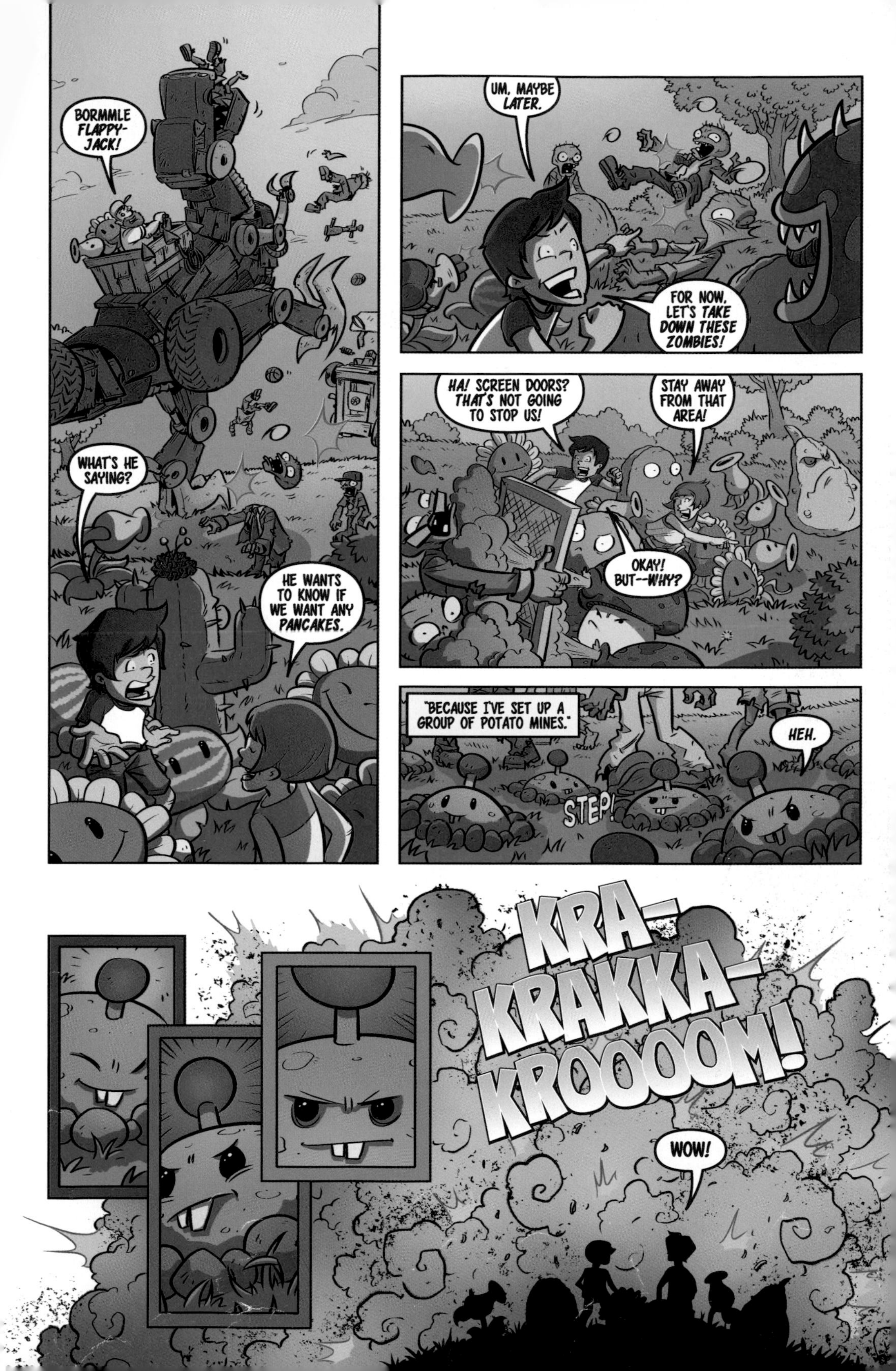
BORMMLE FLAPPY-JACK!
WHAT'S HE SAYING?
HE WANTS TO KNOW IF WE WANT ANY PANCAKES.
UM, MAYBE LATER.
FOR NOW, LET'S TAKE DOWN THESE ZOMBIES!
HA! SCREEN DOORS? THAT'S NOT GOING TO STOP US!
STAY AWAY FROM THAT AREA!
OKAY! BUT--WHY?
"BECAUSE I'VE SET UP A GROUP OF POTATO MINES."
HEH.
STEP!
KRA-KRAKKA-KROOOOM!
WOW!

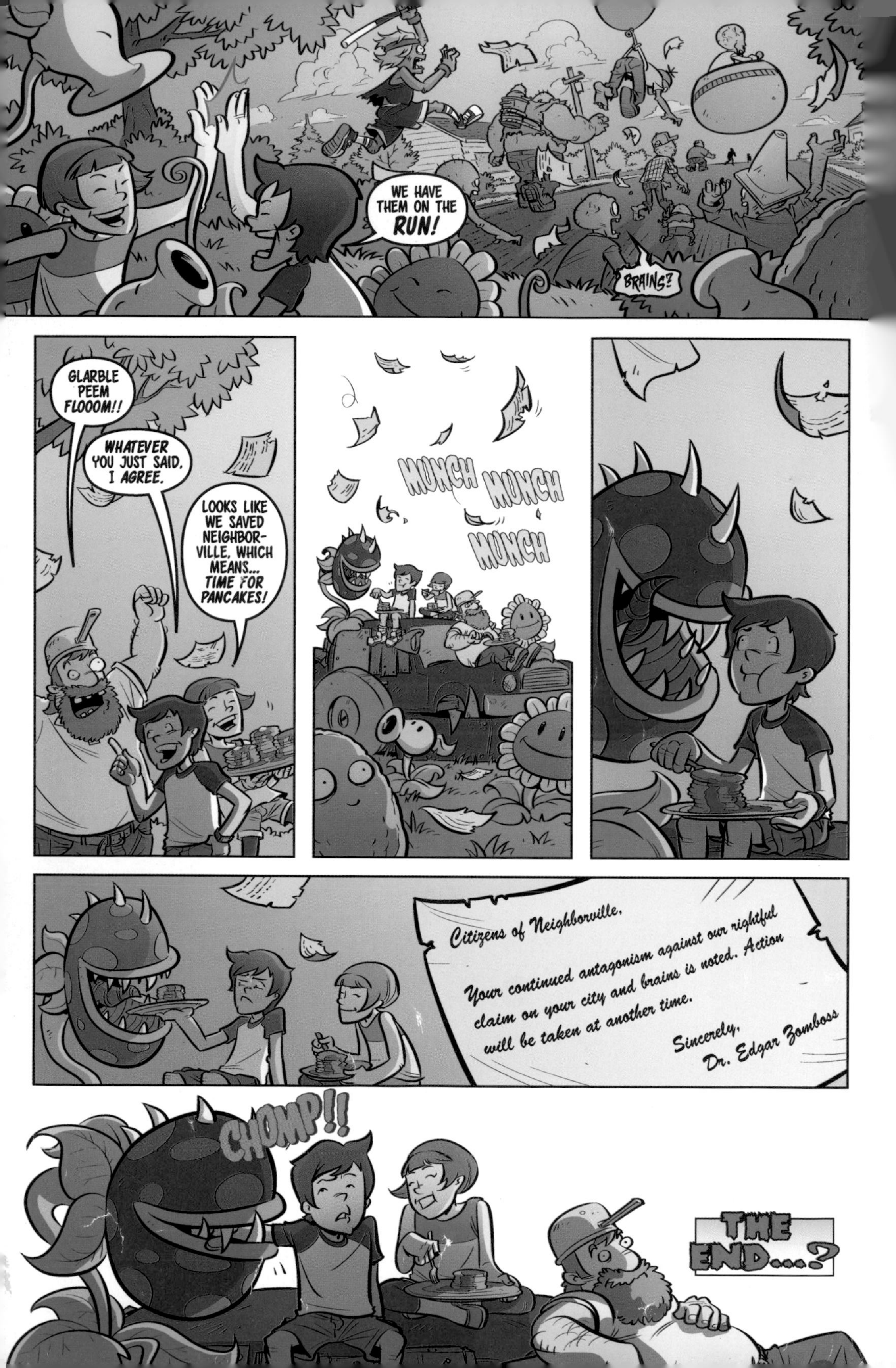
WE HAVE THEM ON THE RUN!
BRAINS?
GLARBLE PEEM FLOOOM!!
WHATEVER YOU JUST SAID, I AGREE.
LOOKS LIKE WE SAVED NEIGHBORVILLE, WHICH MEANS... TIME FOR PANCAKES!
MUNCH MUNCH MUNCH
Citizens of Neighborville,
Your continued antagonism against our rightful claim on your city and brains is noted. Action will be taken at another time.
Sincerely,
Dr. Edgar Zomboss
CHOMP!!
THE END...?

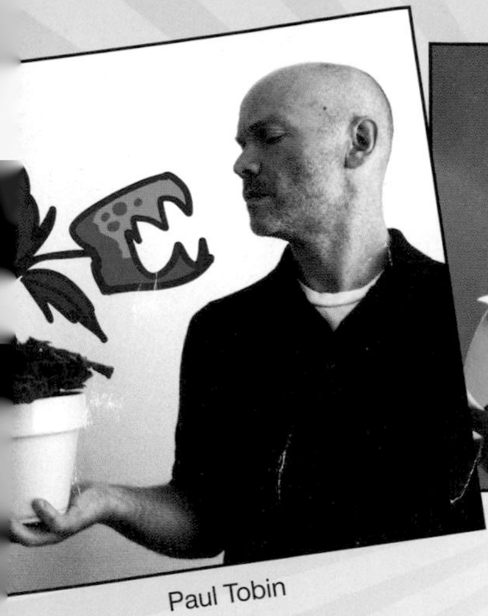

Paul Tobin

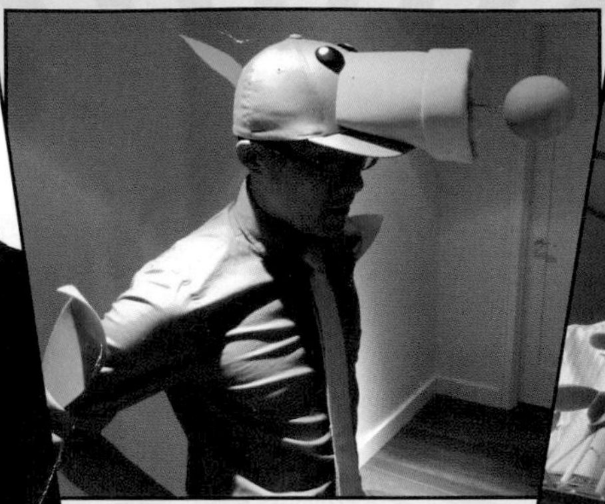

Ron Chan

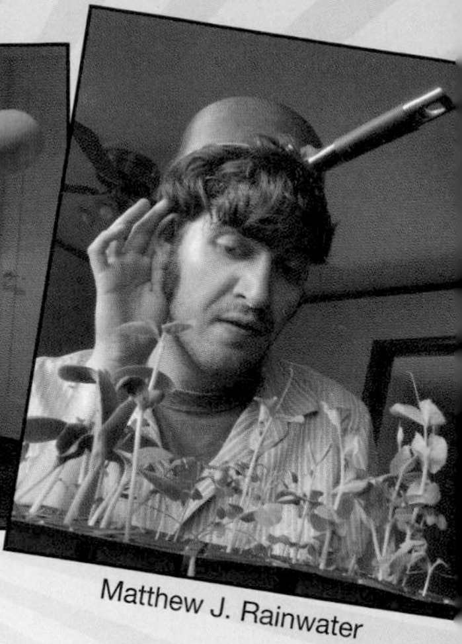

Matthew J. Rainwater

CREATOR BIOS

PAUL TOBIN is a critically acclaimed bald guy who had his first encounter with zombies when he watched the 1973 film *Children Shouldn't Play with Dead Things* on late-night television during one of the first times his parents ever left him alone. They returned to find him cowering in the kitchen with a knife. Paul eventually recovered enough mental stability to go on to write hundreds of comics for Marvel, DC, Dark Horse, and many others, including creator-owned titles such as *Colder* and *Bandette*, as well as *Prepare to Die!*—his debut novel. Paul's favorite zombie-fighting plants are the Cattail, the Snow Pea, and the Spikerock.

RON CHAN was born and raised in Portland, Oregon, and works as a freelance cartoonist, storyboard artist, and illustrator. He graduated from the Savannah College of Art and Design in 2005, and is now a member of the Portland-based art collective Periscope Studio. His comic-book work has been published by Dark Horse, Marvel, Image, Virgin, and Viper Comics. Storyboarding work of his includes boards for 3-D animation, gaming, internal development, user-experience design, and advertising for clients such as Microsoft, Dell, Amazon Kindle, Nike, Konami, and Sega. His first *Plants vs. Zombies* play-through was in 2009 on Steam for PC, and he prefers a Starfruit and Garlic-based defense strategy.

MATTHEW J. RAINWATER is a freelance cartoonist recently transplanted from the warm, humid swamps of Louisiana to the cool, damp forests of Portland, Oregon. A graduate of the Savannah College of Art and Design, Matt has worked on freelance illustration for advertising firms, web design, and independent video games. On top of this, he also self-publishes several comic books, including *Garage Raja* and *Trailer Park Warlock*, both of which can be found at GarageRaja.com. Matt finally beat *Plants vs. Zombies* in 2013 on his PC, and his zombie-smashing strategies tend toward Kernel-pults and Peashooters with a strong Squash and Wall-nut defensive line.

MORE DARK HORSE ALL-AGES TITLES

ChiMiChanGa
by Eric Powell

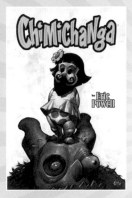

CHIMICHANGA

When Wrinkle's Traveling Circus's adorable little bearded girl trades a lock of her magic beard hair for a witch's strange egg, she stumbles upon what could be the saving grace for her ailing freak show: the savory-named beast Chimichanga!

Chimichanga
ISBN 978-1-59582-755-5

fluffy
SIMONE LIA

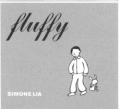

FLUFFY

Fluffy is a young rabbit with a human daddy named Michael. One day Michael decides to take Fluffy away for an impromptu trip to visit relatives in Sicily. Neither bunny nor man is truly prepared for the worldly excitement of a suspected kidnapping in Sicily, and both will be forever changed by the experience.

Fluffy
ISBN 978-1-59307-972-7

USAGI
YOJIMBO
STAN SAKAI
A TOWN CALLED HELL
SAKAI

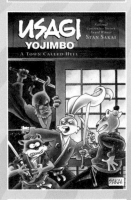

USAGI YOJIMBO

The rabbit *ronin* Usagi's wanderings find him caught between competing gang lords fighting for control of a town called Hell, confronting a *nukekubi*—a flying cannibal head—and crossing paths with the demon Jei!

Usagi Yojimbo Volume 25: Fox Hunt
ISBN 978-1-59582-726-5

Usagi Yojimbo Volume 26: Traitors of the Earth
ISBN 978-1-59582-910-8

Usagi Yojimbo Volume 27: A Town Called Hell
ISBN 978-1-59582-970-2

RICARDO DELGADO'S
AGE OF
REPTILES
OMNIBUS
VOLUME 1

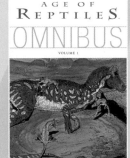

AGE OF REPTILES

When Ricardo Delgado first set his sights on creating comics, he crafted an epic tale about the most unlikely cast of characters: dinosaurs. Since that first Eisner-winning foray into the world of sequential art, he has returned to his critically acclaimed *Age of Reptiles* again and again, each time crafting a captivating saga about his saurian subjects.

Age of Reptiles Omnibus
ISBN 978-1-59582-683-1

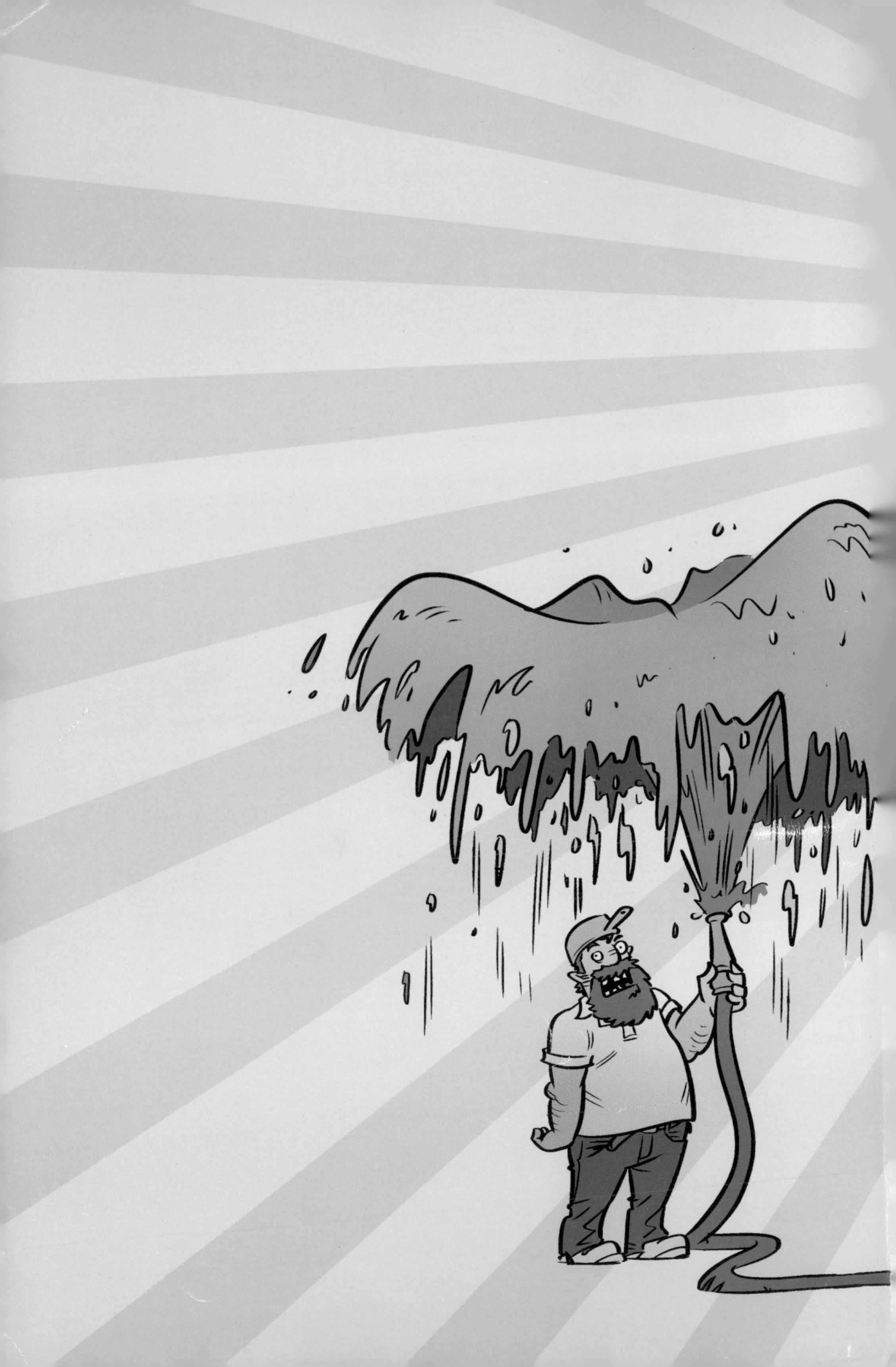

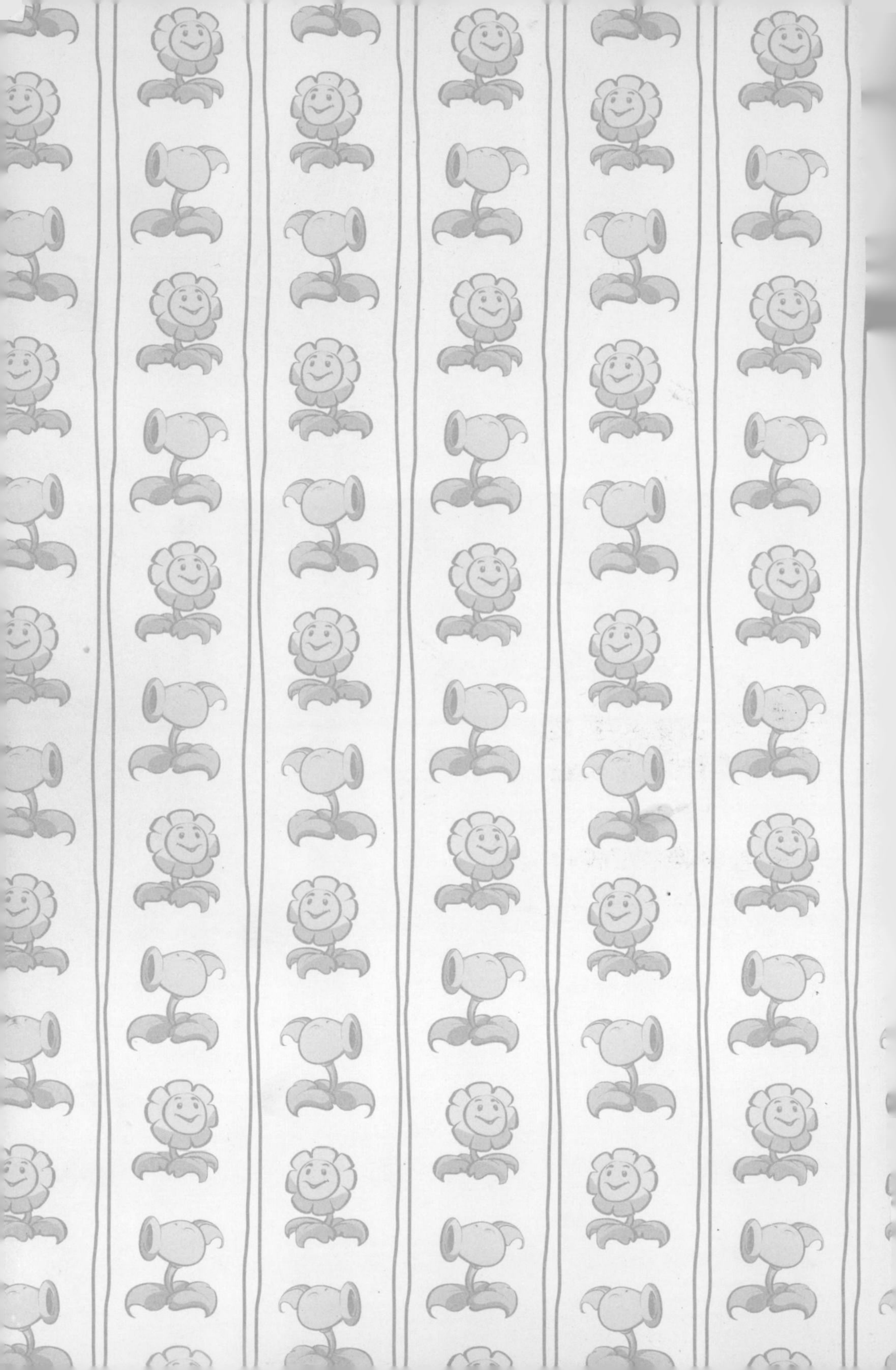